- .... . / -.-. --- -. -. -.. ..- .. –

The Conduit
by Jill Murphy Long

Dedication
To those, who believe there is more…

Acknowledgements
To try—and to be—an artist of any type takes courage, as Einstein once said, and I must add: tenacity.

I am forever grateful to all of the writers, who I have written with and all of the authors I have read and have met in this life, those who encouraged and supported my creative efforts in one way or another. It is because of you that I continue to write. While my road to publishing did start with a traditional publisher and led to my *Permission to…* book series, I do like the instant connection that I now have with my readers due to the changes in publishing.

A big "thank you" goes to my newest writing friends in Portland, Oregon: Katrina, Mel, Emily, and Kirsten, who always answered with my strange questions via texts, emails and in person.

Many thanks to Katrina Joy Plam of kjpcreations.com. Katrina designed three, beautiful book covers that I had to ask my friends on Facebook for input, so I could finally get this book published. Grace M also came to my rescue to help with the back cover and uploading the files.

My new reader in Portland, Oregon, Kimmie. I appreciate you being one of my early readers when I picked up this manuscript, again. Your enthusiasm for my writing made me cross this finish line and I thank you for your time.

Thank you to all of the writers, who I have helped get their books published. It was an honor to work with you and your book. I am so proud of your creativity and persistent efforts. I will put links to your titles so that my readers can find your books.

Also, thank you goes out to my first writing group in Southern California, my loyal crew of creative writers: Sandy, Leigh, Ruth, Rod, and Sam and in Steamboat Springs, Colorado: Elizabeth, LA, Deb, LuEtte, and Joanne—I miss us.

Currently, I'm adapting *The Conduit* to a screenplay. It's so much fun to have such detailed notes (the novel) from which to write a script.

And finally, thank you to you, my new reader, who has purchased my novel. Without readers, there would be no authors. Thank you for allowing me to pursue my dream of writing.

Jill Murphy Long
March 15, 2014

P.S. I'll try to respond to email, but if I don't please know that I'm writing another book or screenplay…and really should stay off of the Internet, advice I tell all aspiring authors:
theconduitbyjillmurphylong@gmail.com

--.- ..- . ... - .. --- -. ...

I don't know what to call the condition I have.

Nor do my doctors.

Initially, I couldn't sleep due to the fact that my dreams would wake me up at morning's first glimmer of pink. From my nighttime travels, I brought home souvenirs like sand in my bed, and purple fingerprint bruises that circled my wrists like bracelets. This morning, I woke with a razor thin, red scratch down the left side of my cheek.

As I stand naked in front of my grandmother's antique floor mirror, I survey for other body damage.

My doctor first dismissed my injuries as simply me being "a rough sleeper". He didn't explain though how the sand got in my bed, especially since Colorado is landlocked. While there are sand dunes here, this tourist attraction is a four-hour drive from my grandmother's house where I live once again, as of just two weeks ago.

However, it's more than my restless nights that have brought me to the nation's best diagnostic hospital, Lucent University Hospital. A month ago, I woke up speaking Portuguese. I knew a few key words from when my grandmother yelled at me, usually to hurry up or be careful, but I was never able to form complete thoughts or sentences in her native language. That night, my college friends in my American Literature's class steered me to the only Portuguese restaurant in town, called Fado, which my brain automatically tells me that it means "fate". They made me order for everyone and the skeptics said they would pay—if I could do what I said I could do: speak Portuguese fluently.

Usually, someone with an ear for language can get the pronunciations for some of the entrées right. I could and did, but what silenced my hecklers was my conversation

3

first with our Portuguese waiter and then the longer one with the Portuguese chef, who left his kitchen to chat about his homeland, our homeland as I found out that night. I wasn't answering in limited words or using tourist expressions, either. He wanted to know how one of his fellow Portuguese citizens had ended up in the states.

Within the first five minutes of our conversation, he realized that he knew of my father and grandfather and then gave his condolences when I told him they were no longer alive. He knew nothing about my mother, except he said she was an excellent pilot.

Pilot? What? Of a boat? A plane? Why didn't I know this? If she's a pilot, she should just fly home now…unless she has suffered the same fate as my grandfather. I let that sad thought dissipate from my mind.

Shortly afterwards, our waiter delivered a complimentary round of *caipirnhas* with the message the chef, my new friend, had picked up our dinner tab. I indulged in the free drink, yet still can't understand my liking for lime drinks. I was raised in the snow. Did I also inherit this taste for tangy beverages?

What first took me to my university's medical center in Northern California was an angry rash on the inside of my left palm and its relentless itch—not my crazy dreams. After a simple skin test, the lab reported that I was allergic to jackfruit, which doesn't exist anywhere in Northern California. It only grows in Asia and other tropical locales I've never visited like India, Thailand, the Philippines, Africa, Jamaica, and throughout Brazil, or so my brain rattled off this information to me. And it tastes like bananas. At the time, I didn't know what this jackfruit even looked like, however, now whenever I think of it, I can see this weird, earlobe-shaped fruit inside my head.

"You taste like banana-flavored, bubble gum," my boyfriend Nile told me once after he kissed me, but the strange part was that I hadn't eaten any of this fruit—ever.

When I told the university doctor I must have eaten this exotic fruit in my dream last night, he looked at me with both concern and confusion. When I questioned him if eating certain foods could feed my new intelligence like my ability to master the native language of my grandmother without any lessons, he politely rolled his eyes.

When I first called my grandmother to tell her about my travels to distant and brand new places at night, I thought she would relate. She's taking a lot of medication and has shared her wild dreams with me, but she didn't relate. She called her doctors.

The next day, she called me and said her primary doctor thought it would be wise for me to see a neurologist. My grandmother went on about how her doctors and their associates were the "most-renowned, medical minds in the country." She was quite confident that they would decipher was going on when I slept or tried to sleep. They would fix me.

I don't function very well on only three hours of sleep a night and my wild intrusive dreams started months ago, so I agreed with her, packed, and left my new friends and my renegade university in Santa Cruz, California. I reasoned I could use the medical help and my bedridden grandmother could use some company. After my mother disappeared, it was my grandmother who cared for me, so I booked the next flight home.

Now, back home in my grandmother's town and enrolled in classes for less than a month, I can sense my new professors are somewhat bewildered by my instant recall of everything. It's almost as if my mind has opened and absorbs everything and anything I've ever learned, overheard, saw, and read. I'm like a walking, talking encyclopedia, or in today's jargon, I'm Google. What do you want to know? I could tell you without going online.

My sports watch beeps at me to get out the door pronto. Ever since my sleep has been comprised, I started setting timers all over the house just to be on time.

If I don't get dressed and across campus in the next twenty minutes, I'll be late for my doctor's appointment. I find my jeans from yesterday, pull on my snow boots, and slip into my favorite ski sweaters, the baby blue one with tiny white snowflakes knitted across the shoulders.

I slip a tiny origami crane made from the foil of a chewing gum wrapper into my jean's pocket and thunder down the stairs, outside, and into the hope of the new day.

[Morse code message: QUESTIONS]

..-. --- .-. .-.. --- .--

     The university's psychoanalyst, my newest doctor now, wants me to remember back to the first night of my broken sleep, a regular occurrence, which hasn't stopped for eight weeks.

     I sit in Dr. Hall's completely beige office: carpet, walls, blinds, chairs, and a couch—I'm so happy she has a couch.

     When my neurologist told me I had to see a psychologist or whatever, I could only think about lying down on a couch with the intentions of achieving my much-needed sleep, but as I look around her office, I find myself irritated by the various shades of this nondescript color, probably meant to soothe, but only looks like cold oatmeal smeared everywhere. Her walls are even textured like oatmeal with irregular bumps and dents…maybe bright colors like ruby, canary, and turquoise, the colors my grandmother has painted our walls are just too stimulating for her anxiety-ridden, sleep-deprived, crazy patients.

     Patients. I'm one of them now, too, but she does have a very comfortable couch. I bounce up and down a bit to confirm this fact and chalk up a point for my new doctor and another reason to convince myself to show up for my weekly appointments.

     Her office is a safe place to rest and I'm not riddled with needles and other, body-testing devices my last doctor Dr. Reid used with too much frequency and had failed to deliver a prognosis or even identify a cause.

     "We don't know," seemed to be his recurring answer for anything associated with my brain—or why it's wasn't working the way it should.

     My newest doctor Dr. Hall is dressed in an immaculate ivory suit. She's busy studying a sheet of paper stapled inside a manila file, but rises two inches off her chair covered in beige fabric to sit, again and smooth her skirt across her lap. Her short platinum-blonde hair bobs about her smiling face. She's an attractive older woman, who's dressed the opposite of me. Dr. Hall is what some would call "put together". I prefer and look like a 'bohemian-urban cowgirl'.

Every Christmas, my high school boyfriend Nile bought me a cowgirl hat. The last holiday when we were still together, he surprised me with the one he knew I wanted: the red cowgirl hat made from felt. I know it's very juvenile, but I love it.

Today as usual, I'm in one of my wonderful ski sweaters with a nod to my favorite season of the year and I always wear boots: snow boots, high-heel, fashion boots, and especially my cowgirl boots, the thicker the heel and squarer the toe box the better. I do wish I could wear boots year-round and almost can because it snows here in the Rockies every month, except July.

"If you want, you can lie down." My shrink smiles at me. "But most of my patients just sit."

Dr. Hall smiles a lot.

I kick off my brown leather cowgirl boots, toss my cowgirl hat to an empty chair, and lie down. I feel sleep coming to me as I stretch out, but my new doctor hands me an expensive, leather journal filled with beige pages. There's that blah color, again. There are light blue lines crossing each page that I know I won't be able to keep my words on.

I pull myself to a sitting position and accept the fancy, fine-tipped pen that she offers, too.

"I'll give you a half hour to be by yourself and write a little." She holds the solid wood door open with her high heel shoe that matches her office and outfit. "Write what you remember about your dreams, what's bothering you, what you see inside your head. I already know about your physical ailments."

The door shuts behind her with a click.

Is this the way psychoanalysts work now? What would Freud say? I thought they sat behind you and took fast notes as you babbled about your life, your fears, your problems, anything and everything—and did not leave the room.

I really don't want to be alone with what I have.

My dreams and the memories of what is keeping me awake at night are just too real almost as if I have lived them. These experiences carry more impact than the typical, lovey-dovey dream about an old boyfriend or rehashing a date gone badly.

My dreams physically accost me.

When Sally the grad student, who works at Dr. Hall's office called me to book my first appointment, she told me the doctor wanted me to keep a dream journal each morning for the next week.

I said I would try.

In soft warmth of morning with a pen in my hand, I usually fell back to sleep because the sun brought safety to me—or at least I felt safe enough to sleep during these daylight hours.

Today, my doctor wants full disclosure of what I've been experiencing in my dreams, what I would rather not remember…

As I put the black ink pen to paper, I begin to sketch an image that I do remember from my dream last night. My dreams aren't making any sense to me, but maybe this latest doctor will see something I'm missing.

I sketch a picture of a little girl's shoe. I think this low-heeled shoe with a single strap is called "Mary Jane".

My drawing needs the color red if it's to be accurate, so I leave my nesting place on the couch to look for a red pen on Dr. Hall's perfectly neat desk. Like all of my professors, she has one in her beige, ceramic pen cup.

I sit back down on the couch and place my journal on the coffee table. I hit the page quickly, putting red dots all over the shoe to make it look like the shoe covered in red glitter that I remember from my dream.

The strap is broken, so I draw it that way and as I draw the second shoe, I can see the little girl, who wore the shoes. My mind takes me, pulls my body back into my dream even though I'm still on Dr. Hall's couch.

And now I remember…each time that I return to wherever I'm going, there is a little girl waiting and watching for me. She wears dirty clothes. Her white blouse is torn at the shoulder as if someone tried to grab her, but she has outmaneuvered her captor.

Oftentimes, she sits against the wall of a dank alley. The soles of her bare feet are as black as her coal-colored eyes. She stares at me, the gringo, who's quite pale from living in snow country and colors her brown hair the color of straw.

Although my eyes are shaped like hers, I wear tinted contacts to make my eyes blue. I guess I was trying to blend into the beach culture during my short-lived time at college on the Californian coast.

With her intense eyes, she stares back at me as if I should know something, but I know nothing. Maybe she is entranced by my presence as if I am from another world and who knows, maybe I am. I am an intruder in her life now with my indiscriminate appearances and disappearances. I can tell by her skittish behavior when I approach her. She's like a cat, unsure if I can be trusted and darts away, but glances back over her shoulder to make sure that I follow her.

From her slight stature, probably due to malnutrition, she looks like a child of a five, but is mostly likely older. I'm guessing six or seven because of her deliberate efforts to make me follow her, yet every time I get close enough to offer her food, she hides behind a young boy with thick dark hair like hers. He's always around like her all-vigilante protector.

When she speeds up the steep alleyway or along a dirt trail that snakes into darkness, she remains in my sight, almost as if she is willing me to follow her to something, to someone…so I do.

I follow her up a twisting path deeper into the city's slums, or *favelas*, as they are called in Portuguese or so my Google brain automatically translated for me.

Each time I show up in this foreign land, it's either in the purplish hue of twilight or in the blackest hour just before daybreak. Tonight, a full moon spotlights the unending stacks of multi-story tenements, all precariously balanced on the mountainside far above the pristine beaches. These shanty town buildings look like a house of cards ready to tumble down into the bay at any moment.

Below, the wealthy stretches across their claimed land, which has been staked for decades and protected behind high walls, surrounding their personal citadels. This disparaging view of such a beautiful seaside city shows a heartbreaking contrast between the rich and the bleakness of poverty that lives in impossible density and yet so nearby. These two, different tropical worlds are a constant truth in this little girl's reality.

I remember trying to read the street signs, but there's not enough light and the white letters have been faded by the sun. I trip over piles of garbage scattered all over the dirt road. We pass a charred, bombed out bus.

Nothing looks like home. I'm beginning to think that I am not in the states, anymore, but this is a dream and dreams can take you anywhere, particularly mine.

My new little friend smiles at me through cracked lips. I search the pockets of my boyfriend's jacket for ChapStick. Why am I wearing Nile's clothing in my dreams? Of course, my brain offers no answer to this question last night or again right now when I ask it.

I remember following this little girl through a cluster of children, some younger than she and without any adults around. They smile while lounging in squalor either oblivious or numb to this state of being. Their blankets are used black trash bags. Their beds are flattened, cardboard boxes where six or seven of them line up and look like they're at summer camp, but without real beds or even regular meals.

When the police show up in their black Kevlar vest and machine guns strapped over their shoulders, they scatter in different directions. The older children, who carry the smaller children run and hide in the alleys. As I pass two male teenagers, I overhear them whispering about how some street kids are being kidnapped and murdered for organs to be sold on the black market.

Now, I wish I didn't know Portuguese.

I watch as the young boy waits for her to catch up or pulls her out of the way of a fast-moving scooter motored by three males squeezed together on the seat made for one. His arm hangs over her shoulder whenever she isn't marching me up some insanely steep, dirt path into the darkness.

We round a corner and end up on a street where a vendor sells coconut water, shrimp-filled pastries, and boiled corn on the cob. The older street urchins beg for money from me or anyone dressed in clean clothes. I pull my pockets of my jeans inside out to show them that I have no money and then jog to catch up with my short companion. She has disappeared into the maze of dark-skinned people and even darker alleys.

My blind following of someone that I don't know and haven't exchanged a single word with might not be a good idea, but the night is only getting darker. I simply go with my gut and follow her.

This might be a trap, but the earnest look on her mud-smeared face tells me to trust her. She needs to show me something and although it may not be a smart move, I am intrigued. I think, this is a dream, right? What can possibly go wrong? And she's a child, so she couldn't possibly possess any evil thoughts or want to harm me…could she?

I look down at my beige pages to see that the entire spread is filled with my scribbling. I didn't think I was writing, just thinking, remembering, yet another talent emerges. I think I'll like this new aptitude a lot, too.

I place my pen to paper and tilt my head back against the comfortable couch to remember more. My right hand hurries to keep up with the speed of my thoughts.

From a young age, I've always kept a diary filled with drawings rather than words. As a child, I wasn't very trusting of the world since it kept taking my relatives away, first my father, next my mother, and then my grandfather. Since I was afraid that someone might read my writings, I drew my thoughts and memories instead. My early efforts resembled a sketchbook more than a diary. On each page, my secret drawings spilled out to the pages' edges, spiraled down in the center, and ran diagonally down to the corners of the paper.

These old journals, filled with my life's sketches, told of my short history to date: nineteen years. I must have started this habit when my mother left with me with my grandparents. I was only six. She had promised to come home…that was thirteen years ago.

I wonder where my boxes of childhood diaries are at my grandmother's house. I know my grandmother still has them socked away somewhere. She never throws anything away.

The door opens.

Dr. Hall enters, balancing a tray with an ornate tin of loose leaf tea, a silver teapot with two vintage teacups on saucers. Between the free office supplies and tea time with the real stuff, I bet these sessions are going to be expensive.

I offer the doctor my journal. I'm both amazed and proud that I could crank out four pages even though I do write big and do not stay on the suggested lines.

We both sip the tea.

She murmurs approval of either the blasé tea or my work.

I grimace and put my teacup down on its saucer. There's no kick in herbal teas. I would rather sip a tiny cup of Turkish coffee with cardamom—

"To help lessen your anxiety attacks, I would advise not ingesting any caffeine."

She puts her cup down to turn the pages faster. "Curious. Very curious." She reads quickly until she gets to the end of my scribbling and then leans toward me, "I want to review your childhood diaries, too. For insight."

She smiles.

"I will deliver them whenever I find them."

"How about this week?" Dr. Hall sits across from me in a chair that matches the couch.

I notice she matches the couch and chair, too. And that's curious…but I keep that thought to myself.

"More like next week. Or the next. You haven't seen my grandmother's choice method for organization. She's a 'piler'. She doesn't file anything, except for her books. They're all alphabetized by author's last name in the seven libraries in her house."

"I see." My doctor is reading my journal pages again, so I settle back to wait to see what will happen next. This is new territory for me, sitting with a shrink.

My grandmother does keep everything, and with me being absent for the last eighteen months, I know she did not recycle the newspapers or magazines—that was my job.

Her piles are now taller and the counters and rooms are filled almost to capacity, which will make my task more daunting. After my grandfather died, she started this habit of keeping things. Everything.

Dr. Hall writes in her spiral-bound tablet that she rests on top of the chair's padded arm. Since she's composing her observation inside her head before she writes, I can hear what she's thinking before she speaks or writes. I know she just wrote:

Tess has a very vivid imagination.

[Morse code message: FOLLOW]

My grandmother sleeps during the day like I do. She's tucked under a mound of handmade quilts despite the flames jumping high in the fireplace across the room. I lean against the door jam and watch gray raindrops slide down the window panes. When I return my gaze to her, she's awake and smiling.

"I'm so glad you are here with me." She holds a fragile hand out to me.

"Me, too." I approach and perch on the edge of her brass bed, holding her cold hand in mine.

"So tell me, how are your classes?"

"Great and kind of boring, but I'll get through them."

"And the doctors?"

"Yours or mine?"

She grins at me.

"They still don't know what is causing my Mr. Toad's wild dreams." I cover her hand with both of mine to warm hers. "How are you feeling? I'm worried for you."

"Good and bad—sometimes at the same time, but what else can I expect at my age?"

"It's not your age. You have never been old or acted old."

"I know. Cancer is not selective or kind to anyone…" My grandmother looks out at the rain sheets and frowns.

I know she doesn't like the rain. She misses her sunny days at the beach.

I don't like the rain, either and would prefer to see fat snowflakes falling from the clouds and covering up the ugly, melting snow that is now peppered black due to collecting a season's worth of cinders.

"What can we do for fun, today? Do you want to play Gin Rummy? Or should I read to you?"

"How about you retrieve one of my photo albums?" She points to her floor-to-ceiling bookshelf on the west side of the bedroom. "I want to show you something."

I walk pass her bureau covered with dusty curios and an antique bottle of perfume that she never wears, anymore. Its essence fills the air with a familiar citrus scent: clean and light, a fragrance reminding me of her, of home, and my mom.

Maybe it is my mother's perfume bottle that my grandmother keeps.

"Grandma? Sometimes, I feel like Mom is here with us."

"I can feel her presence, too."

I touch a slim gold wristwatch. "Is this Mom's?"

"Yes."

I want to ask her more about why my mother went missing, but I'm afraid I'll upset her. I know she misses her as much as I do and in her delicate state, I figure that I'll keep the questions to myself until I'm home a bit longer.

Next to my grandmother's perfume bottles, a tarnished, silver-handle hairbrush is deliberately placed at the feet of Virgin Mary, a twelve-inch porcelain statue wearing a white robe.

My grandmother started to lose her hair due to chemotherapy, but when she moved her hairbrush under Mary's watch, her hair began to grow back despite of the fact she was only half way through her treatments. This interpretation of Jesus' Mother sculptured by a Portuguese artist is buried beneath my grandmother's necklaces. I touch one of the many delicate strands that hang around her neck and trace them down to their gold charms, lockets, and colorful beads, spilling into a shiny pool at her feet.

Every night for dinner, my grandmother insists on dressing up in one of her best dresses and selects a different necklace to wear. She always looks quite regal in her formal dress and jewels, adding a hairpiece to make her taller. She never wears the frumpy dresses that old ladies in the states do. Her dresses are form-fitting with a low décolletage, three-quarter sleeves or even sleeveless. My grandma still has great skin, which has not betrayed her like her body is starting to do now. She claims it was her lifelong diet of fresh fruit, vegetables, and seafood.

Due to my lack of any solid sleep plus my laziness, I'm lucky if I change my clothes for days. That's what jeans are for, right? I reason with myself to justify my apathetic and unfashionable persona.

I stand before her tall bookshelves with hundreds of books; some are as old as she.

"I thought I read a lot…"

Behind me, I can hear her laugh. It is one of my favorite sounds.

My hand touches the gold-embossed titles of the books. In my head, I make a list of these new titles to read and as I linger on one novel, I can instantly hear the story being read to me inside my head—just like an audio book.

The words come out from the spine, through my hand, up my arm, and into my head. By moving my finger horizontally across the book's spine right to left, I can jump chapters. I can't wait to tell my doctors about this new talent. My college years will really fly with my new super ability to "speed read" without opening a book.

"No. Up higher." My grandmother interrupts my experiment. "On the top shelf."

I climb up on the counter to reach the requested leather photo album.

"Not that one, the next, green leather one."

How she remembers what is inside of each of these tomes that all look alike, I'll never know, but to think of it maybe that is how I'm acing my new classes without spending much time on my readings. Maybe I've inherited my photographic memory from her.

With the album tucked under my elbow, I jump off the counter down onto the old Persian rug, which softens the thud of my ungraceful landing.

"Be careful!" My grandmother shakes her brunette hair now streaked with white. "I need you."

I crawl into bed beside her. "I'm still here."

"You turn the pages."

And I do.

On the very first page, my three-year-old grandmother is dressed up like a porcelain doll in a white lacey dress with puffy short sleeves and a wide bonnet tied around her neck. Her hat has slid off her dark, curled-for-the-photo hair. She wears black, ankle-high, buttoned boots and is not posing for the camera like her big sister, but has jumped a few inches off the ground.

The camera has caught her true spirit. This rebel, later to be known to me as my grandmother, tosses a wicked smile at the cameraman, who I'm guessing was her father. I do wish that I had known her when she was a little girl. For even a toddler, she looks as if she is scheming something in that little head of hers. She would have been fun to have as a friend.

The two of them, my grandmother and her father, had their own secret society. She was the son he never had and in rebellion of her frilly, daily wear sponsored by her uptown mother, my grandmother was happy to turn into her father's son whenever he wanted to go fishing, hunting, or kick the soccer ball around the courtyard.

She adored him and told me that she wanted to grow up to be the next, chief of police just like him…until he was killed on duty when she was sixteen.

From that time forward, she simply adopted his habits to keep him near in spirit. She learned to drink like a man, smoke cigars, drive a three-speed transmission truck when few other women knew how, and perfected her aim, knocking cans off the jetty at the beach with his old pistol.

My grandmother also possesses the same unrestrained love of books that he did. I look back over this library in her bedroom. Many of these treasures were his, she told me as I returned an armful of titles after devouring them one weekend. One of the benefits of not being able to sleep is the opportunity of free time to read all night long and in Portuguese. My world of books is wide open now with so many new authors to know from below the equator. Paulo Coelho, I first read his book, *The Alchemist*, in English and then in Portuguese, and moved onto Luis Fernando Verissimo, Martha Medeiro, and Rachel de Queiroz—

My grandmother taps the page to make me turn it.

I turn to the next page.

The pages of her old photo album are black construction paper heavy with sepia-tone photographs that are framed in white borders. Here are my grandmother's memories held in place by little black paper triangles and glued on all four corners of each photo.

"This is my school...I loved school."

Some photos have slipped out of the triangular corners, but my grandmother is already lovingly placing them back into their delicate place.

"This is the house where I lived on the beach." She smiles broadly at telling me this again.

Broad leafy palms tower above her sprawling beach house and shade the rooms from the constant sun. Fortress-like walls surround the backyard's gardens and the aquamarine pool stretches out to their sugar-white beach against the bay. She taps on each picture as in an attempt to bring back the past. I have heard her audio captions that she has narrated before, but I relish any time I have left with her.

The next square photo she touches is a portrait of a small yellow mutt.

"This is my dog, *Cachorro*."

He sits on top of the worn stairs that look familiar to me, almost as if I have sat there, too beside him.

"Doesn't *'cachorro'* mean 'dog' in Portuguese?"

"Yes, but how do you know?" She squirms to pull the pink paisley quilt out from under me and move higher, up under her arms.

"Oh, I picked up a few words here and there, mainly when you yell at me in Portuguese."

"I never yell at you. I'm just loud." She motions for me to turn the pages faster. "There's someone I want you to see." My grandmother stops me after the fourth page and points to a professional portrait of a young woman, who looks like her. She is in her twenties. I look closer. No, she is older than me, probably late twenties, maybe thirty. It's hard to tell.

"This is the last time I saw my sister. We went to the photographer's studio together that afternoon. I have her photo and she has mine."

"How come I didn't know I had an aunt? Is she still alive?"

"She stayed behind. I was the one who left and she was mad at me. Probably still is."

"She can't be after all these years. Let's call her."

"You don't know my sister. Besides, she doesn't have a phone. She's afraid they'll find her if she did."

"You should write her then." I pull the album closer to study her face. "Or email her." She looks like us. I ache whenever I think about family or my lack of any immediate relatives still alive, except my grandma. No siblings and in the immediate family count, I'm missing both parents, both grandfathers, and my other grandmother—

"Hand me another pillow, will you?" My grandmother sits up taller against the brass rails of her bed.

"I've written to her, but she doesn't answer. Wouldn't answer email, either."

"No Internet access?" I give her another fat pillow from behind me. "Do you want me to try?"

"No, you have your studies and you're right, no Internet. I just wish I could see her one last time…"

"Don't be talking like that. You have lots of time and I expect you to be there for my college graduation whenever that will be." I squeeze her hand gently. "How about some tea?"

She closes the photo album and then her eyes—as if deep in a dream.

I lean in to check to see if she is still breathing.

Her eyes fly open and scare me backwards. "My tea, right?"

"Yes, Grandmother, I'll make your *yerba maté*."

[Morse code message: COMEHOME]

The boil of rain on the roof and the pearl-gray sheets falling outside my bedroom window turns my study session into another nap session.

I'll never graduate from college at this rate.

My queen-size bed is loaded with various, body-hugging pillows including a stack of standard sleep pillows plus thick layers of handmade quilts, making it the perfect afternoon study spot or in today's case, a *siesta* session. While I'm afraid to sleep any time now because my nighttime dreams are now finding their way into my daytime snoozes, although I do find myself nodding off behind my geology textbook. I bet most undergrad students do fall asleep if rocks and dirt aren't their majors. I figure a little nap of fifteen minutes will energize, not scare me, so I let my eyes close.

I feel myself falling…and in my dream, a man about my age is beckoning me into a nighttime street party, a happy celebration, and for some reason, I'm not afraid of this bronzed god. He motions me to follow his wide shoulders through the thick crowd and walks with a purpose, so I follow him beneath spectators sitting in bleachers that climb twelve rows high.

We step around others in this jovial mob.

At the edge of the boulevard's curb, I teeter on my tiptoes beside him, looking left as everyone else does. I study his kind face, full lips, and mesmerizing, dark brown eyes speckled with gold.

He smiles.

That did it. I'll follow him anywhere if he keeps smiling at me.

Through my feet, up my legs, and into my chest, I can feel the vibration of a fife and drum band heading this way. I turn to watch the parade in front of me and absorb the intoxicating percussion song that the drummers hammer on their drums.

Yellow, pink, and silver metallic confetti falls from the sky like snow as a very tan man dressed as a Roman gladiator tosses handfuls from his painted wooden Trojan horse. Nearly naked women covered only in feathers that suffice as tiny swimsuits shimmy on stages moved by unseen cars beneath them—my Google brain immediately tells me this fact, but I only believe when the skirts of the floats bellow up and the cars' tires are revealed to show how these dance stages are transported. I wonder if my prescription pills are making me more intelligent or just providing the chemical mix for these unexplainable dreams.

Just this week, Dr. Hall had added Ambien to my ever-growing list of meds.

Their tall headdresses made from violet and chartreuse plumes make these dancers look like Amazon women. This must be where the Las Vegas showgirls get their ideas for their costumes. All of these brunette females are sun-kissed and dance in impossible knee-high, silver boots. I need to get a pair of those boots.

Both the locals and the tourists are spellbound by the energy of the endless parade that snakes down the palm-lined boulevard.

I definitely am not in Colorado, anymore.

Next, strolling musicians tweet repeatedly on their red candy whistles to introduce their float, a gigantic, inflatable balloon in the shape of a black baby's head with a blue bonnet tied tight under his chubby chin. He has a blue pacifier sticking out of his mouth and hangs in the muggy night air above the parade crowd.

After the balloon float, a synchronized dancing group of men, wearing only baggy camouflaged pants tucked into their military boots, stomps down the road to make their music. Their faces and chests are as coppery as the female dancers'.

What do these people eat to make them so fit and beautiful?

I need to eat something in one of my dreams. Maybe I would be fortunate enough to inherit this side effect of a perfect physique with just one meal.

Float after float is a display of joy and an abandonment of restrain. The crowd's roar is indicative of their fierce and loyal support for their favorite dancer troupe. The rousing music pulls me deeper into this dream state where I can now only see straight ahead. My peripheral vision is compromised for some unknown reason.

My ears work, though. I eavesdrop on the people standing behind me to figure out where I am.

"Hun? How long does this here parade go on for?" A woman yells.

"This here parade? Or do ya'll mean the Carnival part?"

He must be from Texas, too. They're speaking English, so maybe I am in the states, but the other voices around me are conversing in Portuguese.

"Carnival!"

"Tonight's only Shrove Tuesday—"

The sonic boom of a silvery shower of fireworks blot his next words and light up the dark sky.

Due to the humidity of the night, sweat drips down my spine. I bump into strangers as I try to dance in the small space allocated, but everyone just smiles and dances, too.

The good-looking male, the one who I'm following smiles at me, again and cracks open a Bohemia beer for me. I have never tasted one of these brews before, yet figure I should try it and clink my longneck bottle against his. He looks familiar and is very easy to gaze at, so I stare and figure it's a dream, I can't really get drunk, right? Or in trouble with him?

He is still smiling.

I could be wrong. I might get in trouble with him.

"Thank you. *Gracias. Danke. Merci. Obrigada.*" I think if I cover my gratitude in a couple of languages, I might get one right. I have no idea where I am.

He wraps his arm over my shoulder and pulls me close. "*Estou feliz que você está em casa.*"

He just said: "I'm glad you're home."

I feign I don't know how to speak his language and simply return his smile, but I do understand him. Where in the world am I? New Orleans? Sweet. I'll have to get a bite of King Cake before I awake.

"*Olá* Tino!" A man pushes through the crowd and pops in right in front of us. "Meet us on the beach later tonight!" He says this invitation in Portuguese, however, my brain hears it in English. As quickly as he appeared, the mob swallows him.

Tino? What kind of name is that?

He turns to me and says in Portuguese, "You'll come with me, right?"

Tino smiles that smile I know I could never say "No" to.

[Morse code message: RETURNSOON]

I stand at the pharmacy counter of the university's hospital. The shiny floor of the corridor irritates my over-stimulated brain, so I look up to be distracted by the doctors, residents, and nurses scuttling by. They're all absorbed in the conversations on their phones, texting as they walk, or talking to a real person, who is trying to keep pace with their racing strides. When did our world get in such a hurry? What's the race for, again? Is there a prize for the fastest?

I pull my mirrored sunglasses down off the top of my head to shield myself from the frantic movement all around me. The newly-minted pharmacist is pouring a steady stream of blue pills into a five-inch tall, plastic orange bottle. He applies the printed label to its front and offers the bottle to me with a slight smile. He's used to adding to my collection of pills that I eat daily. I think I am up to taking seven pills a day.

"Feel better…"

I'm not sure if he meant that as a statement or a question.

My medical file is supposed to be confidential, but he's on the inside and probably has inkling about my case or at least has his own interpretation, which I just heard he said inside his head: "She's a hypochondriac."

Did he really say that? I did hear him clearly, inside my head, as if he spoke out loud. I better check the pages of side effects for my prescriptions, tonight. Maybe this is how I acquired this augmented auditory ability of being able to hear what others are thinking.

He hands me the white prescription bag with the cautionary pharmaceutical inserts already placed inside.

I grab it and march into the throng of people all dressed in matching medical blue scrubs, rushing along with the occasional doctor in her white coat. Through the double wooden doors that have witnessed a century of students come and go, I exit and step into the refreshing air of late winter. The blur of colors and din of babble inside were brewing into a big headache for me.

"Hey Tess!"

This unforgettable male voice makes me do an about-face from the direction of my next class.

"I thought that might be you! My parents told me you transferred."

I smile at my old friend from kindergarten.

Nile looks good, grown up, and now fits into his once gangly body. He flashes me a sheepish grin like he has a secret he has to tell someone and usually does—usually somebody like me.

"Yeah, nothing like transferring in the middle of my sophomore year." I hug my textbooks against my bag of prescription drugs and hope he doesn't ask too many questions about why I am home again at my grandmother's. "You'll have to come by sometime. My grandmother would love to see you."

"Sure. This weekend?" His clear blue eyes reflect happiness. Nile is always happy—never a negative word drops from his lips, at least any I ever heard him spill.

"Call first." I write my grandmother's house phone number on the palm of his hand. She is one of the only people I know who still has a land line and a rotary phone.

"Never did and never will." He moves in closer.

I know he knows our number, but I want to touch him again—after all this time.

"Yeah, I always liked that about you. You just do what you want."

Nile kisses my forehead and lingers like he's inhaling me. "I'm glad you're home." He heads in the opposite direction that I need to go.

I want to follow him and his gorgeous messy mop of sandy blond hair down the crowded courtyard of the campus. I want to be with him, again, but I did heard what he said to himself about me, about us, and think I can wait.

I look up through the bare trees at the sky. There's no sign of spring as promised three days ago by the Virgin Mary calendar that hangs in my grandmother's kitchen. In black ink, the words 'Spring Equinox' did make me think about putting away my much-loved, ski sweaters.

Spring might wake up soon or not. I do live a mile above sea level. The matted lawn on campus offers a slight promise of the upcoming season with small patches of green. All around campus, winter's snowbanks linger in the shadows of the towering, tawny-colored, brick buildings with only one daffodil pushing forward into the diffused sunshine.

Across the wide sidewalk, a toddler breaks free from her mother's hand and races to the solitary flower. She squats and pats its yellow head like it's a puppy.

I stop my hurry to class and watch her cheery antics. To be a child again, living in the untainted wonderment that the world offers daily, although watching her makes me miss my mother. I was about the little girl's age when my mother delivered me to my grandparent's house in the states. For the next three years until I was six, she would come and go until one Sunday when she didn't come home. My memory of her face is slowing fading from my mind's eye. Tears form at my acknowledgment of such a reality, yet don't fall.

My sport watch beeps as a reminder to get to class on time. Ever since my sleep has been compromised, I have to rely on three alarm clocks in my bedroom and two watches on my body to get me to where I need to be. As I stride faster, my bottle of one hundred pills jingles against the cold plastic inside my winter coat.

I smile at the new mom, who waits and watches her tiny daughter.

She smiles back at me.

There is an all-encompassing quietness across campus that now cloaks the plaza. The buzzing of students has ceased as they are now tucked away in classrooms or the "hallow halls of higher learning" what my grandmother calls college. She only completed the eighth grade and remains mad at her parents' decision to make her start working at the age of fourteen.

My ankle-high, snow boots slap against the shoveled sidewalk. I never bother to zip up the backs, so they fit sloppily on my feet and feel more like bedroom slippers. Whenever my grandmother sees or hears me running out the door like this, she yells at me in Portuguese, "You're going to break your neck!"

I can remember her yelling the same sentiment when I was a little girl and paraded around in my grandfather's black leather loafers or my mother's platform shoes made out of cork. I still have her shoes, but I don't wear them.

We shadow each other, the toddler girl and her mother, and me, all walking in the same direction across the wide cement pathway. The little girl meanders in lazy, half-circles while her mother races toward their destination, slowing when she realizes her daughter has paused again to exam a crack in the sidewalk.

I stop and pop two of the little blue pills without water. These chalky pills stick to my throat, causing me to cough and gag. I swallow three times quickly in succession to make sure both of them are down where they are supposed to be.

The toddler looks up at me with concern beaming in her large, doll-like blue eyes framed by thick blonde lashes. Her pink hood of her winter coat slides off her silky hair.

My medicine moves down where it's supposed to go. I head up the cement stairs to my next class, but turn and wave to the little girl.

She waves to me with a blade of green grass clutched in her tiny fist.

As I enter the building, I touch the label inside my coat and can hear the dosage read to me inside my head: "One pill in the morning."

The male voice does sounds like the pharmacist. There's that eerie aural talent again, working without my request. I realize now that my excessive dosage is not going to help my restless sleep patterns, but maybe I'm ahead of the medicine game now by taking a double dose.

I check my watch.

I can't take the elevator as I'm convinced it will plummet to the basement with me trapped inside and I don't need a panic attack right now. If I run up the five flights of steps, I might make it to my class on time. I race across the black-and-white, square tiles and charge the stairs. The next hour and a half will be spent in the dark with a professor almost as old as the rocks he discusses. Professor Wilson is one of those teachers, who definitely knows his subject material, however, he is not the best at relaying the information in an engaging manner.

Nile will probably ace this class since he also loves dirt, rocks, and especially natural disasters. He calls me "volatile" like a volcano and then howls at his own joke. His white suburban upbringing has left him craving danger and has always wanted to switch his major to volcanology. His doctor dad was not very forthcoming with his support of such a deviation in the family tradition and refuses to accept or believe that his only son would make such a departure from his expected destiny in life.

I slide into the one-sided desk and loosen my scarf; unbutton my winter coat and lean back to snooze, hoping my dreams will stay at bay or at least the new medicine will mask the darker moments from my memory when I awake from my nap.

High in this fish bowl auditorium, I look over the heads of brand new college students sitting perfectly erect with pens held ready or with both hands cupped over their three-pound laptops to absorb via fingertips whatever they need to to maintain their 4.0 grade-point averages. Their undergraduate degree is only the first stop on their life plan and perfect scores are mandatory to proceed. This is what I get for transferring. I'm in a freshman's geology class and thought I could slip by and graduate with an art degree in Industrial Design without anyone noticing my missing, yet required science class, but this university's administration did.

Nestled deep into the chair, I pull my legs under me as the ceiling lights in the rafters go from harsh to black. Professor Wilson is preparing to show us another PowerPoint presentation of his recent vacation where he spent the entire week walking the beaches, collecting seashells, rocks, and probably even sand. Without knowing it, he has created the perfect environment for me to snooze. His presentation begins with a panoramic view of gentle, rolling waves calling me to sleep.

I have always liked naps.

Maybe I do belong in a country where *siestas* are the accepted norm.

[Morse code message: FAMILY]

..-. .- - .

Nile and my grandmother are washing the dinner dishes and are holding their conversation high above the clattering of plates and silverware.

I went to the laundry room to get more clean dishtowels out of the dryer, but now here I pause in the foyer before what my grandmother calls her "magic mirror". As a little girl, she would challenge me to ask a question. I always wanted to know when my mother would return, though because I was afraid of the answer, I would instead pose an inquiry about a possible birthday or Christmas present or ask about my grade on my weekly spelling test at school.

Sometimes, I would just ask about tomorrow's weather.

My grandmother would concentrate upon the reflective surface until a vision appeared to her.

I could never see anything.

"The magic mirror is dim, but I think it's predicting we'll see snow showers by morning."

"Grandma! It's August!"

But sure enough, the next morning our mountain town would be frosted in a thin glaze of beautiful snow. All of town's roofs and its quiet roads would be all dusted in white.

My grandmother would wake me with a steaming cup of hot cocoa, the spicy version with cinnamon, cayenne, and a vanilla bean floating on top just like her mother and my mother used to make. Together, we watched the last of the flakes from the freak snowstorm tumble out of the white sky and float onto the surprised, summer grass.

I think this is where and when my love of winter began, the anticipation of something not yet seen, but felt and remembered forever—despite its impermanence. I found it difficult to sleep whenever my grandmother made such a wintry prediction. I loved the chilly morning, the shock of cold from the hardwood floor on my feet, the chill my body felt when I rose to dress for school. I barely ate any bites of my strawberry-jellied toast before dashing out into this magical land of pure snow and its expansive whiteness where I felt nothing bad could happen, trying to hold onto to it before it, too disappeared before my eyes.

Later, I learned my grandmother had a barometer in the kitchen. This weather device did tell her whenever a storm was coming, but she firmly believed in her clairvoyance talents. I did, too because her predictions were correct too many times, both the good and the bad.

When my grandfather never returned, I felt then that my mother might be really gone, too, but oftentimes, I find myself peering into the magic mirror, pass the tallest Virgin Mary statue to see if I could see my mother…like tonight, again.

My grandmother's magic mirror is an antique oval that my mother bought her for her birthday a long time ago. The edge has tarnished with time. Whenever I look into its reflection, I hope to see my young mother, but only see myself.

For years, the mirror leaned on a table inside the foyer until one summer when I helped my grandfather build the altar my grandmother repeatedly had requested. From out of the hall closet in the foyer, we removed the door, reworked the frame, giving it an arched entrance and created a Virgin Mary shrine with a low counter for my grandmother's expanding collection. She insisted her magic mirror be tucked behind all of her Marys to double the protection for our house, reflecting and increasing the number of Marys at the front door. That was ten summers ago when I fell in love with power tools and unknowingly chose my college degree in designing and building things, or 'Industrial Design' as most universities call the program.

During the summers, my grandmother watched as my grandfather and I built my mother a garden fountain in the backyard and that same year, we cobbled together two, wooden chairs like the ones lining the front porches at mountain lodges. Instead of wood, we made them out of old classic skis minus the bindings.

The next summer, we worked with mosaic tiles and built her small tables to complete her summertime sanctuary.

Our grand and last project together was the completion of a sixteen-foot long, picnic table. We would work in the backyard, cutting, sanding, and staining until the first, persistent snow arrived, which was usually over Labor Day weekend, and it stayed on the ground and our work. This early change in weather sent us inside the garage or sometimes, if our project was small enough, to the kitchen table and in the way of my grandmother as she tried to cook dinner.

After the snow arrived to stay for months, each weekend my grandfather and I would tinker with sketches of how to improve any kitchen gadgets that had made my grandmother grumble. She became wary of talking out loud too often because before she knew it, we would have the faulty item dissected into pieces all over the kitchen table.

My grandfather always said, "This is the best way to find out what is wrong and how to fix it. You studied how it was put together."

Maybe my doctors could do this with me—to figure out what is causing my vivid dreams that are now infringing on my daytime reality. I feel like I just step back and forth between this world and that other world, but I do not dare say this to anyone until I know for sure that this is happening. I question though, who will believe me?

Back in my pre-teen years, I spent much of my free time around the kitchen table with my grandfather to block my emotions of missing my mother. One Sunday night, my mother simply left and never returned. At first, we all waited for her to come home, but after almost a year of my crying and questioning, my grandparents told me she couldn't come home, anymore. I didn't understand. How could a mother not come back to her daughter? They eventually let me believe that she had died. I was only seven when this news was told to me. I didn't want to understand what they were telling me. She died? How and when—I was never told nor did I ask. I need to know now and ask my grandmother's magic mirror this question as I wanted to do as a little girl, but didn't.

"Is my mother alive?"

The mirror brightens and glows a golden hue. I reach to touch where the mirror is the brightest, wishing that it is my grandmother just is playing with me, but there is no one near me.

I can still hear her and Nile making the after-dinner racket from the kitchen.

Is this my answer?

Yes?

But where is she then?

I rub my eyes, again and look into the mirror. It retains its golden shine, but the edges are haloed in a rather, silvery hue. I'm taking it in all as a "Yes." Later, as a teen, I did extensive research with the coroner's office in the state and eventually the country's record of death certificates—none could show any evidence that my mother died, at least not in this country. I feel as if she's still alive…and I still cling to this hope.

I don't care that she has been gone a very long time. I want her home with me. Home.

I should ask my grandmother about what she sees now…she has been very accurate about her divine epiphanies and too often predicted the ephemeral history of a relative. I remember listening to my grandmother once long ago as I perched on my knees on the top step of the stairs, my ear between the smooth wood baluster to hear her better. She asked the magic mirror about my grandfather's adamant intent to return to the old country one more time. His plane was schedule to leave in less than two hours, so I felt her panic when she asked the question, "Should my husband be in a plane, tonight?"

My grandmother and my grandfather exchanged heated words after he refused to listen to what the mirror showed and advised.

"I saw first gray smoke, and then red flames shooting through its thick curtain. You can't go. You shouldn't go."

She never saw her husband, again.

Since that black year, my grandmother refuses to board or even look at a plane overhead, fearing she will see it drop like a rock and explode. I didn't tell her when I was coming back from California. I just showed up, so she wouldn't worry about my flight. I toyed with the idea of taking the bus or train, but figured she needed me and I needed her sooner than that. Besides, I would have probably fallen asleep lulled by the purr and would have awoken in Columbus, Ohio; at least on a plane, they check the seats to make sure everyone gets off the flight or at least I think they do.

"Tess?" Nile yells from the direction of my bedroom. "Are you coming?"

"In a minute!" I pick up a stick match and survey the collection of red glass votives for a brand new wick.

These days, I find myself unable to sleep at night, suspended in half-conscious sleep, the dreaded waiting state before my dreams take me away to another dimension, not allowing me to sleep, but to flee constantly from danger.

My nighttime rambles are getting quite graphic to the point that they wake me straight up in bed and then going back to sleep is completely out of the question. I don't like having to spend rest of the whole night alone. I read two or three books a night all in Portuguese and still can't find comfort or an escape from my nightmares and am scared even when surrounded with books that can usually bring me comfort and an escape...I did finish many of my grandfather's books and I didn't think I woke my grandmother when I entered her bedroom to retrieve another book in the middle of the night, but she told me otherwise, the next morning.

She's worried about me, too; I can see it in her eyes.

I needed to find another distraction to get me through the night. Before dinner, I had asked Nile to stay the night.

He smiled his big boy grin, like he would say, "No."

Despite the long year and a half apart and the thousand miles that separated us, we fell back into our relationship. I'm happy to have someone solid, someone real to hold me here in this dimension.

My grandmother has glued a piece of sandpaper to the counter and placed a handful of stick matches in an empty votive. I light a small white candle. As always, I light the first candle to pray for my grandmother's continued resilience to her disease and a quick recovery. The second candle that I light is in gratitude for Nile. Lastly, I watch the brand new wick burn and state my wish to my mother: "Return to me."

I head down the hallway and round the corner to my bedroom. I guess going to get the dishtowels took longer than drying the rest of the dishes.

Nile is waiting for me outside my door.

"I'm scared to sleep alone."

He picks me up and carries me to my room without any additional explanation.

Even with my grandmother just up the stairs in her room and his body next to mine, I just can't hold onto to the fact that I'm protected and untouchable by this iniquity presence that slips under my locked door and through the cracks of my windows.

Yesterday, I found a roll of gray duct tape in my grandfather's dusty garage and taped the cracks around my four, bedroom windows shut. Our garage has accumulated dust because my grandmother avoids it—it used to be his space, her husband's, yet because it reminds me of him, I go in and wander around the quiet space and remember him or sometimes borrow his things like duct tape.

Nile delivers me inside my bedroom. "I like your new window treatments. Gray, it's a cool, calming color."

I sock him in the arm.

He fakes grave injury, grabs his bicep, stumbles across the room to my bed, and falls into the deep layers of the blankets, another tactic of mine to keep me from time traveling or whatever I'm doing at night.

"Good thing, you aren't a theatre major." I jump onto the bed landing on my knees.

"What? Are you saying I would starve?"

"Good thing, I'm such a good cook. I could save you."

Nile surrounds my waist with his long arms and buries his head into my stomach. "It's noisy down here. Guess your stomach likes your cooking, too."

I hold him tight to me. The standing agreement in my grandmother's house is that I'm the cook and she's the dishwasher. Nile helps both of us since he eats the most.

"I don't think I can sleep like this." Nile's voice is muffled.

I smile and release my hold on my *noivo*. "Oh no, here I go, again." I plop back against the pillows.

"Now, what's happening inside that pretty head of yours?"

"You sound just like my grandfather. That's what he always used to say when he saw me thinking."

Now my mind is automatically substituting Portuguese words instead of English, but I don't voice this discovery to Nile because I can't believe it. I shake my head. It's a fluke, a word I probably picked up from my grandmother.

I point and click my remote at the stereo cabinet: Neil Young sings the song, *Cinnamon Girl*.

"Is that an automatic album player?"

"Yeah, it's set up like a CD player and can play six albums."

"Doesn't that kind of ruin the whole experience of getting up and down whenever you want to listen to a new album?"

"I've gotten soft."

"Lazy is a better word, my Cinnamon Girl."

Nile is back to calling me his "Cinnamon Girl" as often as he calls me by my first name. He loves Neil Young as much as I do, so we either play albums from my mom's old collection or he sings to me.

"You're not going to play Neil's vinyl over and over again tonight, are you?"

I do have a habit of being perfectly content to play the same album or a song for hours—it's comforting and puts my mind and body at rest that is until my grandmother or my boyfriend begs for a change. My grandmother likes to listen to symphonies or her "happy tropical music" as she calls it. When I asked her, "Like what?"

She replied, "*Escala Palladio.*"

Of course, I didn't recognize the band, but do know their sound. My mind automatically plays a track for me like the Internet radio station, Pandora, would if you just type in the band's name. In my case, I just think of the band

and here comes the song, playing between my ears. This is another new talent that I do like. Maybe it's my drugs or maybe I just have a good memory.

Luckily, Nile likes the same kind of music I like—even though he calls me "old school" with my ancient album collection of Cream, Traffic, Joan Baez, Carly Simon, and Fleetwood Mac. He knows, however, they were my mother's albums and are one of my few remaining connections to her, so he doesn't hassle me when I get stuck on one and play it for four times in a row.

Tonight, he has brought a few of his CDs.

I flip through the short stack: Train, Snow Patrol, Thievery Corporation, The Dave Matthews Band, and Moby. I could listen to Moby all night long.

He takes away the Moby CD that I clutch to my chest because he knows what I am thinking. We've been together for a while and along with this time comes unspoken familiarity. He knows I want to play this CD at least eight times tonight.

"It's going to be a long night if you insist on the same CD."

I sit back against the headboard and reach for the closest pillow to hug it across my stomach.

"Hey, that's my spot." He grabs my pillow, places his head in my lap, and stares up at me. "So, tell me what's going on? Why the sudden invite? Are you still in love with me?"

"Of course I am." I hold up his heavy head to kiss him. "Nile, I'm not only dreaming in Portuguese, but I can read it and now speak it, too."

"Oh my brainy girl." Nile reaches up and tousles my hair. "Soon, you'll be too smart for me and I'll bore you."

"Never." I squirm down beside him. Although I do notice my vocabulary shooting up a bit each day when I use twenty-five cent words when the easier ones would suffice and now I sound a lot like my American Literature Professor. I wonder if any of my prescription drugs could have aided with my new, instant ability of my brain to act as a Thesaurus on call. At dinner, Nile called me a "maniac" or a "Whirling Dervish" since I'm flying one minute and crashing the next.

My bare feet stick off the side of the bed.

Nile reaches for my goose down feather comfort, the heaviest one on the bed, to cover my toes. I don't even have to ask him, he just knows. Maybe he can read minds, too...no, I know he's just a considerate guy that I'm very lucky to land, again. Chances like this rarely come around twice in life.

"Okay, besides kissing you all night long, what else am I expected to do?" Nile piles my long hair onto the top of my head. He uses both hands to create his bouffant masterpiece, but the conditioner that I use makes my hair slippery and the thick strands tumble down. He gives up.

"A foot massage would be nice." I put my ice-cold soles on top of his bare feet.

He shrieks.

My grandmother pounds her floor with the kitchen broom's wooden handle. Our household tool is seldom used for sweeping, but is often used for sending messages back and forth between the people upstairs and those below.

"It's only Nile, Grandma!" I yell to the ceiling.

"Only if you bring them up to room temperature." Nile gets out of bed and digs in my top dresser drawer. "What's wrong with you? You never had cold feet in your entire life."

He exchanges a look between me and a two-foot tall, ceramic statue of Virgin Mary on top of my dresser. She's one of my favorite Marys, dressed in a turquoise hooded cape worn over her tangerine-colored gown. "Why is Mary everywhere at your grandmother's house?"

He throws a thick pair of rainbow-striped, toe socks at me. "You don't really wear these out in public, do you?"

"My grandmother is convinced Mary has kept her safe all of these years. Besides, I think she's beautiful. I want a turquoise cape and orange dress like hers someday."

"What? To match your toe socks?"

I send him a sweet smile.

"I'll see what I can do." He charges the bed and belly flops next to me. The old bed doesn't take the landing of his six-foot-four, two hundred and twenty pound body very well and it shudders across the wooden planks.

My grandmother thumps my ceiling from upstairs, again.

Nile giggles. "She loves me."

"We both do."

He leans in for a kiss that I know will last a long time.

I can see it in his eyes. Actually, I hear his idea first inside his head. I didn't realize guys thought about their actions, their next moves, I just thought it was all hormone-driven, but Nile is definitely not "all guys". Either way, I won't say no to any of Nile's ideas, tonight, but only after my foot massage.

[Morse code message: FATE]

.... .. -.. . ...-.

After getting quite dusty from climbing around on my hands and knees in my grandmother's crowded attic, I found the box of my childhood diaries. By the looks of my drawings and the few words, I probably started keeping my memories when I was in first grade—about the same time my mother disappeared permanently from my life. My drawings were a way to deal with my unsettled thoughts and all of my questions stagnating in my little head without answers plus I'm sure my vocabulary at the age of six was a bit limited, so I articulated my feelings through pictures.

Four of my grandmother's twelve dining room chairs are being stored up here and all of the seats are covered in the same plastic when they were shipped from the furniture store. I pull the plastic sheet off one of the chair and there is still more plastic wrapped loosely around its seat. She leaves the plastic on everything and it drives me nuts and this includes the lampshades on the lamps downstairs, which are probably a fire hazard, but she never turns on the lights, so maybe not. Plastic rug runners are all over the carpet in the living room, the room we rarely enter. Like most houses, it appears to be a trophy room or a museum in that you can look inside, yet cannot enter. My grandmother told me that these plastic runners between the hallway and the living room and dining room are like directional paths to her. To me, they're like treacherous roads when I run through the house in my socks.

Under the gable window where I sit on the plastic-covered seat of the dining room chair, sunlight streams onto my lap. I paged through a dozen entries from my diary, remembering what I tried so hard to forget. Each night and sometimes even during the day, I'm being reminded of my past life or perhaps of my second life that I could have lived or am currently living. No wonder I'm so tired in this life—no time to sleep in either. Dr. Hall is going to love this trip through my memory.

I feel a clunk under my feet. My grandmother is hitting her bedroom ceiling with the kitchen's broom. She must have heard me rearranging the attic and knows of my location, but then again, she always knows where I am. I stomp the floor to respond and kick up dust particles that flicker across the beams of sun.

With a tall stack of diaries clenched in my arms, I round the circular staircase to the landing outside her room.

"Grandma! Look what I found!"

Now I sound like I am only six—or like Nile when he's excited.

She waves me to come inside her bedroom. I have to waltz around my white crocheted, hammock strung out between the wooden pillars in her bedroom. Last weekend when I awoke in a pool of sweat and twisted sheets, I surrendered to this new remedy to cool my body down: lounging in a hammock in a skimpy nightgown. Since my grandmother is weak due to her condition and stays in bed most of the day, I had tied up the string hammock in her room. She told me she had carried that hammock with her when they moved to the states.

My grandfather shook his head, asking her, "What are you going to do with a beach hammock in the snow?"

He would have been happy to see what we have had done with it now.

My grandmother had laughed as she watched me curse the P-shaped hook that fought me as I twisted its sharp point into the thick wood without any success. The wooden beams eventually worked very well to support my new napping place and habit, but I had to resort to a hammer to make the hook grip into the grain.

"Você está teimoso como eu!"

She had yelled, "You're pigheaded just like me!" This instant translation available between my ears is usually very helpful.

I tumble my diaries onto her yellow chenille bedspread and hop up on the bed beside the stack. My grandmother is anticipating the warmer days of summer the way I do my snowy weeks of winter. She had asked me to change her bedding to welcome her favorite season. I'm still holding onto winter and my inventory of quilts in case of one more cold night, but the warmer nights lately make me believe she is right, again.

"Show me something pretty." My grandmother nudges the diary closest to her.

"You're asking a lot since I was just a little kid."

She peers at the pile of old notebooks and points at a purple one. Of course, it's purple; everything I owned in my elementary-school days was purple.

I open the notebook to the center spread and there's a bridal veil with words flowing in and around the fragile fabric I had sketched.

"Oh my." My grandmother touches her forehead.

"What? You don't like my art? I told you it would be juvenile. "

"It's just that you wrote in Portuguese."

"I did?" I pick up my notebook and spin it, so I can read aloud the words written in purple pen across the entire spread and there it is: *A uniäo de Anita Maria Santiago del Regis Carmo Mão de Ferro e Cunha de Almeida Santos Abreu."*

"That's your mother's birth name. And you spelled all of her names right. How old were you when you did this? Do you remember?" She reads the first words: "A marriage of—"

"Little. Maybe Mom had told me how to spell her names."

"No, here in the states, she only let us call her Beatriz Johnson or Betty for short. No one was to know her true name."

I'm a bit stunned to ask why—why my whole family is a mystery? What had happened to my father? We never talk about him.

As if my grandmother heard my internal questioning, she responds, "Your father, too was brave like my husband and fought against the drug cartel and winning every one of his court cases until he could not, anymore." She looks tired as she sits back against the pillows. "They took down everyone that got in their way."

My sport watch sounds. Fifteen minutes to get to Dr. Halls' office. I have a feeling this conversation with my grandmother could take a long time.

"Can we talk later?" I kiss her good bye.

She nods. "But that's all I know. He divorced my daughter, so to me, he died before he did."

Oh, wow. No wonder his name is not spoken around this house.

I scoop up my diaries, race down the stairs, grabbing my Army green, canvas bag and dumping my memories, my past life, inside, and dash out of the front door. Two bikes lean against the side of the house. One night last week when I couldn't sleep, again, I decided to tune up the beach cruisers even though the nearest beach is on the Gulf of Mexico and probably more than nine hundred miles south.

My brain instantly confirms my assumption. I shake my head to stop it from processing other random thoughts like the history of the bicycle.

Most of the time, Nile thinks this new skill of mine is great, except when I know all of the answers, then he says it's annoying.

I click my helmet under my chin and jump on my pink Schwinn bike and pedal hard. The wind throws my hair back away from my neck and calms me a bit as I head to my appointment. Secured over my left shoulder and across my chest is my courier bag with my childhood diaries, which perhaps holds the answers to my mysterious dreams—if nothing else, its emblazoned pink neon, peace sign across its front makes me smile.

When I arrive, Dr. Hall is not in yet. I was able to get here on time despite the afternoon foot traffic of meandering pedestrians and their wandering dogs on long leashes or unstable tykes on trikes crisscrossing the bike trail.

I plant myself in my usual spot on Dr. Hall's couch and flip open another of my childhood diaries. There are more words written in Portuguese: *Corcovado, Tijuca, Cidade Maravilhosa, Cristo Redentor*. I do recognize the young handwriting as mine, but wonder why I wrote such words. What are these messages from my younger self to my older self? Have I always time traveled, but didn't know I was?

Dr. Hall has arrived. I can hear her muffled words coming under the closed door from the reception area. She's trying to unravel my nighttime dilemma. Even though her words are difficult to comprehend, I can tell by her tone of voice as she speaks to her assistant Sally that my situation is far from ordinary and isn't a quick fix. When I passed by the receptionist's desk just minutes ago, I saw my file folder with red words stamped on the outside. On the manila folder, right next to my name blazed the words: URGENT CARE.

I'm too young to have such health inflictions.

I stretch out on her wonderful couch and drop my winter coat on the carpet.

Dr. Hall has left a brand new journal on the glass coffee table for me. On the first blank page, my doctor has taped a small piece of paper flush against the binding. She wants me to rate my quality of sleep each night. Along with a space for the dates are my options to check one or all of the following: calm, restful, full, heavy, broken, restless, light.

Is she kidding? If my shuteye could be described in any of these first four options, I would not be here. I check the last three adjectives: broken, restless, light—because my nights have been just that. I heavily underline the word 'restless', which my sleep has been since March fifteenth. My mind does not stop processing at night like most, well-adjusted people. It races into overdrive and stays there in the middle of the night until the break of day, but not before flying me through vivid scenes. I try to locate a familiar sight, sign, or person—but I can't and still do not know where I go. I'm beginning to think this locale of my dream is not of this country.

Each morning, I wake up with a massive headache, which only a hot mug of *yerba maté* seemed to negate. My grandmother somehow knows this infusion could help even though she prefers to sip it in the afternoon. From her bed upstairs, she yells, navigating me through her cluttered counters and shelves in the kitchen. I locate her magic brew of dried leaves and stems. She keeps her precious *yerba maté* in a blue ceramic, airtight square container on the counter behind a stack of old newspapers right next to our old-fashion, white porcelain farmer's sink. I popped open the heavy lid and sniffed. Her tea of choice looks like dirt with broken twigs and pieces of autumn leaves.

She swears this is the stuff that keeps her going even though the doctors initially only gave her less than six months…two years ago. The thought of death makes a coldness settle over my body, so I cover myself with my winter coat.

I run my hand over the cover of my second, brand new leather journal, the price of seeing a $150-an-hour shrink. For some reason, I don't have to pay anything. My grandmother mumbled something about the benefit of being a full-time student. Again, she pushes away my question when I asked about paying all of these medical bills for exams and testing, and now my weekly visits to a see a head doctor. I think someone in my family has or had money, but here's another question still not answered by my grandmother. When I do ask about the rubber banded, hefty roll of one-hundred dollar bills that she keeps in the coffee ceramic container next to her curative tea, she simply says, "Money does grow on trees."

I don't know if she has the expression mixed up or just doesn't want me to worry about money. When one day last week when I ran upstairs to ask her about another roll of money I found under the bathroom sink behind the stack of toilet paper, her response was, "Your grandfather took care of us."

"So, money's not an issue, then?" I stood there, stoking the fire in my grandmother's fireplace to warm her and her room.

"No, it is not. What is an issue is when you can't have back what you really want."

"Grandpa?"

"Yes, my husband."

"I'm so sorry, Grandma." I went over to her and wrapped my arms around her small shoulders.

"It's okay, I have you."

"And Nile."

"Yes and Nile." She smiled, but sadness showed in her eyes.

I return to the last page in my first journal. To help me recall last night's dream, I reread a section where I remembered riding up and over choppy waves in a black bay of balmy ocean water and how I fought against the strong undertow; my arms and legs tired quickly. My silver evening dress made of a thick heavy fabric pulled my body down like a dive belt. As I thrashed the top of the water to close the distance to shore, I felt as if I was being pursued, although could not make out a silhouette of anyone behind me. After five attempts to identify my pursuer, I was convinced he dodged my glances by going underwater every time I turned to look or maybe he was just getting pummeled by the wave sets as well.

In my journal, I make a question mark by this passage to talk to Dr. Hall about why I thought someone was pursuing me in my dream.

As I reread my words, an uneasy feeling overcomes my body. I pick up the new journal and my hand moves across the page, writing in greater detail than I had originally remembered of that night. With my eyes close, my hand with the pen recalls my dream without any of my conscious help. I fall deeper into the memory. My right hand takes down all the details almost as if it's taking a transcription.

The night ocean spat me out onto the wet sand.

Under a moonless night sky, I crawled like a sand crab across the small beach and into the cover of the tall grasses at the bottom of a dune. Up and over the closest sand dune, I scrabbled toward a makeshift shack made from driftwood, nestled at the bottom of the next dune.

With my eyes still closed, my hand continues to scratch the pages of my new journal. I know I am in this world, in my doctor's safe office, yet I'm being pulled back into this other world.

This beach area is void of people and structures, except for the soft, welcoming yellow glow that slips from beneath the door of the shack, which is also built from driftwood. I feel as if the light is beckoning me closer with its illusion of safety and warmth. Or maybe it is the presence behind me that is ushering me forward. Due to the incessant crashing of waves, I cannot hear the presence of another human, but suspect I am not alone. My wet dress rides up around my hips as I crawl faster through the deep sand. Why am I crawling? It's dark and no one can see me and this is a very slow mode of transport—

My eyes flash open. I am annoyed at my own dream and its lack of logical action. I write questions for Dr. Hall:

Why don't I stand and run?

What am I afraid of?

I make two big question marks in the margin.

My eyes close, again. My hand speeds to keep up with the movie playing out in my mind's eye. I move down and across the narrow valley between the dunes to close the last ten yards between me and what I perceive to be safe…and I stop writing; I can't remember, anymore and open my eyes to stare at my doctor's beige walls.

Dr. Hall enters and smiles at me. Her arms are loaded with my files accumulated by Dr. Reid and reference books to help her decipher my ailment that keeps me from sleeping like a normal person. Her leather briefcase hangs off her shoulder. She balances a tall, 'To Go' cup of coffee in her free hand. "So, how's it going? Can you remember?"

"More than I want to."

"No, that's good, Tess. We'll be able to make progress with more information."

"I woke up with sand in my bed this morning."

"Have you been to the beach, lately?"

I turn my head to look at her to see if she is kidding. She's not.

"No. And my grandmother's house no longer has a sandbox in the backyard. It's now a vegetable garden, well, when there's no snow on the ground, it is."

Dr. Hall knows Colorado is a landlocked state and while there are sand dunes, I haven't ever visited them, but would like to. I heard you can ski the sand dunes like a mountain slope.

"No, I'm not around any sand, and especially not in the winter." I feel as if I'm only talking to myself in these sessions, anymore.

She nods and says to herself, which I still hear, of course: *Okay, so no nearby access to sand.*

My doctor takes her seat across from me with her glass coffee table between us. I look twice at the glass vase placed in its center. Yes, it's filled halfway with seashells and just water. I look closer; there's no sand at the bottom of the vase. I bump my knee against the table, which hurts.

My knees are scratched up, too from last night jaunt, so I pull up my jeans and show her my latest injuries from dreaming.

She jots a few words on the Steno tablet she uses every session. Her interior pages are light purple, the color of the dots found inside white orchids. The lines of her paper are of a darker hue of the same color. I can't seem to escape the color purple in my life.

"I think these scratches are from crawling across the beach last night."

My doctor just hums a comforting sound in response, offers no explanation, but just sips her latte.

I'm really surprised that she didn't write 'Nut Case' instead of 'Urgent Care' on my file. I would have, particularly after I shared with her last week that I believe my mind adventures are real.

And here I am, in a room colored beige, waiting for my psychoanalyst to say something, anything to explain what I'm feeling, or possibly experiencing in another dimension of time—and living, but now she's too busy enjoying her latte.

[Morse code message: HIDEHER]

-.- -. --- .--

I stand before a gorgeous man, who's probably my age. It's night again, and again I am not at home in my bed with Nile. The man wears a white dress shirt with just two buttons closed across his chiseled chest. He's in dark jeans and barefoot like he just walked away from a photo shoot for a magazine ad. He stands across the bonfire from me. His eyes have not left my body.

I look away.

His intensity pulls me back to his gaze.

Do I know him?

Should I be afraid?

He smiles. He looks like the same man that I followed around through the thick crowd at the parade a few nights ago or maybe it was a week ago.

Where are all of his friends or at least the guy, who invited us to the party? Is it even the same night? I can never tell the order of time or the amount of time lapsed in my dreams. Time all blends together. I do know it's very warm wherever I keep going and tonight, I'm on a desolate beach with him.

I make the mistake of returning his friendliness with a slight smile.

In a few quick steps, he's standing beside me, eating a piece of fruit of which he offers me a bite. I don't recognize the strange fleshy lump. He seems to be enjoying it and is still offering me another piece.

I accept and only stare at it.

He laughs at my hesitation. "You love jackfruit as much as I do." He speaks in my grandmother's native language and motions for me to eat.

I try it and I do like it. It tastes like banana-flavored, bubblegum, but it makes my throat itch. I motion for something to drink. He opens a small cooler just a few steps away and comes up with two Bohemia beers.

"Same beer?" I hear my words in English inside my head, but they come out in Portuguese. I switch to English and say out loud: "At least you're loyal…"

"Of course, I am." His shoulder-length, dark hair blows around his face. He unsuccessfully pushes his locks back over his forehead just for the wind to blow it back into his face, again thirty seconds later.

I question if this is a good idea to eat and drink with a stranger, yet his sweet smile keeps me hanging around and nursing the beer, which is erasing the itch in my throat.

His skin is the warm color of milk chocolate probably from spending every day in the sun all of his life. His hair and eyes are shades much darker than his skin. I feel like I could eat him up—

What? What am I thinking? What about Nile? He's a stranger. I'm a stranger in this city, on this strange beach, and I'm drinking beer. Can I get drunk in a dream?

With a branch, he pokes at the small fire and makes the flames jump higher before our bare feet. When his voice reaches my ears, his foreign words are immediately translated into English. "I want to take my time in living my life."

He pulls me down onto the warm sand beside him. The fire shines on his animated face.

I shake my head to stop this dream and bring me back into bed with Nile or into my doctor's office where I last thought I was lying, but as I look up, the sky looks so surreal like a velvet blanket speckled with brilliant diamonds stretching from one side of the bay to the other.

I am definitely not in my bedroom.

Night has engulfed the surrounding mountain range, making it impossible to delineate where this earth stops and the next begins.

"What kind of confused face was that?

I smile and then take a slow sip, not much of answer, but I'm afraid to speak, not knowing if my words will be in Portuguese or come out in English.

"Maybe tomorrow I'll find my way…to where I am supposed to be, but right now, here with you, I see no reason to hurry away the night." My companion of the evening touches my beer bottle with his and smiles. *"À vida."*

"To life," my brain translates for me, but my mouth blurts out a question that I have been holding in my head and it's in English: "Are you real?"

"What a strange question. Try me." He peels off his white shirt to show off his sun-tanned chest and tight stomach. He definitely looks real and he speaks English, too. Now he is really perfect.

I reach out to touch his skin, but stop as an image of Nile appears in my head. This is just a dream, right? I'm not technically cheating on Nile, am I?

I am, aren't I? I hold onto my bottle of beer with both hands.

"Why do you think you came back to me? Our young hearts speak the truth. You are for me and I am for you. Always."

He takes my beer away and digs a hole in the sand for it. His is empty already and he places it sideways on the beach.

He smiles and touches me on both sides of my chest.

I lean back into his hand on my back and away from the one that cups my breast. The heat of his hands sears my skin in spite of the red flannel shirt I wear over my bikini.

Bikini? Where did I get one of these skimpy Brazilian suits? No wonder they are so inexpensive. There's hardly any fabric to this white crochet swimsuit. I pull Nile's unbuttoned shirt closed over my bikini and scoot away a bit, but not too far. Why am I always wearing something of Nile's and right now?

"My name is Tino. We should be formally introduced before…" He brushes my long hair away from my eyes. "…you know."

"I'm Tess."

"I know." Tino pulls me into his lap to face him. Inside his embrace, it feels so natural like I have been here before with his lips on mine, his hand on my breast. Do I know him? Could I have known him from an earlier dream and just blocked the memory because of guilt?

Tino stops kissing me, "Where have you gone?" He gently taps my forehead with his. "I was kissing my girlfriend of four years and then she disappears. Just like that. I thought we would be together forever."

"Forever? How can you know? We're only nineteen, right?" I brush sand out of my long hair. It doesn't work.

"Love knows no age." Tino pulls my hair into a ponytail and ties it with a long string of dried seaweed.

My mind is replaying previous conversations: I swear I had this exact conversation with Nile…and then a book of poetry opens in my mind. I read to Tino, "Actually, the saying is: 'Love begets love, love knows no rules,' and I quote Virgil."

Or maybe I'm quoting my grandmother quoting Virgil.

"I like my saying better." Tino kisses me again for a long time.

I pull back to study his face. "Four years? I thought we just met?"

"It is you, who likes to play this 'pick-up game,' remember? So, I am picking you up. Play along. You also said you want to swim in the ocean, so be ready."

I kiss him, again to confirm what he just said about the girlfriend part. Yes, we fit together; there's none of that initial awkwardness with someone new for the first time, the worry about getting it right, doing it right. With Tino, he's just right. I roll back onto the sand and pull him on top of me to feel all of him, not just his lips and hands. My shirt falls open and he unties my top. Our skin meets and heat runs down my spine to where his hands now touch me. He's above me, so I hold onto his hips tight with the inside of my knees almost as if I'm trying to hold onto Tino, and my life. We dance on the beach for a long time, both of us taking turns to bring the other to happiness. The fire is out by the time we finish. I have sand everywhere. Tino pulls me up off the ground and carries me into the night ocean. This time I am not afraid of the water. I have Tino.

[Morse code message: KNOW]

.-. . - ..- .-. -. - --- -- .

I sit at my favorite coffeehouse waiting for Nile. It's tiny, which means to me it's cozy. The walls are painted in a rich mocha color and its contrasting red leather chairs are clustered into inviting corners, making it a great spot to linger—even once your mug is empty. This converted house is an attraction for all types of coffee drinkers. To my immediate right are three men each with a thick gold chain circling their ropey necks and sporting various lengths and trims of gray mustaches. They hold court in a loud and animated discussion while downing multiple espressos. They take turns ordering a new round. They must be brothers or old friends, who are starting to look like one another.

In front of me are two women, exchanging thoughts, ideas, and recipes in a rapid volley of whispers. They sit tight with their sloppy ponytailed heads leaning in towards each other, drinking foamy cappuccinos during their precious and probably infrequent hour together.

A female teenager sips black coffee, scribbles all over her manuscript, and every time the bell on the front door rings, she looks up to see who she can add to her story. She doesn't seem interested in the male college student that just entered. He runs his hand back and forth over his crew cut and surveys the chalkboard menu above the display of gifts for sale. When he picks up a pre-made sandwich wrapped, the sound of waxy paper makes my stomach growl even though I had just finished my lunch. He peels back the paper on the turkey and pesto sandwich and eats it while he waits to pay.

The writer taps her pen against her stack of paper and looks up again at the newest customers, tourists, who enter and stand right beside her. They're talking for everyone to hear. The writer smiles and appears to writing down the dialogue of whoever sits too close to her and carries on conversation at full volume, but the offenders don't seem to notice that they're now in her story.

It's Thursday, my day to meet Nile for a caramel-topped or chocolate-laced coffee drink and stare at each other like we used to do in our senior year of high school when we both ducked out of our last class of the day. I skipped geology. He missed art class. We were both mortified at each other's choice class to skip, but that was how the day fell. Nile loves realistic, earthy things. I love anything to do with art and somehow, we managed to connect.

Back on that fateful and last Thursday together, he couldn't believe it when I told him that I was leaving our cold snowy state for the boiling hot California because he knew how much I loved snow. What he didn't say was he couldn't believe I was leaving him.

But I was. I was afraid of falling in love too young and wanted space. Now all I want is Nile and his love no matter what our age, so I couldn't believe it when I returned home to find out that he wasn't dating anyone.

We both believe that we are the lucky one.

At the front door, a toddler waddles into the coffeehouse slowed by the weight of her winter coat and boots. I watch as her mother steps up to the gray-swirled, white marble countertop. She orders two hot drinks with frequent glances over her shoulder to confirm her tiny daughter is safe. Meanwhile, her daughter is in the process of de-dressing, yanking off her orange- and yellow-striped stocking cap by its tassel. She pulls at her mittens with her tiny front teeth and tosses them to the dark granite floor. Next, she tugs at the Velcro closures on her orange puffy coat and lets it clump onto the ground like a kicked up rug. This three year old unwraps her pink scarf as if she's a Parisian woman with years of experience with such fashion attire. Off comes her fake, fur-lined boots and up she climbs into the oversized suede chair. The little customer waits for her mother to deliver something yummy. She catches me watching her and flashes a shy smile.

The linen lampshade imprinted with the outlines of autumn maple and oak leaves immediately takes her total attention. Her tubby hand reaches up to touch the glow on the fabric. She smiles as brightly as the light bulb beneath. As she peers around the bottom of the lampshade, her little mind seems amazed to find the light source. She smiles again at her discovery. Her mother arrives, carrying two mugs of hot cocoa topped with whipped cream and a small plate displaying a perfect, peanut butter cupcake with two forks.

The little girl kind of reminds me of Nile and his ever-present curiosity, although, I do wonder why I'm always watching toddlers.

Dr. Hall has her own explanations that always seem to circle back to losing my mother at such a young age. She said, maybe I am trying to be that little girl again or attempting to see what my mother would have been like at that age if only my three-year-old mind could remember.

I think I just like to watch toddlers when they see their world for the first time.

Someone kisses me on top of my head. I look up to see my boyfriend smiling at me.

He sinks into the chair next to me. Every time I see him, I feel a rush of adrenaline pulse through my body down to my knees. I wonder how long he'll be able to do to this to me. Forever, I hope.

"Hey, sweets. Thanks for saving me a seat." He looks around the crowded coffeehouse and smiles at me, again.

Although he does not know it, he's my main reason why I transferred. With all this craziness going on inside my head, I needed him in my life, but I don't know what to tell him or where to even begin to explain what's happening to me. I think he understands, though. Medical minds are inherited in his family's DNA whether he wants one or not.

"What? You don't look very happy to see me." He moves out of his coat and pushes up his sweater sleeves up to his elbows.

I lean over and disperse his doubt with a long-lasting kiss that makes my feet tingle this time. Or maybe it's my medication.

No, it's him.

"Let's go back to your place." He wraps me in a huge hug.

So much for our fancy hot drinks, I think, but don't say as I follow Nile as closely as I can out of the coffeehouse.

He races me down the sidewalk out of town. He leads, blocking me from passing him and then I fake a left, and pass him on the right to be in the lead. Nile cheats and picks me up and spins around to put me behind him and runs down the dry, crooked sidewalk with tree roots busting up the cement slabs.

We had played this game a lot as little kids, racing each other back to my house all summer long. His house was off limits due to his mother's regular migraines.

Today, we run through the silent afternoon to my grandmother's house. He beats me to the front door, doesn't stop once inside to shed his coat, but drops it on the stairs as he takes two steps at a time on his way to say, "Hello" to my grandmother first.

"You win, again, however, let it be noted that I let you! Again!"

He just laughs and knocks the door to my grandmother's room.

I stop before my grandmother's collection of Marys in her altar just inside our front door. The tallest Mary in my grandmother's collection is a wood-carved statue painted white. She wears a white gown tied with red sash. Her hooded cape covers most of her brown hair. Virgin Mary points to a red heart painted on the top of her gown. The creator of this three-foot tall statue added a sheen of blue glitter all over her clothing to give her a surreal glow.

I admit, it's a little creepy with her heart painted on the outside, but there is something serene about her facial expression that makes it okay for her to wear her heart on her dress. This Mary stands in the very center of the altar.

When my grandfather and I started to build the altar, Nile came over to help us. Almost every afternoon, my grandmother pulled Nile away and into her kitchen with the sweet aroma of brownies. She did her best to erase the missing mother syndrome from which I suffered and for Nile, too since his mother was often unavailable to his emotional needs due to her headaches and desire to be left alone.

My grandmother knew the chocolaty warm treat would help us forget just for a moment plus she thought it very "Americana" of her, especially when she added chocolate chips to the batter and sprinkled the top with powdered sugar after the brownies cooled. She chattered away in her country's tongue—nothing that I could understand at the time and her words were particularly lost on Nile's ears, but when she said, "brownies" in the middle of her comforting monologue, we happily waited in anticipation of such goodness to be pulled out of the oven. My grandfather would also stop work and join us for a mid-day treat.

Over the years, my grandmother has added new Marys to her altar that also shimmer and glow without any lights. She told me she always wanted to have the same welcoming here in her new house as she had in her first home, the one on the beach.

I stare into her old magic mirror behind the tallest Mary and close my eyes, willing an image of my mother to appear when I open them.

"Please come home," I whisper to myself and to Mary.

My grandmother said when she concentrated before this mirror and with Mary's help, she could see the future. Recently, she told me, "The future is good."

I open my eyes.

The mirror just shows my sour face, so I'm still waiting to see what this good can be that my grandmother believes.

Around the curved alcove, my grandmother had me hang a flat circular piece of cobalt glass with the evil eye in the center to ward off such spirits from entering our home. Four crescent moons hammered out of thin silver metal cross the higher portion of the back wall. She once told me they honor the decease of her immediate family: her father, brother, husband, and my uncle Regis, her only son. I turn my eyes away from death.

One of the shorter Marys wears a heavy gold crown with brilliant fake jewels placed every other quarter inch. Her head is tilted to maintain its balance on her head. This ornate, three-dimensional figure looks as if she could step down from her pedestal and walk away from her holy shrine. As a little girl, I waited and watched, but she never did move. Maybe Dr. Hall is right, I do have an overactive imagination.

Shortly after my mother's unexplained disappearance, I would kneel night after night before this picture of serenity and pray for my mother's return. When I was eight, my grandmother finally allowed me to light the votive candles that lined her altar. I thought this action would increase the intensity of my wish so that Mary could clearly hear my prayer and do something about it—even though my mother never came home, I still returned every night before bed. Now as I near adulthood, I still return every night before I go to bed and continue to grasp at the hope she might return someday, when she can, however, I think my dreams are showing me another way to live and believe in my future.

Can my mother and I ever be reunited?

I pick up a stick match and strike it on the piece of sandpaper glued to the counter; it's getting worn out and I should look for a new piece in the garage later. As I light the votive in front of the tall Virgin Mary, the holy mother of Jesus, I wonder about the powers mothers possess. Can mothers communicate with loved ones after they depart? Is my mother trying to communicate with me? Is that what all my crazy dreams and the beeping I hear in my head is all about?

The first night I arrived at my grandmother's house, I had heard an incessant beeping and have heard it every night since, although I'm baffled as to what and why I can hear and no one else seems to notice. It's a bunch of short electronic beeps followed by a rapid succession of longer beeps and then with a silent gap in between each sound. It doesn't make sense and before I can jot its sequence onto paper, my dreams usually sucks me away into dark alleys or even darker waters.

Maybe if I revisit my grandmother's collection of photo albums, I can learn something she's not telling me about my family. Maybe the answers are in the photos or in the sand in my bed, the latest souvenir from my dreams, or maybe Dr. Hall has my answers or will soon, but I think I'm confusing Dr. Hall despite the fact that she's a very intelligent woman. Maybe my answers are not to be found at doctors' offices.

I scan my grandmother's altar, again and this time, in the background of the altar, there are three, ten-inch tall statues of nuns reading the Bible and dressed in sober black habits.

When did these new additions arrive? I make a mental note to ask my grandmother or Rosalyn.

Rosalyn, my grandmother's home nurse, is coming down the steep stairs. She gets to go home early today because Nile and I are here. She has been helping my grandmother since my departure to college in Santa Cruz. My grandma thought my California university was a renegade college because the professors there did not offer grades; they just awarded a 'pass' or 'fail' mark. She still shakes her head about this and is very glad I'm back at a 'real' university, or she told me over tea last week. I just hope she likes my 'real' grades as much.

Over the months, Rosalyn had become much more than just the help. She is family, a tiny Japanese woman who's strong and always dressed in ironed blouses and slacks. After our town lived through a five-hundred and fifty-inch winter, she finally agreed to wear the snow boots that we bought her instead of her usual sandals with socks. No wonder she and I get along so well, she doesn't mind winter, either.

"Hi, Rosalyn. Is Nile entertaining my grandmother, again?"

"Yes. He is quite amusing."

[Morse code message: RETURNTOME]

.-.. .. ... - . -.

"Dah-dah."
Pause.
"Di-dah-dit."
Pause.
"Dah-dah-dah."
Pause.
"Dah-di-dit dit."

Ahhh! The same annoying, beeping noise that I heard the first week I arrived wakes me, again from my morning slumber.

I can't tell if the sound is coming from outside my bedroom window or from inside my head. Is it a car alarm? Or an army of lawn caretakers with their noisy equipment?

The other day, I told Dr. Hall that my ears ring a lot, especially at night when I'm trying to fall asleep. Now, I have both beeping and ringing in my ears.

Is it someone's home security alarm?

No wonder I'm grumpy these days. My grandmother even commented on my altered state or there lack of happiness.

Could this noise be a woodpecker?

I thought they tapped, not beeped.

My grandmother does insist I fill the birdfeeder in the backyard on a weekly basis. Maybe I'll stop doing this chore and then this persistent din will stop.

Or maybe the maddening beeping is just a pesky neighbor with irritating habit of hammering at six in the morning! I pull a pillow over my head to block my ears, but I can still hear the persistent noise. My question's answered. It's coming from inside my head. I peer out from beneath my pillow to double check and hear no outside sounds just the electronic beep inside me.

Now I know I'm going crazy.

The pink of daybreak brightens the early hours faster in a land where there are no clouds. Usually, I like watching the sun wake up, but can't enjoy this moment right now with the constant beeping playing inside my brain.

I roll over and grab a small tablet Dr. Hall gave me to keep on my nightstand and jot down the reoccurring sequence: "Di-dah-dit. Dah-dah-dah" followed by three longer sounds. It repeats: one, two, three times—then tap, tap, and then…blessed silence.

I'm too tired to figure what it could mean. I'll hand it off to my shrink. Maybe Dr. Hall will know what to do— if anything's to be done. I close my eyes in frustration and drift off into an agitated sleep.

I wake again, minutes or hours later, I'm not sure. My grandmother is standing over me. She's holding my mom's wristwatch in the palm of her hand. Either, she is very worried to have climbed out of bed and down the steep stairs to make it here to check on me, or I'm dreaming, again.

"You have to stop it, Tess. Stop going into these dreams." My grandmother's voice is right beside my head. She places my mother's wristwatch on my nightstand.

I squint to make out the appearance of my grandmother leaning down close to my ear. "Grandma?" I pull myself up into a seated position. "But I can't."

"You can't? Or you won't?"

I'm not being pigheaded like she used to call me, especially when I was younger and insisted on doing things my own way. I have to ask her what I think I already know. "Grandma, do I know a Tino?"

I really don't want to know the answer because in my heart and by the way my body acts—even if it's just a dream, my body knows and remembers him.

My grandmother seems to be losing her energy to stand and sinks onto my bed. Her face becomes pale and her hands shake as she attempts to force out her next words. "Tino is the eldest son of the police chef, a childhood friend of yours." She pushes her thick, white-streaked hair back from her face.

"His real name is Antonio. You couldn't pronounce Antonio when you were little, so his name to you, and all of us, became Tino."

"So, I do know him?"

"Yes, the same way you know Nile." She shifts on my mound of blankets to find comfort.

"He's my boyfriend? Wasn't I just a little kid when I knew him?" I rub my eyes. They always seem to be half open these days and today, they don't want to face what feels might be true. What to tell Nile? Do I have to tell Nile?

"Love knows no age, Tess." She places her hand over her heart.

I reach out to touch her, however, I can't. I hope I'm only dreaming again, fearing what she may say next.

"Stop asking question. Accept what your life is now. You can't change the past."

I sit up in bed and reach towards my grandmother, but my hand passes her through like she's a hologram. I pull it back, shocked.

Did she die?

Is this her ghost?

I fly out of my bedroom and up the stairs to find my answer.

[Morse code message: LISTEN]

70

. ... -.-. .- .--. .

As Dr. Hall places the tea tray on the coffee table in front of me, she glances at the open journal across my lap. Immediately, my mind starts to search for an answer why these tables are still called 'coffee tables' when the last thing we do around them anymore since the fifties is drink coffee—

"Can you use words instead of drawings? Or along with your drawings?"

In the center of the next page, I see a drawing of a white marble statue of a man holding his arms wide open as if calling to his people.

I don't remember drawing Jesus.

I nod and accept the delicate teacup in my hands. Her office is as chilly as the outside weather; I hope this small token of warmth will jump start my body temperature as well as my memory.

"And can you write in English when you jot down details about your dreams? I will have an easier time interpreting your dreams if I don't have to use an English-to-Portuguese dictionary all the time."

Sally knocks and enters with a manila envelope, which she hands to my shrink.

"Thanks, Sally." Dr. Hall pulls out the papers. "Your EEG test results."

I didn't like that test with all of the goopy electrodes attached to my scalp and the flashing strobe lights that were highly irritating even with my eyes closed. I shake my head to erase the memory as if it's an Etch-a-Sketch and as if that's how my mind works now…it does work, though.

She scans the pages. "Everything looks fine. Good. Normal."

"Why then can I hear what others are thinking before they speak? Like for example, what you're thinking inside your head?" I pull up to the edge of the couch to gauge the reaction of my doctor, to see if she believes me.

"And why not? We, our bodies, are an electrical force field and our thoughts are also electrical, so if you can tune into this frequent, of course, you can hear them." She rapidly writes on tablet.

What? She's finally hearing me and maybe believing in my "superhuman abilities" as Nile calls them?

"Also, people give away what they're thinking with their body language. You might be better at this aptitude than most."

So much for believing me…everything has to have a logical reason in Dr. Hall's world, but because she is a doctor and because she is a shrink, however, I thought she would allow for more latitude in the possibilities of answers.

Carefully, I print the translations. Beneath my Portuguese words wedged in between and around my drawings in block letters that looks like an architect's handwriting, I write:

Follow
Come Home
Return Soon
Listen

Dr. Hall looks at the new words and then to me. She takes a seat in the comfy chair across the low table from me, waiting for me to stop writing, but I can remember, so I keep writing in Portuguese, but switch to English, moving into last night's dream. I write as fast as the images appear in my mind. The words in my journal seem to speed before my eyes.

Dr. Hall moves over to sit on the arm of the couch beside me.

Over my shoulder, she reads my words out loud: "At first, I thought I could blame my tossing and turning each night on my love of MSG-laced Chinese food or drinking too much red wine. Initially, I didn't think much of my entertaining dreams and did enjoy the live picture shows in my head. These nightly movies were kind of like a private showing of an indie film on a faraway set. I had hoped to take a trip next to Bollywood or even Australia eventually, but my excursions rapidly darkened in tone."

"Why did you stop writing?" Dr. Hall asks.

I can hear her question, however, my dream is alive again and I am under its control. I continue to write.

She now silently reads over my shoulder.

I can hear my own voice as if reading the voiceover to the movie screening in my head. I'm running down a wet alley filled with shadowy figures that watch me as I pass them. I can't detect who they might be since I only see black profiles, but I know they are men. Every corner I turn down is another dead end, forcing me to run pass them again, trying to find an escape. It's an aggravating situation. Someone has left the group and is running after me. I duck into a thicket of tall thorny bushes under the pretense I can disappear in this shrubbery and from my pursuer. Their thorny branches reach at my face and scratch at my bare forearms.

I feel blood slide down my left cheek in a straight line.

From the second-story window, the pulse of salsa dance music leaks from the open windows and matches the racing tempo of my heart. My dream is so real, so alive that even in the black and gray shadows of night the apartment buildings create a steep, colorful canyon for my passage. Under each flood of light from the street lamps, brightly painted stucco walls are illuminated in the darkness. The colors of indigo, flamingo, and cantaloupe pool down the walls in single wide swatches between the blackness of

73

night. I attempt to quiet my breathing, to stay unnoticed in the thick row of bushes. I don't dare move to wipe the blood dripping on my face in fear any movement will give away my hiding spot and I'll be found.

When I can't hear the slap of shoes against the wet pavement anymore, I step out of the shadows and round a corner into an affluent neighborhood of sprawling homes. From shadow to shadow of the thick palm trees, I jump into their dark corridors to remain invisible, but then stop in front of one of the houses painted a tropical green color of honeydew. This sprawling, two-story house that looks somewhat familiar is guarded by a ten-foot high, black, wrought-iron fence. The courtyard is lit to an almost, daylight-intensity by floodlights, which are cornered under the eaves below an expansive, terra-cotta tiled roof. Its double gated entrance is closed and locked, wrapped tightly shut with ropes of chains.

I grasp the closed gates and bang them back and forth in my attempt to enter its safety.

I'm locked out on the street and feel as if I have been in this predicament before...

The heavy chains clamor against the rails, encouraging the approach of fast slaps of shoes, once again. I dash away from the light and hope and pray the alley's darkness will erase me. When I try to look back over my shoulder to see who pursues me, my head refuses to turn to the left, so I run faster.

Dr. Hall has slide down beside me on the couch and is reading my words as fast as I put them to paper.

I look to her for input.

She shakes her head and covers my hand with hers.

[Morse code message: ESCAPE]

..-. ..- - ..- .-. .

There are no streetlights down the alley behind my grandma's house, yet delicate snowflakes tumble throughout the evening from the thick clouds, which light up our backyard's white lawn with its crystalized deepening presence. Our neighbors scrape their plastic shovels repeatedly across their driveways in an attempt to clear the black asphalt, although their efforts can't keep up with the velocity of the white dust landing and covering the area that they just emptied of snow. Scoria tossed from a bulldog of a snowplow impedes their process, adding small bumps of volcanic rocks across the new smooth paths of fluffy snow.

I'm not afraid of this alley and its familiar noises that come around with wintertime.

I gave up shoveling an hour ago, reasoning that the storm wouldn't stop hurling flakes at me before morning plus Nile arrived and dragged me inside saying, we weren't going anywhere tonight anyhow, so why fight nature?

I like his reasoning.

He also ran away with my snow shovel.

Besides, my grandmother is anticipating our Pacific Rim creation full of shrimp and vegetables over Udon noodles. She likes when we serve her entrée as soup in a big bowl that warms her hands as she tips the final drops of the broth to her lips.

"No chopsticks, please," she said when I presented the plans for our dinner earlier in the afternoon.

In the warmth of the small kitchen, this crowded space is filled with my grandma's 'must keep' things: old magazines, newspapers, and books: new, old, and borrowed from the public library. She is one of the few people I know, who ordered a library to be built into the only available wall in the kitchen. Here lives her cookbooks, both the brand new ones signed by celebrity chefs made famous by their television shows and her splattered cookbooks that she brought over from the old country. Grandpa was mad she brought so many. The boxes weighted down his plane, cookbooks filled with local recipes and many others about the history of food, tea, wine, and coffee.

Rosalyn's cookbooks also now live here in my grandma's kitchen on their own special shelf.

My grandmother also keeps anything she can buy "on sale" at the grocery store and usually orders Rosalyn to buy in bulk, and in my opinion that's just too many and too much for only two, full-time residents, my grandmother and Rosalyn. Now, however, that Nile is a frequent diner and I'm home again, we're beginning to eat up some of these mega purchases, mainly Nile is.

"Tess are you ready to amaze your grandmother, again?"

"Yes, I always amaze her in the kitchen."

Nile ignores the disasters on every countertop. He clears enough space for his wooden cutting board to chop the carrots into pinwheels as if he's five-star chef at his own restaurant, showing off for his kitchen staff. He even throws me a big toothy grin as if he's reading my mind or maybe he's just reading my body language. "I know you can amaze her and me with your cooking, but you just scare her when you wave a knife around and there's a difference between amazing and scaring."

Next, he tackles a softball-sized, Spanish onion. This big bad vegetable always makes me cry—although I never cry for emotional reasons like I probably should.

"That's why you shouldn't talk to her with a knife, waving it around." He laughs at his own joke.

Tonight, he's the master chef and I'm happy to be his sous chef and follow his commands. My sleepless nights make me very listless and when following a recipe is involved, I rather sidestep any leadership requirements, so we have a chance at dining on something edible.

"Rosalyn is joining us, right?" He slides the perfectly diced onion into the sizzling wok.

"No, not tonight. She promised that she'll join us again, soon."

Nile is skilled at making the best, one-pot dishes with his yin and yang way of replacing the required ingredients with whatever's available in our kitchen. The aroma of Nile's Japanese-influenced dish wafts through the house and reaches my grandmother.

She bangs the handle of kitchen broom on her floor, indicating she approves of whatever we're creating.

I arrange a small bowl of wasabi peas, rice crackers, and sesame sticks, and pour two short glasses of red wine.

"Steady. Do you want me to carry that upstairs?"

I look him as if he has paid me a horrible insult.

"What?"

"I'm very balanced."

He laughs, again. He knows I'm a klutz.

Nile helps me assembly my gift to my grandmother on a bamboo tray. I wink good-bye to him as I make my way upstairs.

Nile shakes his head and then covers his eyes so not to have to witness the potential crash.

My years of experience, first as a waitress at Denny's, the diner from the seventies that's still around in some parts of the country, and then summers at fine-dining establishments helps me to navigate the crowded hallway of my grandmother's home without spilling or dropping anything. Her accumulation of furniture and yard sale treasures like end tables and floor vases and her love of houseplants make our house a permanent obstacle course. As I travel up the steep stairs to her room, I don't look at the tray in my hand because I know if I do, I'll spill—it's an old waitressing tip that really works. I just haven't told

Nile my secret…one of a couple secrets that I'm now hiding these days.

With the tip of my cowgirl boot, I tap against the half closed door. I love my authentic boots. My new friends in Santa Cruz didn't quite know what to make of my fashion statement of wearing boots with short-short, white shorts at the beach. I glance at my square toe box and note that the sand did do permanent damage to the leather. Did I bring sand home from the beaches of Northern California?

"Come on in." My grandmother smiles and pulls herself up higher in bed against her collection of various pillows. "I was expecting you."

Nile can't understand our need for twelve or more pillows on every bed, couch, and at least two on for every chair including the dining room chairs.

I told him that we like to be comfortable.

My grandmother likes to collect handmade quilts, but isn't too keen on making one of these heirlooms herself. One summer, she tried it only to have the piles of fabric squares collect dust. Maybe that's where all of these pillows came from over the years; she had made pillows out of her largest quilting squares.

I pull down the legs on the tray and place it in front of her. "Nile is making us another one of his marvelous feasts."

"I know. My nose never lies to me." She clinks my glass and looks me in the eye. "To you, Tess. May you find your happiness."

"If you ask me, this is a pretty good arrangement. I have you and Nile and I will be almost done with my studies in another—"

My grandmother sips and then shakes her head.

"I thought you liked California wines."

"No, it's not the wine. Tess, I'm worried for you, your health. You need to fix whatever is going on inside your head and do it now."

I take a long sip and say nothing. I want to tell her about where I think I am going in my dreams, but don't want to worry her any more than she already is worrying.

Nile clunks our floor from the kitchen with another broom there for that exact purpose.

I stomp the floor, holding my wine glass high without spilling as drop. Now he knows I am coming back downstairs to help.

"What were you looking at?" I point to the open photo albums on her bed.

"Oh, I was just remembering the first house your grandpa and I lived in when your mother was born." She pulls the album over so I can see the house. "Over on *Vinte Quatro de Maio*."

I lean against the side of her high bed and examine the rambling house hidden behind wild vines of blooming, trumpet-like purple flowers. White wicker chairs with padded floral cushions dot the covered front veranda. Beside the potted plants on each step, there's worn path in the cement. On the middle step, a black cat lying in the sun stares at the camera. Her dog sits in the shadows above the cat. "I've been there."

"That's not possible, dear. You weren't born and then we moved uptown to a high rise off the beach, and then here to this snowy town."

"I have sat on those steps and played with *Gato*."

"How do you know my cat's name?"

"You must have mentioned it before. Don't you name all of your animals their species' name?"

"Yes, I do. You better go help, Nile." She smiles and closes the album. "Thanks for the treats."

At the bedroom door, I turn back to her. "I swear I have been there, Grandma. Weird, isn't it?"

"Maybe you have..."

[Morse code message: FUTURE]

..-. .. -. -.. -- .

Today, Dr. Hall hypnotized me to get me to talk more about my dream and answer her questions. She had videotaped the session.

Thank God, this test didn't require any needles.

Now, she looks a little bit shaken; little did I realize this dream that I told her about wasn't the 'light' versions captured in my journal.

"Do you want to watch the video?" Dr. Hall asked me.

I nodded, kind of afraid to see myself in this altered state.

She hits 'play'.

We both watch 'a prone me' on the couch, eyes closed, looking like a stiff. I want to say this to my doctor, but she probably wouldn't think it was funny. I think it is.

I start talking on the TV monitor, so I sit up and pay attention.

"I didn't end up in the angry ocean at night in my last dream because I was out for a midnight dip with my beau."

It's weird to hear my own voice. I don't sound like the 'me' that I hear inside my head when I speak to others.

"Someone else was with me. Not chasing me like I had initially thought, but guiding me to safety."

I watch myself stretched out like a sloth, eyes closed, motionless except for my lips.

"I question your allusion of perceived safety in a dream. The reality of such a concept." Dr. Hall is talking to the "me" on the couch and pushes the microphone closer to the edge of the coffee table.

"The beach shack was a safe zone. My intuition was correct even while dreaming or time traveling or whatever is happening to me at night."

I sound like I'm wide awake, but have not opened my eyes or moved.

"Let's go back to the start of your dream, so you can maybe remember the ending."

When I speak again on the monitor, my voice sounds sleepy and my words are slow: "The evening started out with a small group dressed more for the opera rather than a sunset cruise."

I start to remember this dream and look away from the television, hoping my doctor doesn't notice. I'm not watching the "me" on the screen, but remembering seeing the women on the yacht. No matter what their age, they dressed with an edge of sexiness. I found it refreshing that they did not let a number stop them from being fully them—when in America, society degrades and calls older women "a woman of a certain age".

These Latin women don't let anyone tell them when they must cease being a woman, a sensual being. They're proud of who they have grown to be, they apply makeup to enhance their natural beauty, select clothing without any regard to "age appropriateness" but only to heighten their perfections and show off their best attributes, their breasts, backs, necks, legs, or calves. This picture that is floating again before me was a refreshing one—much different than the future of what awaits me as an older woman in North America where I'm expected to disappear, say nothing, and do less as my years come to pass, satisfied to be just a spectator instead of an active participant in life.

"Tess, you have stopped talking. What do you see?"

I hear Dr. Hall's voice in the video and I return to listen again as my voice starts: "I remember the women's sparkly jewelry, their towering hairpieces and extensions all adding a certain glimmer to their presence. They attracted admiration from both sexes."

"Do you hear anything else? Is anyone talking to you?" My doctor probes. "Do you recognize someone, anyone?"

"The music playing is a song I recognize. I don't know its name, though—I think it's the one my grandma calls her "happy tropical song" and there's champagne delivered as frequently as the songs change."

"Did you drink any champagne?"

"Yes, a couple of tiny glasses. Could the alcohol in my dreams affect the medication I'm on? In reality?"

I can hear my psychoanalyst scratch this question onto her tablet; she doesn't know the answer either.

"Continue, Tess. Who else is there?"

"Important people. Friends of my family. And my grandfather with my mother. My mother…" My thinking was getting slower and thicker from the endless glasses of champagne and I couldn't find my tongue to call out to my mother. I remember that I ached to talk to my mother, to reach out to her…

Would she recognize me at the age of nineteen? She hadn't seen me since I was six.

She was dressed in an ethereal gown that floated about her without a breeze. Her long dark hair framed her tan face and painted red lips. She wore no other makeup and didn't need it.

Dr. Hall pauses the tape with a click. "Why do you think this woman is your mother?" She is now asking me, the live body in the room, not the one hypnotized on tape.

"I know she was my mother." I tell Dr. Hall. "I have studied my grandmother's photo albums for years and even though I never did know her at the age of forty like she appears to be in my dream on the yacht, I know it was her."

"Are you ready to continue?"

I stare at the frozen image of me on the monitor and hear the click, again to play the tape.

My sleepy voice continues to tell the story: "I stood back to see if my mother would recognize me, but it's a dream, but maybe it was my choice whether she would or would not know who I was. I know that I should have approached her and yet again, I experienced a sickening sensation of not being able to move, as if I was sleep walking and without any control over my feet. At that moment, a waitress swirled between us, concealing my mother across the deck from me. Clusters of elegant couples closed up the space and sampled tidbits off the waitress' silver tray. As a heavy night cloud covered the fading colors of twilight's pale orange and lilac, I lost track of her. When I moved again to see my mother better, she was swallowed again up among the laughing people aboard the expensive boat."

I can hear my doctor talking as if she speaks through a thick wall made of cotton: "Tess? Then what?"

"I remember being swept into the fray and handed off to one partner and then to the next male. The ocean's small swells hit the portside of the vessel making me sway in my high heels."

I can hear Dr. Hall's gentle voice, encouraging me to continue. "What happened next?"

"I cannot see her. My mother."

Again, a tremor involuntarily courses through my body as it did then even though, right now, I'm sitting on my doctor's beige chaise lounge.

"The face of my next dance partner is not friendly. He turns his grin into a sneer as he grabs my wrists and pulls me closer to his chest and pinches me hard in his grip leaving tiny purple bruises like a bracelet around my wrists. We swirl in the illusion I'm his partner in more than just a dance, especially when other men try to take me for the next song. He holds me like we're an intimate couple and maneuvered us dangerously close to the back of the boat where the double engines mow the black ocean into a white frenzy."

As I sit here on her couch, I flinch and try to break his grasp. I remember the host beckoning everyone inside even though the song isn't over, down the steps into the lavish galley. Couples follow each other.

"Tess, I cannot hear you." Dr. Hall's voice betrays her attempt to shield her frustration from me.

My voice starts again on the video.

"The yacht's engines find a higher gear and motor forward with a bit of a jerk. My dance partner wraps his arms around me, forces a smile at me, and then offers a sincere one to the other married couples, who nod to us as they depart from the deck to go below. As the last man in a tuxedo smiles at me and ducks his head to head down the tight stairway, I feel myself spinning out of my dance partner's embrace and over the railing of the yacht.

I'm free-falling.

I splash into the dark waters, sinking fast due to the heavy fabric of my evening dress.

To be underwater at night, at first appears so peaceful, the initial silence and then the warm comforting enclosure of the black water.

Within seconds, panic shoots from my stomach to my throat, compelling me to attempt some movement in order to stop my downward plunge. I scissor kick towards the faraway, glass-like surface.

I watch myself on the monitor, despite the fact my body was lying in my doctor's office, I remember the sensation of gasping and breaking through the surface of the water to gulp oxygen.

"Are you okay?" Dr. Hall gets up and leans over me.

I must be acting it out again, here in my doctor's office.

The 'me sitting on the couch' nods at the same time as the 'me lying on the couch'.

"Between the rise and fall of the swells, I can see the outline of the ship traveling back to the dotted white line of the harbor. The lights on the shore appear to be pulling away as the waves grow bigger and slap down around me, taking me with their perpetual motion out to sea."

I start to think about what's happening here and the more Dr. Hall probes my mind to make me remember like asking questions about my dream's beginnings, their endings creep up into my brain and in greater clarity and detail. I realize these moments spent somewhere else in my unconsciousness or in an out-of-body experience are not the joy rides like they were when they began…as a sunset cruise.

I'm becoming more and more aware that somebody doesn't want me around or want me to return to my grandmother's house. Somebody wants me to perish, although at this point, I keep these suspicions to myself. My head doctor doesn't think my dreams can be an altered actuality, so why would she believe someone wants me dead?

Dr. Hall is talking, again. She sounds as if she is underwater. Her words are slow and thick. "Te-s-sss-s? Ca-nnnn yo-uuu h-earrr m-eee? Yo-uuu ca-nnn waaa-ke uu-p nn-ow."

I tell her "okay", but I'm not sure if she hears me. I can't seem to pull myself from this other world and back into the healthcare service building, and onto my doctor's couch. I remember swimming as fast as I could toward shore. After flaying around for the better portion of fifty yards without much distance gained, I realized if I dove and swam beneath each wave, my progress actually improved. My heavy dress isn't helping my efforts to save myself.

Up and out of the rollers, I lunged for a huge breath and down just beneath the water's surface, I pulled and clawed my way through the endless waves. I swam with my eyes closed due to the burn of the saltwater. When I thought my arms and lungs and legs couldn't or wouldn't move one more time, a huge wave plucked me up and spat me out onto the wet sand. I coughed out seawater and rolled up into a crouched position on the wet sand, afraid and cold.

I look at the video is which switched 'off' and realize she didn't hear any of that, so I tell her what I think is important. "I think the presence behind me, guiding me toward the shelter, is female."

I watch the confounded expression on my doctor's face.

"How do you know this?"

"I can smell her perfume."

[Morse code message: FINDME]

.-.. --- ... -

On the way to my doctor's appointment, my grandmother gives me bills to mail. While I was there, I thought I should empty her post box, too. As I stand at the counter tossing away junk mail for hearing aids, coupons for denture toothpaste, and fruit-of-the-month club offers, I sense someone at my elbow, correction below my elbow. There stands a little girl to my right, who is less than three foot tall. The tears in her shiny eyes are on the verge of spilling over her brown lashes, thick and long enough to make any female adult jealous.

I tear up a business letter for a pre-approved credit card and throw the little pieces of the application into one garbage can and the rest into another. I look down at the toddler, again. She hasn't moved.

"Where's your mother? Or father?"

No answer. She doesn't even blink, just stares at me. In her eyes, shines the universal look of fear. She's lost and afraid.

I sort the envelopes a little faster, wondering what to do. She probably knows she shouldn't talk to strangers, but at my age, I could be someone's very young mother.

"Is she in there?" I look through the double glass doors to the postal counters. What is her mom thinking? A little tyke like this can't possibly open such a heavy door or even reach the handle...I move over to the doors and hold it open for her. She bolts inside.

I watch the door swing shut and wonder if I should have yelled, "Does she belong to anyone?" But it's a friendly town and she'll be safer inside there with kind, older people waiting in the long line, and hopefully her mother is in there, too, feeling like an idiot if she indeed left her child in the lobby alone.

A shiver runs down my back. I know how the little girl feels. I've been left alone as a child and I think it was frequently.

I immediately sensed what was going on inside that little girl's head, the fear, the total panic, the isolation, and the feeling of having absolutely no idea of what to do next. Beside the words playing out inside other people's heads, I can also feel their emotions…talk about being truly empathic. Yet such a young brain as hers cannot be expected to process what to do, she only understands what has happened: Mom is gone. I am lost.

Lost. I must have been lost a lot as a kid or maybe even after I landed in the states. I'll have to ask my grandmother about this sense of trying to find home and why I can't…or maybe Dr. Hall will have some insight to my search for home, for my mother, which is regularly heightened when I find myself around young children.

[Morse code message: LOST]

- .-. ..- - ....

I think I hear my doctor's voice through the wall in the reception area, but it's Sally, a psychology graduate and Dr. Hall's receptionist. "I thought you discounted her dreams as just "having a wild imagination"?"

"Originally, I did think that she lived in some fantasy world due to the fact her mother died when she was a little girl, but the more I look into the physical side effects of her dreams, I think I can pinpoint it to a cause, her regular complaint of seeing visual snow or floaters."

"Tess does have an obsession with all things winter."

"Yes, I know, but she said that she has been seeing these clear floaters before her eyes her whole life. I think this is a result of her anxiety about her missing mother and when her adrenaline levels are raised, she sees the visual snow." The doorknob turns. "Is she here yet?"

"She's parked her in her usual spot with a cup of tea."

"Thanks, Sally."

Before my shrink can close the door and maybe because I want Sally to hear what I have to say, I blurt: "I don't have MS."

"Tess, I just want to rule out some possibilities. Another condition that produces visual snow is the inflammation of the optic nerve, which is caused by Multiple Sclerosis." Dr. Hall places her briefcase on her desk. "I want you to see a specialist to rule out this disease."

I stretch out on my doctor's couch and place my journal over my eyes.

"Or I can prescribe medication to help. I can set up an appointment right after our session. Will this work with your class schedule?"

Of course, I only sleep in my classes, anyhow and somehow manage to know all of the answers, so I don't have to be there physically.

Dr. Hall still doesn't believe my intelligence has expanded. I should ask her to test my I.Q., however that would only distract her from her mission: to find out what's causing my agitated nights and distant travel without a plane ticket. This new truth, the concept of time travel or at least the very possibility of living a parallel life is what the medical field, even at this teaching medical hospital, doesn't seem quite ready to embrace. I'm not sure if I do believe it one-hundred percent either, but what I see and where I go feels very real.

Are my dreams showing me my alternative life? Time does stand still and I seem to be the one, who's jumping back and forth between continents and the different ages that I have been so far in this life and that life.

I want to tell my psychoanalyst I do believe these 'happenings' are occurring in my other reality. The fact that I'm asleep when these events happen and when I return to consciousness and only remain as a vague recollection of such events is irrelevant. They still happened. What about the souvenirs I wear home such as the purple, fingerprint bruises circling my wrists like bracelets? And it's not from Nile—as Dr. Reid initially implied that I had a bad boyfriend. If he only knew Nile, he would know how very wrong he was.

But how do I explain the sand in my bed?

This morning, I woke up with a razor thin, red scratch along the left side of my face. Doesn't this mean something? Is this tangible evidence I do indeed go somewhere and it is a real place, but the question that I still can't answer is: "Where?"

Dr. Hall lifts the journal off my face, "Can I confirm an appointment with one of my associates, an ENT specialist at the Otolaryngology Foundation in Denver?"

"Oh, sorry. Yes. I thought I had said, "Of course" out loud."

"No, you're talking to yourself, again. Remember, I can't hear you like you can hear me."

Oh? So, she is starting to believe that I can hear other people's thoughts or maybe she is convinced I do have superhuman hearing.

"Can you go Thursday afternoon?" Dr. Hall is busy at her desk, shifting through papers while dialing the phone.

I sit up and sip my tea only to find it stone cold already. How can this be? Bone china is pretty, but pretty ineffective. My mind starts to think of a new design made from a slightly, thicker ceramic to trap the heat and keep the beverage warm for a minimum of fifteen minutes before it becomes undrinkable, but that wouldn't be bone china, would it?

"Tess, Thursday?"

"Yes."

I can see the new cup design in my mind's eye and am tempted to sketch it in my journal, but again, my doctor would want to know what this means; it just means I want to stay in today's universe. My brain can't process how thick the walls of the cup need to be anyhow, so I dismiss the assignment. I open my journal to a Post-it Note sticking from the top.

My head doctor, Dr. Hall, now wants me to list any liquids imbibed for during each 168-hour period. These are the possible number of hours available to everyone in one week, my Google brain tells me quickly and unlike everyone, I spend most of them awake.

The other day when I was zapped of any energy due to my lack of sleep and was feeling sad, again about my mother still being gone, Rosalyn told me a Japanese legend that her father had told her. If I believed and did the work, my wish—any wish could come true. She said I had to make one thousand origami cranes by myself.

I started folding that night.

From the possible and normal, fifty-six hours of nighttime sleep available to most people, I can only find shuteye without any interruptions for about twenty hours a week, not counting my naps. I did the math in my head rather quickly in comparison as to how my math brain used to work before discovering I possess expanded capabilities in all academic realms. Twenty hours? No wonder I'm burning through concealer makeup. Nothing seems to hide my darkening circles under my eyes. I even tried cucumber slices like they suggest in women's magazines, but Nile found me prone on the couch the other day, took the vegetables off my eyes and crunched on them next to my ear to wake me.

So, here I am, back in Dr. Hall's monochromic-colored office meant to pacify, yet it only agitates me in my constant state of sleep deprivation. Maybe it's the fact that I'm sitting a psychoanalyst's office, not the color of her walls that's getting to me.

I can't be crazy, can I?

How should a crazy person feel?

Does a crazy person even know that they're crazy? I leave that question alone…

I open my journal to see Doc Hall has provided a Post-It Note on each page for each day to list my beverages and alcoholic drinks.

Drinks? I'm not twenty-one yet, but guess I shouldn't lie to my doctor. I do indulge in an ice-cold beer—even in the artic hold of winter and for some reason, I create a little plate of ice cubes for my can of beer.

This balancing act always makes Nile yowl with laughter, especially when I try to carry it across the kitchen to the tiny table where he camps regularly with his homework.

I drip the whole way across the linoleum floor holding his can of beer on a small tray and then back again with mine. With a piece of thick paper towel under each of my slippers, I then skate around to mop up the droplets of water and at the same time, wash my grandmother's floor.

Nile just shakes his head, but this is how we conclude our study sessions late in the week with beer and a mopping session—at least my grandmother's kitchen floors are cleaned once a week.

I sit up on Dr. Hall's couch rather than stay in the position she usually finds me. She's right. This method of telling her on paper of what's going on in my head is much easier than staring at each other each week. I find it difficult to talk about myself and particularly about my problems, which are growing into a never-ending list. I prefer to call them "talents" and some definitely are, but when my mind allows me to travel to faraway cities and dumps me in dead-end streets, dark alleys, or in a black ocean, I want someone in the medical field to make these distressing adventures stop.

At first, I didn't tell anyone that I could understand what my grandmother was saying one day when she babbled in her native tongue. It was like a switch was turned on inside my head and I had always spoken Portuguese. I know that I inherited her coal-black eyes and her thick brunette hair. I found photographs of my mother and me when I was about six; I was her clone and she was her mother's, however, being out in hip California where every woman was a blonde with blue eyes, I colored my hair and also changed my eye color thanks to tinted contacts. My dark hair didn't take kindly to the dye and now looks like dried out hay. I still kind of liked my new look, but my grandmother wrinkled her forehead when she saw what I did to my hair. Her eyesight must be failing because she didn't say anything about my choice of eye color.

Lately, I've been too tired to go get my hair colored, so I'm letting it grow out to what it is normally, dark brown. Since I'm always rubbing my eyes and knocking my contacts out, I'm back to being Nile's dark-eyed, "Cinnamon girl", too. Maybe it's due to my lack of sleep or my diminished field of vision without contacts that I walk into things and give myself the bruises and cuts in this world.

After that first day I saw Nile on campus, he later told me that my hair looked like I had spent too many days at the beach in the saltwater. He likes me better as a brunette, I think, even though he would never say either or…what I want to look like is up to me.

The first night back at my grandmother's house after finally unpacking my five suitcases, I found myself sitting at my late grandfather's old upright piano where he often played Beethoven's *Moonlight Sonata*. He didn't live in the states long, only about eight years before he went on a trip to the old country and never returned.

My grandmother doesn't like to talk about that dark time and waves my questions away whenever I try to find out more about my shrinking family. She had said, "I'm your family now and you are mine."

I sat on the creaky, piano bench and played his favorite song like a true master and without any sheet music. I wouldn't have been able to read the notes, anyhow if I had any. I never took any lessons.

Is it possible to absorb a talent like my instant professional ability to play music through my grandfather's abilities? Is it encoded in my DNA because of him and therefore, I can play masterfully without belaboring childhood lessons?

By my third perfect rendition, my grandmother hobbled to the top of the stairs to see if his ghost played the haunting song. I sprinted up the stairs and hustled her back into bed, wondering if music could indeed heal?

I sit up taller on Dr. Hall's comfy couch. My Google brain is not providing any answers on this genetic topic racing around my mind at the moment, but perhaps there isn't an answer available from the medical world as of yet. I need to know if along with the usual physical attributes found on the bodies of future generations, if talents are transferable, too? I write this question in my journal for Dr. Hall to read and answer later.

Next, I make a note about my lack of sleep. My body and mind are so tired from my broken sleep at night. Since I'm scared to sleep alone at night, I find it easier to nap during the hours of sun, and of course, I feel safer, too. The upside of my daytime catnaps is that my mind actually seems to sleep, too, most of the time, although not always. No dreams, just quiet sleep I've been craving after months of little or no REM sleep.

In the brightness of daylight is when my time travels or whatever to call them, usually don't interrupt my downtime unless prompted by Dr. Hall with hypnosis or the same question she seems to ask again and again: "Then what happened?"

This query gets my mind to replay last night's dream or a recent one, however, they don't always rewind in sequential order.

Unfortunately, I can sleep almost anywhere during the day. I know my professors think I must party all night long, falling asleep as they drone on about early Greek philosophy or the world's constant state of upheaval somewhere on the planet due to wars, but when called upon, I awake with the correct answer about what is happening or what has happened the Middle East, China, or Korea.

This never fails to irritate them.

I'm not called upon much, anymore.

At this point in my real-life experiment of 'What do we know of the mind?' I'm a true believer of learning through osmosis.

Nile believes, too since I can be found face down on my open textbooks during much of my study time and then I ace my exams with perfect scores.

The afternoon sun sneaking through the bamboo blinds in Dr. Hall's office is making me sleepy. I find myself slipping into a very still dream state where I do finally sleep without any danger seeping into my space.

When I awake from my short nap, my doctor, who normally is not flustered by any of my recent news or the discovery of a new talent, is sitting in her beige chair across from me. She rapidly reads my journal, flipping the pages and bobbing her silver, high heel shoe, which I have learned from watching her body language, this foot action is a sign of her anxiousness and inability to provide with the right answers to herself or me. Her left pointy toe aims at me. This woman has more shoes than the Philippine's First Lady. Dr. Hall should also open a museum with her shoes like Imelda Marcos did. My Google mind always seems to run off on these tangents more days than not.

Dr. Hall reads the last page of what I wrote today. She shakes her head and says "Interesting" a lot, looking up at me, trying to digest my scribbles in two languages and elaborate sketches.

I still illustrate my dreams and sketch in color since my nightmares are so bright, not the black-and-white slideshow like they used to be. I catch the emotion in her pale hazel eyes before she returns to reread the pages of my journal. They give away her thoughts, so I listen to her monologue inside her head. She's worried about me—unlike the previous times. I lean closer to hear what she is thinking. It sounds like she's whispering inside her head. I untie the thick, braided laces on my snow boots like I'm tightening my boots, but do this only to hear her better.

She wears shoes made for spring; I'm still in winter boots because my feet are always cold these days. I should tell Dr. Hall about my circulatory problems, which have become Nile's problem as well. Like a prima donna, I make him warm up my hands and feet. I don't think he minds, though since I pay him back in other ways.

When I first found out I could hear what others said inside their head—inside my head, I dismissed this knack as the gift of women's intuition. However, as my intelligence expanded into brand new subjects never taught to me, I now pay attention to what I did just hear and don't label it 'a gut feeling', anymore. Whenever I'm with my friends in the middle of a fast-paced conversation, I am guilty when accused: 'You just read my mind!' because I just did.

This truism has become a fact, at least for me. My brain can answer the person's questions before they ask me, making our conversation a bit weird. Close friends of mine had just laughed and discounted my ability to know what they're thinking was based on being in classes together since first grade. I know my confession of this aptitude would only encourage a constant barrage of "What am I thinking right now?" from my friends. I would be kind of like their Facebook page without having them post what they're doing right now. I could just say it out loud for them and their Facebook friends. I wonder if I always had this ability and just didn't recognize it. These days and weeks, though I'm just too tired to keep up old friendships, so I avoid this situation and unfortunately, them, too.

Right now as I eavesdrop on Dr. Hall, she is thinking that my case is quite outside the normal realm of schizophrenia—what? She can't be serious. Me, a schizophrenic?

As she writes the word on her tablet of purple-lined paper, I watch the word appear upside down from where I sit and still can't believe she believes this possible diagnosis. And as if any psychological disease can be classified as 'normal', I want to add to her internal monologue, but know she can't hear me, my internal words.

I look away from my doctor. Her intense face is reflected in the framed universities' certifications hung around her office. I can hear her voice inside her head better this way. She's checking off what my condition is not inside her thoughts:

Bipolar?

No.

Acute stress disorder?

No.

Paranoid? Delusional? Extreme anxiety?

All no.

Dr. Hall pauses…alcohol or amphetamine dependency?

No…

I shake my head and turn back to my doctor to see that she too, knows my problem is neither of these two dependencies.

She studies her clear polished fingernails.

I can hear her admit to herself that perhaps for the first time in twenty-two years of practice she might not be able to provide a solid diagnosis.

"I think we need to do more testing."

How can she honestly say that? She just booked me into another doctor appointment this week. Did she not read through the seven-inch stack of test results that neurologist, Dr. Reid, conducted during the first couple of weeks after I returned home? He had already did every blood test, CAT scan, EEG, brain MRI, and others body-imaging examinations. Can there really be any more tests to do?

I'm half listening probably because I already know what she's going to say and due to my chronic lack of sleep, which is making me lethargic and at the same time frustrated because no one can find an answer to why I can't get my vivid dreams to cease. I need my sleep.

I have heard, "We just don't know…" much too often from my doctors these days.

"I want you to spend the night in the university's sleep lab to rule out any psychosomatic causes for your nightly scars."

There's my answer: a night in a sterile laboratory. Maybe I'll sleep soundly or experience even more lucid dreams under observation. As if I am not getting enough sleep as it is, she wants to tag my skull with hundreds of electronic pads attached to long colored wires, which already are making me feel claustrophobia just thinking about being tied up all night long.

She interrupts my thoughts, "This type of test might show something that you are amiss in saying or writing."

"Okay, when?" I slump back into the once comfy couch, finding it now hard against my spine. I swing my feet, and despite the fact I'm almost an adult, still cannot touch the ground. Here I am three years old, again—and wish I was. I would have my mother with me and I wouldn't have this problem, but then again, I might have always been in this quandary—living in two worlds and just didn't know it.

[Morse code message: TRUTH]

.--. .-. --- -- .. ... .

Nile's eyes brim with big tears.

Rosalyn and my grandmother sit in the king and queen chairs at the dining room table and stifle their laughter from behind their cocktail napkins. This time, my grandmother has set the table with the pink ones that read: Born to Party. Forced to Work. Evidence that she's still holding a grudge against her parents about starting work young and foregoing any fun she assumed came naturally with attending high school.

The platter of blackened red snapper over a bed of Jasmine rice is almost gone. The dish was laced with chili peppers and spices not known to Nile's tongue and is definitely out of his comfort zone of acceptable heat. He fans his open mouth and sticks his tongue out at me.

"Nice. Remind me not to take you to a fancy restaurant."

He downs his tall glass of milk.

"Nile? You don't like my dish?" Rosalyn bites into a shiny red pepper and chews without any reaction.

Nile's eyes grow larger as he watches her swallow the deadly vegetable or at least that's what he's saying inside his head.

I hear him say it to himself. I reach out to my boyfriend and cup my hand over his.

He's trying to speak, but the heat still lingering inside his mouth makes it impossible for words to get out.

"Rosalyn, Nile loves your cooking." I squeeze his hand.

Nile nods.

"But it's the spiciness that's got his tongue." I pass him my glass of iced water.

Nile accepts it and points to the glistening, half eaten, evil pepper on his plate.

"Rosalyn, since you created this culinary masterpiece, Nile and I will handle dish detail." I push back from the table to collect the dinner plates.

Nile picks up the glasses and our salad plates, but avoids the serving platter.

My grandmother bursts out laughing.

Rosalyn laughs, too.

Nile frowns, but a kiss from me on his cheek changes that.

After the dishes, I suggested going outside to cool down his mouth since he swears it's still on fire. Tonight promises us a full moon for our twilight picnic. Spring is definitely making its arrival known with its increasing warmer evenings. Nile and I can camp outside wearing just a sweater until the night chill descends and sends us indoors. I like the crispness of the coming darkness with its temperatures in the forties.

Nile is not too thrilled about this nighttime picnic—he's another summer person, yet pacifies me and agrees to sit outside in the cold. He pulls on his knitted cap and ski gloves and holds the back door open for me.

I think his extra clothing is overkill, but lead him outside by one of his gloved hands.

I want to feel the weather down to my fingertips and on the tip of my nose. I know winter is almost over, summer will arrive and the freshness in the air that only winter can bring will be gone.

Nile watches me savor the chilliness that is settling in around us as the sun sinks behind the neighbor's house. He shakes his head, convinced I'm losing all faculties and stands to stoke the fire burning inside the *chimenya*. Rosalyn had given us hers once she moved into a condo downtown. She had said, "With only a second-story porch, I can't use it, anymore. It's against the CC&Rs."

I'm glad my grandmother made the offer for her to use it here and she does and so do I. I like this self-contained fireplace because Nile has to sit very close to me to feel the heat and if we fall asleep, there is less danger of its sparks jumping out on the lawn and burning down the house.

Nile just stares hard at me when I say what he thinks are just ridiculous sentiments. He comes from a very stable family with three older brothers and a younger sister. His parents own titles of prestige. His dad is a doctor. His mom is a lawyer. They have been married thirty years, are happy together, and both employed by the university. That pretty much sums up their life, according to how Nile sees it. "Nothing ever changes in my world."

He lives the polar opposite life of mine. Everything that I thought to be true is changing in my world.

"I brought a flashlight or a "torch" as the English would say." My Google mind tries to tell me, but I already knew that one. I click it 'on' and 'off'. The spotlight lights up Nile's face.

Nile laughs. "And what game do you want to play with a torch?"

"Where's Waldo? But we'll call it, "Where's Mary?"

"We're going to drive the neighbors nuts with a beam of light flashing all around the backyard."

"I know." I pour hot chocolate from the red plaid thermos that my grandmother must have purchased in the seventies. I'm surprised it still works, but the steam following the hot liquid proves it is very functional in spite of its birth year.

Nile accepts the blue-and-white, enamel metal cup. "Since when do you camp?" He lights up his cup with the flashlight.

"My grandmother did. This is from her camping collection."

"How many collections does this woman have?"

"If you count her books, flamingos, gnomes, photo albums, necklaces, and pillows…six?"

"You forgot her Virgin Mary collection. You know, the ones we're trying to locate tonight." Nile slurps his chocolate soup. "I don't know about all those others, that's just one too many. Except the photo albums. Those are good books to own."

"Just wait until you're her age and then I'll do a count of your collections."

"Don't bother. I'm not a hoarder."

"She just doesn't want to lose any of her history, so she keeps everything." I sip from my metal cup that's heating up my hands due to its contents. "I started using old magazines from the bottom of her endless stacks to make my origami paper cranes."

I pull one out of my pocket to show him.

Nile takes it from my palm and makes it fly through the air and land on my head. "Really? I thought you had to use pre-cut, perfect squares of special paper to make the folds hold tight."

I sit very still so the paper crane won't slip off my head. "I like how the glossy, four-color ads and the black-and-white articles make for interesting looking birds."

Nile sips his hot cocoa. I can hear him thinking about folding the slippery pages.

"Can I help you make your one thousand cranes?"

"No, according to the Japanese legend, the person who's making the wish has to make them all. I do appreciate your offer."

He takes the bird off my head and puts it in his pocket. "I'll string them up for you and hang them from your ceiling in your bedroom, so they look like they're flying. I'm sure your grandpa has fishing line stocked away somewhere in the garage." He clinks his metal cup against mine. "Good luck, but hurry up and fold faster, would you? I want to meet your mom."

"Yeah, only 644 more to go until you maybe can meet her."

Nile makes a sad face. "Hey, what about your new game? He throws his arm around my shoulders and pulls me to him. "I was hoping it would be something like 'Truth or Dare' or 'Spin the Flashlight' or even 'Strip Poker'?"

"You could never handle that last suggestion outside. You're cold in July." I kiss his check. "But I'll reward you each time you spy Mary." I kiss him on the lips for a long while.

"Okay—got it!" Nile scans the backyard with the beam of light tracing the top of my childhood swing set, across my old sandbox, which is now Rosalyn's dormant vegetable and herb garden. She took over the tending to the garden when my grandmother bemoaned the fact that we would have to buy produce at a big box, supermarket chain. Now each summer, Rosalyn grows enough for us, for her needs, and Nile's family.

It's a big sandbox.

Nile draws the beam of light up the stone wall separating the backyard from the alley, along the side of the garage and circles it up to the pitch of the garage's roof. "There's Mary number one. Pay up."

I take his cup from his gloved hand and place it on top of the mosaic table beside me. I reach up and hold his neck, slowly kissing him for minutes.

Nile pulls away to breathe and then smiles, "I like this game."

He continues to run the flashlight over the pieces and parts of my childhood in the backyard. The light stops on the budding Japanese maple tree that I used to swing from and climb all over as I got older and taller. My grandfather had planted the delicate small tree in the shade of the other trees for Rosalyn when she moved to the states shortly after my mother and I arrived. He wanted her to feel at home even though she had never lived in Japan. I guess in retrospect, we have always known Rosalyn.

Over the years, she told me short stories about her family immigration during the campaign by Brazil to get cheap labor to help on the coffee plantations after African slavery was abolished in 1850. South America first enticed Italians and other Europeans to come live and work below the equator with the promise to pay their passages.

Rosalyn tsk-tsked aloud when she told me what her father told her. "When they arrived, they found the pay to be subpar, the living conditions as bad as it was for the Negroes. Bosses equally as racist. This false promise of a better life resembled modern-day slavery just the same. Italy shut down Brazil's efforts to lure more immigrants with the passing of a law, prohibiting the subsidized immigration."

Over our "family dinners" together: my mom, grandmother, and me, Rosalyn loved to entertain us with stories of how her relatives escaped the great poverty in the rural populated countryside after feudalism ended. I thought she was really old then when she said that, but later realized she meant her relatives.

"My family was part of the first wave to arrive in Brazil. As early as 1908. They continued to come to the land of coffee."

Rosalyn only drank coffee, not tea like my grandmother.

She sips her coffee as she continues at the end of the meal, telling me a history I know I'll never know of my family. "My great, great grandfathers were smart business men. Instead of working the coffee plantations, they had saved enough money from working their plots of land to buy the coffee plantations!" She had covered her mouth and laughed.

I'm glad my mind has decided to keep these morsels of family history stored in my head. Rosalyn has been with my little family for a very long time. I just can't remember how we meet. I'll have to ask her to help me find this memory in this foggy mind of mine.

In the darkness of the oncoming night, the tiny buds on the Japanese maple tree are visible, however, this mature tree knows to wait for more consistent, spring-like days and nights to leaf out fully and into its usual greenery that shades a corner of my grandmother's backyard from mid-June to early October.

Nile moves his aim and spotlights a little plastic Mary in the nook of next tree, a grand cottonwood. Mary leans against a primitive birdhouse I built when I was nine. My grandfather had supervised my operating of the power tools. My grandmother worried, especially when I handled the skill saw.

My grandfather applauded my straight cuts and my grandmother stopped worrying. I was kind of a serious kid, unlike now. Maybe hanging around Nile again has made me regress back to our kindergarten antics.

This Mary wears an ensemble of all crimson: a long dress with a hood. In autumn, she's the same color of the leaves.

"Found the second one!" He waves at her with the flashlight. "Hi Mary!"

I reward him with a peck on his cold cheek.

"Wait! That's it?" He clicks off the flashlight. "I quit."

"Oh, come on, there's always the grand prize." I turn on the flashlight and put it back in his hand. "There are more Marys to find."

He runs the light across the bottom of the white garden fence. "You need to earn your keep and paint that fence for your grandmother."

Its peeling white paint reveals the weathered, wood grain beneath. I should paint the fence for my grandmother this summer. "If I promised to wear my bikini, will you help me?"

"Of course! Hey, I feel like I should call you Tom Sawyer from now on."

The beam of the flashlight shines over the cement fountain in the middle of the garden sanctuary. My thirteenth summer seems like eons ago and while Nile started to hang around that summer more like a boyfriend than a friend, I remember it as the summer of when my mother became a fading memory. I had a hard time remembering her face, slowly it slipped from my mind's eyes and only by staring at old photos of her could I see her again for a little bit.

For her birthday that year in case she returned, I asked my grandfather to show me how to make a garden fountain and a small table with a mosaic-tiled top like I saw in a magazine. He wanted to make matching one for his wife, so mother and daughter could have tea together, again one day. We had old wooden tables, but the snowy weather had damaged their surfaces. I thought tiles might last and survive our winters a little better.

He agreed, took Nile and me to the library for to check out design books and then to the hardware store to find our materials. Many days later and just-in-time for my mother's birthday, we had finished the fountain that bubbled water in its center and two, small tiled tables with metal legs that have turned a green patina.

The birds took an instant liking to the fountain, so I guess it resembles more of a birdbath than the fountain that I had intended.

The next summer, we added two new chairs to the garden sanctuary. This special space we created for my mother's homecoming continues to wait year-round. It does looks better each year and becomes more overgrown due to the freak snow storms in September, which turn into rain and usually reappear often in late spring, too.

This waiting for my mother's return is wearing on my hope…and me. I vowed to myself to make fifty more paper cranes before I go to bed tonight, or if I wake up in the middle of the dark scary hours like I usually do.

Nile is now running around the backyard in his frantic search for another Mary. He backtracks to the fountain's waterless basin. In the center where the water normally cascades into the bowl, there stands a dry Mary. When she arrived to live in the fountain, she wore a canary yellow gown with a white cloak, but the constant rain of the fountain throughout spring, summer, and autumn has turned her mossy green. I think the heavy snows of winter have only solidified the fur coat provided by Mother Nature.

He holds the beam of light over her head so she looks as if she on stage and then dashes back to me, crawling onto the blanket beside me.

"This is starting to get a bit creepy." Nile attempts to climb into my lap, but there isn't enough room. He slips off me and back onto the blanket. "They're everywhere!"

"What can someone of your size be afraid of?" I remove the flashlight from his hand, turn it off, and straddle his lap.

"Everywhere I look, this woman, these women are staring back at me."

"You're cute. What do you expect? Women will stare. Besides, she doesn't really stare. "

"Yes she does!"

"Mary, Jesus' mother, has more of an all-watching, all-knowing look."

"Exactly. And it gives me the heebie jeebies."

"You're safe with me." I kiss his forehead and lean my forehead against his.

"Look! There's another one!" Nile points to the top of the alley's wall. "More Marys!"

Under the street light where he points are five Mary, little Marys, all lined up like songbirds do, equally spaced apart from one another. I wonder if my grandmother is more mobile than she lets on to us or maybe she directed Rosalyn from her second-story window. What did she use to anchor them up there? Why haven't I noticed them before? Is danger approaching our house from the outside? Maybe I should be afraid like Nile is? He's kidding, right? I look into his eyes for the answers.

"The neighbors now do officially think the ladies of this house are cuckoo." He hugs me, locking down my arms, so I can't swat at him.

"They already knew that many years ago." I fall back to the ground, pulling him with me.

"Can we go inside? The wet grass is seeking through the blanket to my jeans."

[Morse code message: PROMISE]

-... . .-.. .. . ...- .

On a sunny afternoon with a perfect Colorado blue sky above, stretching up to the peaks of The Flatirons and east pass the state line and into Kansas, I arrive at my weekly psychoanalysis evaluation to simply conduct a monologue with myself, again. At this point, this is what I've concluded is going on in these sessions that continue to provide very few answers.

Dr. Hall only repeats herself today as she does on other days, simply saying, "Tell me more."

So I do, in my usual prone position on her wonderful couch: "Many nights, I deliberately wake myself up because of the pending danger playing out in my mind—like the nightmare I had of flying off a blind, twisting road above a body of water. I'm the passenger in a brand new hunter green, Range Rover."

Why I can remember the color of the car is baffling because it was another moonless night. How many nights in a row can pass without a moon or at least a hint of the orb? I guess I my visits to this other place are not occurring in sequential order of the Georgian calendar, which governs us up here in the snowy Colorado Rockies and the rest of the real-time world. Or maybe I'm not showing up on a regular basis, in this other world—or perhaps chronological time is irrelevant in my dreams.

I realize, at this point, I'm only talking to myself and resume telling my thoughts out loud for the benefit of my doctor. "Someone else was driving. I couldn't recognize who it was because my head wouldn't turn to the left. I think my driver was a woman."

"How do you know?"

"I could feel her presence, a slight stature. Narrow shoulders, definitely not a man's, but there was a man with us. In the back seat. Behind me."

110

"Did you recognize him?"

"I couldn't see him, but had a feeling that I did know him, too. He was about my age."

"And what age are you in your dream?"

"Probably sixteen." I think to myself, Why would knowing my age matter and as if that single fact would help me or my doctor figure out 'the why' or 'the where' of these crazy travels? This was the summer I got a pixie haircut—cutting my long hair to the bottom of my earlobe and I do remember my hair not sticking to my neck.

"I remember flying high above the calm black bay with absolutely no way of getting out of the car before it shattered the still water below. Someone had removed the interior doors' handles and the children's safety locks on the power windows were jammed."

I remember again the feeling of pure panic taking over my entire body.

"Our speeding car was unable to take the centrifugal pull of the bend in the road and it veered away from the safety of the cliff's embankment. I searched the front seat area, the floor, and the glove compartment for anything to break the window, and just as I looked up, I watched helplessly as we soared off the sheer cliff, suspended for an absorbent amount of sickening time above the expansive bay. I didn't feel like dying that night, not even in a dream. I thought I was screaming, although I don't think any sounds came out of my mouth. I banged my fists against the cold glass and then tried again to see who sat beside me as we hit the water."

I straighten my legs and cross my ankles. In the retelling of my dream, I had curled up into a ball.

"Then what happened?" Today, Dr. Hall is the one who's writing furiously in this session.

"When I awoke in the early light of morning, I was in my bedroom. My nightgown clung to me as if I had taken a shower in it. Only when Nile woke up and found me on the floor and touched my back did I realize I was soaked from sweat, not the ocean, and from living through such a terrorizing ordeal in both my mind and in my body."

I tremble again and feel chilled even though I'm in Dr. Hall's office and not back in the cold water. The memory of saltwater splashing in my eyes each time a wave crashed over me makes me rub my eyes, now.

"Are you seeing snow, again?" Dr. Hall sits across from me in a brighter outfit today. She wears a business suit the color of the inside of a cantaloupe and that includes her high heel shoes. This happy brightness hurts my head. I turn away from her.

"Yes, and as much as I love the real thing, these little halos and trails of light in front of my eyes make it impossible to read. I just can't concentrate. Everything goes all blurry and jumps around a lot."

"Don't worry about your finals."

"I am worried about my exams. I can't see to read and won't be able to take the written exams"

"I've spoken with your professors and most of them already knew something was up, so you get to take a verbal test due to your skewed vision. Unless your vision returns, then you get to do the fill-in-the-bubble, paper test like everyone else with a number two pencil. Okay?"

I'm relieved, but I do have it easy. If I get stuck in my tests, I can just pull up the answer in my brain and my teachers wouldn't even know.

"Dr. Hall, from what I researched on a couple of Internet forums, it seems as if many sufferers of visual snow cite a variety of illnesses or conditions that can cause this visual disorder like Lyme disease, autoimmune disease, or even chronic exposure like dehydration, over-acidification of a body, or the prolonged use of a VDU."

Dr. Hall stops reading her notes and looks up at me. "VDU?"

"Visual Display Units. A fancy acronym for computer monitors, e-readers like the NOOK and the Kindle, iPads, you know." I had hoped that Dr. Hall would be thrilled to hear these possibilities and take Multiple Sclerosis off the list.

"Unfortunately, Tess none of these claims have been confirmed by scientific study."

I guess the docs are a bit slow in believing anything new without twenty years of clinical studies, unlike bloggers and their followers and that would be me, who will and want to believe everything they read online—even if it's in electronic, black-and-white, it must be true.

[Morse code message: BELIEVE]

... .- ...- . ...-.

I feel myself plunging deep down into a tunnel of suffocating water. Everything is silent, except for my screaming inside my head. To stop my spiral tumble into the ocean, I extend my arms out like Jesus on the cross. Useless. My body sinks south, deeper into the salty water. I mermaid kick my legs and feet together to bring some upward motion to this insane dance with the ocean. I look up to see how far I will need to go to break the water's surface. It's a long way and looks even farther away due to the night's sky.

Am I suspended between life and death, right now?

I experience a temporary hold or rather a floating sensation and realize that I am no longer falling deeper into this body of water. My feeble attempt to move up through these layers of water is working, but only if I alternate my mermaid kicks with the downward thrust of my extended arms. This method of swimming directly toward the black horizon is a slow process. I try not to panic as I watch the line between ocean and the sky move very slowly, but closer to me. This is also the same line between living and dying. My lungs are searing with intense pain due to the lack of oxygen. I exhale as slowly as I can, blowing out bubbles as I sneak glances upward to gauge how much farther I need to go before I run out of air.

The lid of this bay seems so far away.

I close my eyes and kick and pull at the thick water above my head, reaching for the blessed oxygen just outside my watery prison. I don't think I will make it. This ceiling of water is not within my reach.

Is this what it feels like to drown?

A sudden feeling of apathy overcomes me. I stop fighting the water. I know, now, I will not make it.

114

Before my world fades away, I feel a hand on my back and forearm. Someone is pushing me upwards. The hands I feel are strong, wide like a man's. Again, I try to see who my savior is, but can't move my head or open my eyes.

I feel myself being propelled upward and finally, I break the water's surface. I gasp. I sputter briny seawater from my mouth, coughing while trying to tread and stay above the choppy ocean waves. A random idea enters my head moments after I return to life: If I'm going to keep ending up in the ocean at night in my dreams, I better start going with Nile to his water polo practices. I shake my head and grin. I didn't die in my dream. I'm alive—this time—but might not be the next.

As oxygen feeds back into my lungs and brain, I realize how ridiculous this nightmare is, although it doesn't change the fact that I feel like I almost drowned.

There is splashing next to me about three yards away, and when I can finally move my head to see the person that saved me and even with his slicked wet hair, I know he's the same male I met at the parade, on the beach, and according to my grandmother is my boyfriend, too, or my other boyfriend, Tino.

Tino rolls his eyes like he can't believe he's alive and then he takes two strokes toward me and holds me in his arms and kisses me hard, out of gratitude for life, both of ours, rather than lust.

My mind tries to figure out how we came to be here—bobbing along in the night water and breathing, again. I kiss him back, but it's a short one since the ocean is tossing me around again. Were we thrown from the Range Rover? But I thought I ended up in the bay after the sunset cruise…or maybe I ended up in the bay both times.

Breathe, I focus on just breathing. I take another huge breath.

Tino does the same thing and then lets go of me.

I feel a swell of panic again to be left alone in the choppy water, which is getting colder with each passing minute. Across the swell of the incoming wave, I yell, "Thank you", but he's gone, swimming toward a rescue boat that's zooming out of the harbor and towards us. Now I feel reassured he wasn't leaving me, just wanting to make sure we were seen.

I have no more energy left to exert to follow him, so I stay put and float. I wonder how long I clawed my way to life again. My legs and arms say a very long time due to the burning and heavy sensation that I feel in them now, then I remember–the Range Rover rocketing off the road, the lingering sensation high above the water, and then hitting the black surface like an explosion, yet without any flames or smoke—just silence as glass-colored bubbles headed toward the bay's surface as we dropped deeper into bottomless water.

I scan the watery horizon for the driver. There is no one. My heart hurts. The driver was a woman and something is telling me that she was my mother. She couldn't have died in my dream, could she? Or is this real life, my life in another place? Or in another time in my life? Can I possibly be living two lives at the same time?

But someone must have seen our car dive into the bay and called for help. I say, "Thank you" aloud once again. I can now remember the sequence of the horrible plunge into the bay. We tried to open the doors and the windows before hitting the water to escape before it filled with water, but we were locked in and the electric windows were jammed. The driver must have somehow got the sunroof to open just before our car crashed into the bay. Someone pushed me up and out of the car as it dropped deeper into the bay. We fought the gravity under water, insistent on pushing us down to the bottom of the ocean. We raced against the seconds to make it out of the Range Rover before it sank with us stuck inside and without any chance of a successful rescue just delivery to a watery tomb.

I scan the mountaintop surrounding the bay and can see a white statue, glimmering due to its own soapstone hue. This grand statute must be very tall to be able to see it from this distance. Could it be a statue of the Virgin Mary? And how ironic would that be? My grandmother's choice saint for protection, is also this seaside city's choice, too. Yet this imposing figure's stance above the port seems to be more masculine and perhaps he watched over the driver, Tino, and me to ensure we lived another night.

I, too hold my arms stretched wide from my side like he does to making floating a little easier while I wait for the boat to pick up my rescuer, Tino, and then come to me. I refuse to believe the driver died, so I scan the immediate fringe of the nearby waves and swim in a small circle. I think I see the outline of a head bobbing on the waves. The boat moves in close next to rescue her. I'm so relieved for this person whether she's my mother or not.

Where am I?

I study the edge of the white, outlined port and look up to the top of the mountain, again to study the all-white gleaming sculpture. The statue looks like the one visible from Interstate 70 in Colorado on Lookout Mountain, but there are only vast farmlands after the high rises of Denver. There's no massive body of water, except small, artificial lakes for boating and ice fishing. I can't be in the United States, yet this is a dream and how often do places and people show up in the right order, the right place, let alone in the right latitude? In my hallucinations, this seems to be the rule. Nothing makes sense.

The drone of an engine idles across the water fifty yards away from me.

The rescue boat shifts into a higher gear and moves closer to where I am tossed about between the rolling waves. The time that it takes the boat to get to me feels like an hour or longer…maybe I did bob here for hours. I keep getting slapped in the face with waves of saltwater. I drank some by accident, which is not alleviating my thirst. I'm so thirsty. I could go for a gallon of my fresh wonderful, snow water that flows out of the faucet at my grandmother's house.

I am pulled into the rescue boat by a pair of strong arms and hands. They wrapped me in wool blankets and place me on a bench beside Tino. The night sky is calm above us unlike the activities taking place down here on this watery stage. The boat heads back to the dock where the ambulances' lights puncture the darkness with its intermittent strobe lights of flashing red and blue and white. I watch as the medical people work on a patient, who's on the deck of the speeding boat.

It's our driver.

Tino wraps his arm around me.

I let my head fall back against his chest and listen to his breathing. I blink and try to see between the medics if I know the woman that the medics are working desperately to save.

Could she be my mother? Would I recognize her at the age of thirty-seven and with wet hair and in the shadows of night?

She needs oxygen, so one of the paramedics is placing the plastic mask over her mouth. She is shivering, another medic slaps heat packs against his thighs to make them heat up and lines both sides of her body and her chest with them. He covers her with two more, thick gray blankets.

I can no longer see her face. I try to stand to see her better, but a paramedic sits me back down again.

As I look up at the innocent stars piercing the dark heaven in numbers too high to count tonight, I think about home in the Rockies. Maybe Nile and I will try to count the stars as soon as the snow melts and the night are warm enough to lie on the grass together. I always liked sleeping outside, holding hands and counting the stars until we fell asleep—like we used to do when we were barely teenagers. This memory within my dream warms me. I close my eyes wanting to awake there in summer—in the future—with him…

Wait, was it Tino or Nile? My dreams and worlds are running together.

I remember that Tino and I used to lie on the beach and watch the stars cross the sky overhead. My Google brain interjects and tells me I'm wrong. The earth rotates, not the stars, however, then it continues to say due to gravity every object in space moves—I cut off the automatic transmission all about the earth, the moon, and the stars and that is starting to sound like my professor's lectures…

Why can't I picture or remember who is or was beside me staring up at the stars? Could it have been both of them in different summers since one lives above the equator and the other south of it?

I look up again and this time it's Tino, who kisses my salty lips beneath the stars.

[Morse code message: SAVEHER]

-.- . . .--. .... . .-. .... .- ..-. .

Nile rolls across my wide bed over the mountain of quilts and slides off the side to crawl across the braided rug. He reaches out to me, touching my soggy nightgown.

"What the heck?" He snatches the top quilt off the bed and covers me.

His whole face reads of concern. He whips my nightgown off over my head "Is it raining over here?" His instinct is to resort to levity when he's freaked.

I force a small smile at his attempt to lessen both of our worry about this predicament. My body is shivering to stay warm. I curl my bare legs up against my chest to trap in any heat. My teeth are chattering uncontrollably as I try to talk. "No. Went for. A swim. Again."

"Where? In the bathtub?" Nile hugs me with the quilt. "Let's get you off this cold floor."

I cling to his neck as he sweeps me up from the hardwood floor.

Nile buries me under the mound of quilts and goes to adjust the thermostat control on the wall. "You know, you'll have to tell Dr. Hall about this—whether she'll believe it or not."

"You'll have to come with me."

"I could, but what if she thinks I'm in cahoots with you on that pill inventory you've started?" He slides in next to me, using his body to warm me. "What is in your collection here on your nightstand?" He leans over me to reads the labels: "Valium, Ambien, Lexapro, Lunesta…"

"I want to stop taking them."

Nile sits up on one elbow. "You have to take at least the sleeping pills, Tess."

I shiver "no" with my whole body.

He loads three more blankets on top of me from the stash that I keep neatly folded at the foot of my bed on the long bench. "Your poppy flowers need a fresh coat of paint or will you persuade me to do this, too?"

My brain automatically adds his suggestion to my 'To Do' list, but know I won't do it anytime soon. One summer while I waited for my mother's return, I had painted red poppy flowers around the perimeter of this white bench. Rosalyn must have moved into my bedroom after I left for college. Winter came early that year I left for college. It comforts me to have it in my room and reminds me of my mother for some reason that I can't recall.

Nile worms around beside me. "I think the weight of these extra blankets is making my feet fall asleep. They're stretching them straight out from my ankle bone, making my legs even longer!"

I smile at him, although can't find the energy to laugh at his joke. However, I think he might be right. This could happen to a body part or a whole body due to the layers of the blankets. Maybe that's why I'm so lethargic and it's not the prescriptions I digest daily.

I tremble again and question the fact, why has my core temperature has radically changed over the last couple months? Me, who has never been cold in my entire life, now can't ever get warm these days. My feet are icicles most night and days, too.

Nile teases me about the fact that I'll be wearing my Nordic ski sweaters into summer this year. Unfortunately, his joke might be closer to the truth and another one of my realities in this life. My body's chills and the inability to regulate my body temperature is a very real sign of being sleep deprived.

Nile pats my blankets down around me like he's making an apple dumpling.

I stop him and hold his hand to anchor myself in this room. I'm afraid of slipping away, again. "My new pills, Lunesta, aren't helping me to sleep much, anyhow. Every time I crack open the lid to my pills, my stomach revolts. I really think it's the combination of all these pills that intensifies my dreams."

"Or maybe I shouldn't stay over so much."

I open my cocoon of blankets and invite him into my space. "I actually dream less when you're here."

"Yeah, you just go for ocean swims at night."

I tuck my chin under the layers of quilts. "I promise to stay here with you, anymore. I'll just sleep in my classes."

"As if you have a choice when and if you stay or go." Nile wraps his arm across my stomach and holds onto my hip. "Bet you're real popular with your professors. You fall asleep as soon as they begin to lecture."

"They probably think I'm cheating, somehow because I always wake up with the right answer whether or not I finished my homework."

"Have you told them anything about your predicament? Or should I say your hyper-intelligence?"

"They do know something is up, particularly when they ask a question about something that we turned in at the start of class and my paper is absent."

"Houston, we have a problem here."

"No, Nile, it's just that I now know stuff. Like the way you know your memories. It's just in there." I point to my head, make a gun out of my fingers, and then pull the trigger.

"Stop it." Nile takes the pretend gun from my temple. "You better not leave me, again."

"I think the pills are helping me in that area, though, of being smarter."

He punches a fat pillow to make a dent for his head and turns on his side to face me. "So, what happened this time?"

I close my eyes not wanting to feel hopeless and soggy again, but I had to remember something, anything to figure out where I was. Dr. Hall said if I could zoom in on a detail, we might be able to answer the "why?" or even the "where?" of my nighttime travels. She still calls them "dreams" or in the more graphic and threatening situations, she does mumble the word, "nightmares".

Due to the length of time of which I've been experiencing such travels, I'm convinced at this point I am living a parallel life. I'm not sure if I voiced this out loud to Nile before, so I take a deep breath before I say, "I think I'm living a parallel life."

He looks like he believes me or wants to because he cannot explain either why I woke up on the cold floor drenched like I did indeed go for a midnight swim in the ocean.

He pulls back the quilts and licks my shoulder. "Yup, salty.

"Like saltwater or just salty like sweat?"

"You taste like the ocean, Cinnamon Girl."

With that revelation, I know I need to find my own answers. Maybe Nile will go to the library with me, not that I need to—I could just ask my Google brain to help me figure out where I am traveling to, but there is something about being surrounded by books and holding onto something real like a book that I find soothing.

"Come to the library with me, today?"

"Oh that place where they store all the of the universe's knowledge?"

I elbow him under the covers. "How dare you talk smack about libraries!"

"Yes, of course, I'll follow you anywhere, but haven't those professionals you've been calling with your hundreds of questions given you the answers you're looking for?"

He's right. In my recent discussions with physicists at MIT, Berkeley, and UCLA, I'm starting to understand quantum physics a bit more than before all of my mental tripping started. Also, after digging through my grandmother's photo albums and within my own brain's ability to tap into instant knowledge, I found some proof including a handful of physicists scattered around the globe that do believe in this reality.

Actually, there are believed to be four levels of parallel universes, but I don't dare say any of this to my psychoanalyst. They lock up people in mental institutions for such declarations and I'm not taking my chances. I need to be here for my grandmother.

Nile touches his finger to my lips. "Your lips are moving, but you're not saying anything."

I kiss his lingering finger. "Sorry. Thought I was. I was just trying to piece together what I have been experiencing to figure out where I'm going based on what the physicists said to watch and listen for." I pull his arm across my stomach and hug it. "It was night again, a warm evening, probably sometime, somewhere in the middle of summer. The ocean was so warm, at least the first two minutes."

"Was I with you?" He smiles.

"I wish."

He pulls his arm away to place the palm of his hand on my cheek because even my face is cold.

"I was in dark water with three-foot high waves randomly thundering down on me, dunking me under again and undulating without any rhythm. I tried to pop up above the swells to see a landmark on the shore."

I remember the mountain where the statue stood looked like a hunchback and was bare of any trees. I know where this is, but do I dare say it out loud to Nile?

"I should have been with you. I'm the best at treading water."

"Yes, you are Mr. Water Polo."

"Maybe I could go "pro"." He folds his arms back behind his head, lost in his dream. "Nah, I don't think there are enough groupies in water polo."

I slug him with a pillow.

"Hey! You're the one for me. How many times do I have to prove it to you?" He places a pillow over my arms to keep me from clobbering him, again. "Besides, the chlorine wreaks havoc on my hair."

His hand travels down across my hips, back and forth with his light intoxicating touch.

"So you're the one for me?" I play with his gorgeous hair to straighten it, only to watch the stretched lock that I pulled straight pop back into a loose, springy curl. Women would pay tons of money to have hair like his. I left my hand wander around his wide chest and then to his tight stomach.

"Yes. Your grandmother told me that we are forever. She seconded my heart's vote, so that's that and you know it, too."

"She says a lot of things, some right and some not." The edge of the blanket is tight near my face, only my eyes show. "Forever? How do you know? How does she know? We're only nineteen."

"She told me, 'Love begets love, love knows no age—" Nile has wrapped his leg over my thighs and pulls me against him.

"The ancient, Roman poet Virgil said that and it was, "Love begets love, love knows no rules…"

"I like the way she said it and I think she's right on this one. Besides, either way it says the same thing, "age", "rules", at least in my opinion." Nile rolls over onto his stomach.

I feel cold again and scoot against his side.

Nile returns his hand to my body, exploring as he talks; his mouth and body acting completely independently of each other. "And then, what happened in your travels? Did you swim to shore?"

"No."

"No? Oh! My! God!" He hides his face in the blankets. "You died! Agggh!"

My grandmother thuds the handle of the kitchen broom on her floor, my ceiling.

I cup my hands to yell up to my grandmother, but Nile takes my hands away from my mouth.

"Don't bother. She knows it's me crying, not you."

"Oh, does she?"

"She said you never cried as a little girl or cry now, so she knows it's me making the ruckus."

He's right.

I don't do the female, water-work thing. "I didn't die this time."

Nile gives me the extremely, wide-open, eye stare that says, don't ever say that out loud, again!

"Sorry. But I'm here now and all I can remember is seeing a white statue high on a mountaintop."

Nile pops up in bed pulling the blankets with him and off me. "Like our Mother Cabrini shrine on I-70? I swear you can see her for fifty miles! She must be four hundred feet tall." Nile spreads out his arms wide like Jesus. His wayward hand knocks me across the mouth as I sit up to recover the blankets.

"Ouch. I fall back onto the pillow to garner additional sympathy and attention.

It works.

He pulls me on top of him. "Oh, sorry!" He places a delicate kiss upon my lips and stays awhile. "It's not swollen…yet. Hey. You taste like banana-flavored, bubble gum. Give me some."

"Oh. That." I hold my breath and try to figure out why I taste like jackfruit, again. This whole debacle with being allergic to jackfruit is what initially took me to my university's medical center in Northern California. When I originally received this diagnosis, I didn't even know what this fruit looked like, however, now I have seen it, tasted it, and eaten it with Tino…it feels weird to be thinking of him right now while I'm with Nile here. Tino always tastes like banana, bubble gum, too, but then again, he's usually snacking on his favorite fruit. "I'll save some bubble gum for you next time."

I don't have a rash like the last time, but Nile is right, I can taste the banana flavor inside my mouth. I scan my brain to see if jackfruit is added as an extender to any food products in the United States. My instant mental research comes up zero, so I'm beginning to believe whatever I eat in my dreams, I can bring back home. I wonder if the doctors at this teaching hospital will be open to such crossover possibilities.

"Nile, I think your Mother Cabrini standing high on Lookout Mountain is actually a statue of Jesus Christ."

"What? Then why does the brown, national park service sign on the side of the freeway say, "Mother Cabrini Shrine?" Tell me that! Oh, you will because you know now everything." Nile sulks and buries his face in the crook of my neck, but starts to kiss me with force. I hope he doesn't leave a mark like he sometimes does. My grandmother gives me dirty looks, but never says anything. How could she? She encourages him to stay the night. I think she worries about me after she's gone and wants him to be in my life now and then in the future.

"Do you want me to tell you?" I climb on top of him and try to merge into him by lying perfectly flat. There is more warmth between us this way.

"Yes, I guess." He wraps his arms around me.

"Mother Cabrini is there at the base of Jesus, but she's made out of black marble and is shorter than me, so I would never be able to see her between the slaps of the waves." I whisper into his ear.

Nile squirms and begins to move slowly under me. "How can you see Jesus if your ocean swims all happen when it's dark?"

I close my eyes and wait as another salty wave hits me in the mouth. "The statue is illuminated by many lights." I squint. "Actually, the old lights were replaced by LED projectors that save energy and can change colors and zero in to light up Jesus' face or hands or whatever."

"How tall is your beacon of safety?"

"The statue alone is almost one-hundred feet tall plus the pedestal it stands on, which is another eight feet or so."

Nile rubs my back and moves down to my butt. "Aren't you warm, yet? I'm baking."

"I'm still chilled."

"Yeah, your butt is still ice cold."

He rubs my butt now in an attempt to warm up me, all of me, and it's working and sit up on top of him.

"How tall is the Jesus at the Mother Cabrini shrine?"

"Just twenty-two feet tall."

Nile holds my hips. "Maybe you're in Colorado all this time in your dreams. You're looking at Jesus at the Mother Cabrini shrine."

"What about the salty water?" I let my hands slide down his chest and push them back up again, giving him a chest massage.

He groans. "Okay...you're back in Santa Cruz."

"The ocean is in the wrong place." Finally, I feel a bit warmer.

"It's a dream, Tess. Of course nothing is right or where it's supposed to be." We rock like we're in the ocean.

"It is in my dream. Besides, Nile, it's still winter here and it isn't winter where I am going. Unfortunately."

"No, you mean, fortunately, it is not winter. You would be an ice cube in no time floating in the ocean!" Nile pulls me down to kiss me, to stop me from talking. In defeat of in trying to follow any logical patterns or clues in my travels, I melt into him again for several minutes.

"Colorado doesn't have an ocean." I let out a contented breath. Finally, I feel safe here with Nile. He holds me on top of him, gripping my butt in his large hands, not letting me slide off of him.

"What about the wave pool in Denver? That could explain it. That's what you are floating in. We should go as soon as they open."

"The wave pool isn't filled with saltwater." I breathe in Nile. His scent is Old Spice Energy body wash. It reminds me of home in the Rockies.

"It would be great to be able to swim in saltwater rather than chlorine. Much better for my skin and hair." Nile fluffs his chlorine-kissed locks. "I should call the manager of the wave pool with this great idea!"

"Nile, I think I know where I'm going."

He pulls the blankets over our heads. We're together under a tent.

"What I saw from the water was the statue of *Cristo Redentor* or Christ the Redeemer in Rio de Janeiro. I'll have to check my journal again to see what I sketched as a little girl and compare it to the image I see in my mind's eye from last night, although I can't tell my doctor until I'm sure."

"I still think you're seeing Jesus." Nile touches my check again with the back of his hand this time to see if my body temperature has returned to normal. "The Jesus statue here in Colorado."

I snuggle against his bare chest. "The American statue of Jesus isn't anywhere as tall as *Cristo Redeemer*" My voice is muffled even to my ears. "Ironically though, Christ the Redeemer's open arms are symbolic for "peace" however, where he stands is anything, but peaceful with the cartel ruling the streets and the government."

"Just because it's on the Internet doesn't mean it is right or true." Nile places his hand on my forehead. "Yet, I message for peace was heard, today, so your mom could come home already."

He looks into my eyes to see if I'm getting sick. Even though he's fighting his family about becoming a doctor, too, I can see he is already one. It's in his nature. He might take the long way around, but I see him as a doctor, a pediatrician, one who's great with children. He makes them laugh during visits and he'll bring his yellow Lab to his office…

Can I really see into the future now, too? Now, wait a minute…I can see him giving a lecture to hundreds of young, students and other medical professionals in a gigantic, jammed-packed auditorium? He's a world-renowned neuroscientist? Not a pediatrician? Not a volcanologist? I better keep that insight to myself.

But if I can see into the future, why can't I predict when my mother will return or at least when these disconcerting dreams will end?

"Your temperature feels normal, again." Nile pushes my hair back from my eyes. "Did you date your childhood journal entries?"

"No because that would have taken the fun of this mystery." I grin.

He places his knees over my legs locking me down and pulling me even closer. "Are you sure you're not in Colorado? Never mind. Of course, you're sure. Tess, Tess, Tess, what am I to do with my itinerant girlfriend?"

"Keep me safe."

Nile locks his arms across my back. "This should work." He kisses me again slowly as if we have all night.

We do.

[Morse code message: KEEPHERSAFE]

.-. . -- . -- -... . .-. -- .

I'm following my little guide as she departs from the tram and walks out of the terminal.

The sign at the top of the mountain issues a warning about the dangers of rock climbing *Corcovado* Mountain. I'm glad this time that I can read Portuguese, although I'm not going to be climbing these rocks anytime soon—even if I could climb it in a dream and still be safe. The walls of this mountain are nearly vertical. I glance over the edge to confirm what I saw on the tram ride up and step back. It's a bit frightening and the last thing I need to do is fall off a cliff by my own violation and not due to some evil presence in my dream.

This tourist attraction should be swarming with people, yet we are alone. The sun is starting to slide down toward its watery bed, so maybe we were in the last tram up for the day.

She's off, running up the final stairs, so I climb up after her. I hit the two hundred and twenty-third step towards the statue of *Cristo Redentor*, which is perched high above us. I know there are that many steps because I can hear her counting them in Portuguese.

"...dois cem e vinte e um... dois cem e vinte e dois...dois cem e vinte e três!"

She's out of breath, but smiling at me. This is the first time I have heard her speak and her voice is soft and sweet like an old soul.

Above us, a sunset streaked in brilliant shades of orange is diffused by a sheer curtain of fog rising from the bay. The solid white statue of Jesus with his arms stretched wide stands directly before us.

My Google brain tells me that his reach is more than ninety feet tip to tip.

This eerie sunset fog has ascended on us and is reaching up to Jesus' face. I can feel the fog's moisture on my bare arms.

To keep up with my little guide, I climb over a low metal fence meant to keep the tourists off the small plot of grass, yet a piece of barbed wire left behind from an earlier rendition of this guard fence rips across my shins. I wipe away the momentary pain and slow my stride to check where I should step next. I'm wearing shorts again, not my normal daily attire of jeans. Blood drips down my shins.

My little friend stops and looks at me, worried. I smear the blood off my leg.

She takes my hand and leads me to sit on the edge of the low wall at the feet of Christ the Redeemer. The long shadow from the statue darkens with each passing minute of the oncoming twilight. The humidity of the evening is tinged with a coolness now, a relief from the day's earlier hot mugginess.

My little friend scans the mountaintop as if she was expecting someone. Someone, who she knows won't break her promise, or I hope, won't break her little heart.

Together, we watch for someone to burst through the thickness of now what has become ground fog, too. I'm not sure who we're anticipating, however, by my friend's posture she is definitely sitting in a state of heightened anticipation.

She watches the top of the cement stairs that we just climbed. At that moment, I realize I don't even know her name and lean toward her to ask, but she sits up taller as a head of a person appeared first, then shoulders, and the waist as this person climbs up the last steps and into our view: a woman.

From a park light that just clicked on, her large, hoop silver earrings shine against her dark hair. She wears a white dress with small, red poppies embroidered around its square neckline and hem. Her red sandals slap against the sidewalk as she towards us.

My little friend points to the lady, who is approaching us—in case I didn't see her.

What does she mean? Should I know this woman? All I do know is I feel surrounded by a sense of peace, something I have been missing in my dreams, and in my real life for a long time…so, perhaps I do know her.

The woman smiles a bright smile with perfect teeth. She could be a model.

"Tess?"

The little girl jumps up and dives into the woman's arms.

Is the little girl's name Tess, too?

At this moment, I realized this little girl does look a lot like me.

The woman stands, picking up the child in her arms and says, "Remember my name: *Anita Maria Santiago del Regis Carmo Mão de Ferro e Cunha de Almeida Santos Abreu.*"

I repeat her name as I watched her leave with my little friend. *"Anita Maria Santiago del Regis Carmo Mão de Ferro e Cunha de Almeida Santos Abreu."*

Together, the woman leads the little girl in saying her name aloud. Her tiny voice echoes the woman's words: *"Anita Maria Santiago del Regis Carmo Mão de Ferro e Cunha…"*

The woman stops and places the child back on the ground, but holds her hand, creating a linked silhouette of two against the misty night sky. I want to follow them, although I'm rooted to the ground without the physical ability to stand for whatever reason.

I can hear the little girl repeat the woman's name: *"Anita Maria Santiago del Regis Carmo Mão…"*

I watch them disappear down the stairs and fade into the darkness of night. She says her name again to the little girl: *"Anita Maria Santiago del Regis Carmo..."*

The more I repeat her name, the less I remember. I say what I can remember out loud: *"Anita Maria Santiago..."*

"Who is that?" Nile rubs my feet.

Since Nile and I had chosen the living room for our study hall today, we're prone on the couch, laying toe to head. Nile has been reading one of his fat books about volcanoes while I'm still deep in the memory of my last night's dream and don't want to answer Nile, right now—

He bites my big toe.

"Ouch!" I jerk my foot away and accidentally kick him in the chin.

"Ouch!" It's his turn to recoil and sulk.

I get up on my knees to rotate and lay beside Nile, wrapping my arm and leg across him. "Sorry."

He pretends to give me a dirty look and holds his chin like it still hurts.

"Did I knock out any teeth?" He smells like the sandalwood soap that I gave him with as a Thursday present last week just because. I bury my nose against his neck and inhale more of him. I kiss his neck and move up to find his lips.

He taps me on the head.

I pull back to see him bite both his lips over his teeth. He mumbles, "Would you still love me if I didn't have my teeth?" He talks funny like this.

I laugh at my old man. With my hands, I force his mouth open and peer inside. "No. I probably couldn't. Teeth are very important to me."

Nile smiles with all of his teeth like the Cheshire cat. "So, what did she say next?"

I roll onto my back and on top of Nile's outstretched arm to remember the woman in my dream. "I didn't think I was talking to you."

"You were talking out loud like you usually do and I was listening like I usually do, so tell me, what did she say?"

"She said to remember her name. Nile, I think she was my mom, the younger version of her, the age she would have been when I was six. I vaguely remember what she looked like since that was about the time when she disappeared—"

"Was she really your mom? Can you be sure? Her real name? I knew it! Betty Johnson couldn't be your mom's real name." Nile leans up on his elbow and dumps me to lie flat on the couch without the warm pillow of his bicep. "Tell me you remember all of it!"

I look up into his wide eyes and say, *"Anita Maria Santiago del Regis…"*

"That's a really long name."

"There's more. I just can't remember."

"More?" Nile lies back down. "Wow. Are you sure she was your mom?"

"I think. She looked like the pictures my grandmother has of her from when we first moved to Colorado."

I sit up beside Nile. We barely fit on the couch together.

"I have to remember her name: *"Anita Maria del Regis Carmo de Almeida Santiago*…oh, wait. Dr. Hall has my diary with her full name. I remember seeing it…and my grandmother will know—"

"Something's not clear to me. Was she calling the little girl, "Tess"? Or was she speaking to you? Or to both of you?"

[Morse code message: REMEMBERME]

A snowstorm turns my college town white, again but this time in June. Being a winter person, I love its unexpected return while most of my fellow students and professors bemoan the delay of warmer days and nights. As I cross campus, sunshine streams down between the snow clouds to light up the last of the falling flakes that glitter like silver metallic confetti. I stop, captured by the instant beauty of the world, but if I dally, I'll be late.

The new snow crystals crunch under my boots. I slip and slide across the iced sidewalk that no one bothered to shovel. Three inches is not enough danger to warrant any additional hours on the timesheets of the maintenance crew, however, in the last five minutes I have witnessed two people go down on their bums, cursing their lack of balance or the slippery surfaces or the university's negligence to keep them safe.

Safe. That's a harbor I can't seem to find these days. Even with the emergence of a brilliant blue sky above me that seems to be intensified at 5,430 feet above sea level and the delicacy of fresh snow that traces the thin aspen branches, this very environment I love and crave brings me little comfort these days. I continue to feel palpations in my chest for no apparent reason. Sometimes, I know my anxiety is caused by my lack of sleep, my worries about flunking my classes, or my concern for my grandmother's health, and all of these thoughts gather at the bottom of my throat, making it difficult for me to swallow or breathe.

Lost in my anxiety again, I slip on the black ice and almost go down hard onto the sidewalk, but I right myself and laugh out loud. At least I can still laugh, but these moments never last long enough.

My geology professor passes by me, tipping his head and smiling at my momentary lapse of coordination.

He's wearing some kind of extra-sturdy, hiking boots with slip-proof soles and trudges forward without any trepidation, unlike the majority of people out in the weather today.

"Professor Wilson?"

He stops and spins to face me.

"Is it possible to trace the origin of sand?"

"Of course. Bring me a vial."

He's off again in his purposeful trek to his science building. I think he lives there.

Dr. Hall suggested I request the assistance of my other professors on matters beyond her knowledge. The sand-in-my-bed incident continues to baffle me, so on impulse I didn't think it would hurt to ask Professor Wilson for his input. I just hope he has an answer that makes sense. Otherwise, he will think I'm crazy, too.

Nile skates toward me on the ice like he's an ice hockey player born in Canada.

I slow my walk and veer away from his approach, afraid he's going to slam into me. He does, body checks me and wraps me in a huge, spinning hug until we both slow to an upright stop.

"Nile! You crazy man!"

"Yup that's me." He plants a big kiss on top of my red felt cowgirl hat. "Ouch." His lips temporarily stick to my snow-frosted hat and then he moves to kiss me full mouth. "So any spectacular dreams last night?"

"Rather not relive it and dispel my illusion of safety." I link my arm through his and look around hoping Dr. Reid saw us, but there no one else out today except us.

"But they are so entertaining." He skates down the sidewalk pulling me along in his crooked dance.

"I'm glad I can be your amusement."

"Oh come on, Cinnamon Girl." Nile stops in front of me. "They're just dreams. They can't mean anything."

"You might be right." I pick up my speed and march ahead of him, feeling a bit annoyed that he doesn't believe me, either.

Nile slides to catch up to my deliberate long strides. "Did you ask if you can change your sleeping pill prescription?"

"I did and now I'm afraid my cocktail of brain pills that the doctors have me on is only adding to my psychedelic nighttime trips."

"Can I have some?" He presses his cold cheek against mine. "I'll keep your feet warm when I sleep over. Promise."

"No, no drug sharing." I take his warm hand in mine. "In fact, I stopped taking the Valium. Plus Ambien didn't seem to be working, either. Every night, I'm off on a trip somewhere anyhow. Dr. Hall wants me to stay on Lunesta now."

"You're catching up on your sleep in geology class or so Professor Wilson mentioned to me." Nile parks me in front of the building that houses the mental health offices. "Here you are. See you tonight."

"Oh, yeah? Did I invite you over for dinner? Again?"

"No. Your grandmother did." He skates away to his next class. "I told you she loves me!"

I watch Nile lumber away from me and find it reassuring to have known him since he was a little kid. He was one of my very first friends when I moved into my grandmother's house.

I only wish I had known my mother beyond the age of six. If I could, I would go back in time to meet her when she was my age, at nineteen, to get to know the woman, who would become my mother and if I could, I would travel into the future and meet her as an adult in her forties, the age she would be now if she hadn't…my eyes grow glossy with tears that refuse to fall. Maybe this is actually what I am doing in my dreams. She is the woman that keeps reappearing in my nighttime ventures as often as the little girl does.

But what I can't figure out is am I there in the lower latitude observing them—or am I just dreaming about our limited and fractured time together?

Am I being shown what my future would have been like if I stayed in Rio? Maybe that is and was my fate and I am living in both worlds.

Could I be living two lives?

I need to talk to Rosalyn. I suspect she has been with or has known my family for a longer time than I actually know about and she might know something that could help me figure this all out.

My sport watch beeps, indicating I only have three minutes to get to my emergency appointment with Dr. Hall. She had called and insisted on seeing me today. I guess snow and icy roads are not a deterrent to good doctors. I dash up the steps and duck inside behind other students. I forego the ancient, gold-plated elevator with its open, black melt basket and run up the stairs, fourteen landings later to race inside Dr. Hall's office, out of breath, and lean against the reception desk.

"You made it. And with thirty seconds to spare." Sally smiles and sips from a funny-looking teacup, which resembles a small round gourd. "You want some?"

"Sure, but no caffeine. I'm not allowed to do that drug, but can take anything from a plastic orange bottle."

"I have a great new tea for you to try."

"Oh no. What country are we visiting this time?"

"South America. It's *yerba maté*." She pulls the silver straw made of metal out of the gourd to show me its enclosed spoon peppered with holes to sip the muddy tea. "You'll like it!"

"That's exactly what my grandmother says. Why is everyone insistent on giving me the same remedy?"

Dr. Hall pushes through the heavy wood door. "Oh good, Tess, you're here. Follow me. Wait until you hear this." She waves a manila folder above her head like a victory flag.

I only hope it is good news. Honestly, I feel like surrendering right about now.

"I'll bring your tea in." Sally motions for me to follow my doctor.

Inside her office, Dr. Hall goes behind her desk and opens my file. "Sit, sit. Make yourself comfortable."

I sit and slip off my snow boots and winter coat.

Dr. Hall is rifling through the thick stack of paper anchored with a silver metal clamp at the top. "I was afraid of this."

"I thought your flag waving meant you had good news." I will my doctor to say something positive and have the answer to all of my questions—and hers. I don't know if I have this new power to redirect reality, but thought it wouldn't hurt to try.

"Tess, I had the lab rerun your blood work." She sits before my open file and glances up at me. "I didn't prescribe Chantix."

"Oh. That." My new power did not work. I didn't hear her statement coming first from inside my head like I usually do before she speaks. I sit back against the couch for support. "My doctor at my college in California thought it would help me kick my nasty habit."

"Yes, I know what it does." She taps the page. "I'm concerned about its side effects, especially when mixed with the other meditation you're currently taking."

"I don't want to be addicted to nicotine, anymore."

Sally knocks and steps in with two steaming gourds of her specialty tea. "Dr. Hall, *yerba maté* is okay for Tess, right?"

Doc nods. "Thank you, Sally."

Sally hands us the tea and backs out the door, closing it tight behind her.

"Tess, Chantix can explain a lot of things about your case." She reads to me, however, my brain is ready to work now and is already ahead of her mouth, hearing the problematic symptoms of taking Chantix now even before she reads the list of printed words in front of her out loud to me: "Anxiety or panic attacks. Feeling very agitated or restless. Seeing or hearing things that are not there, or hallucinations. Feeling that people are against you, or paranoia." She pauses.

I can hear her voice inside her head and then with a slight delay, I can hear her speaking voice, both are very clear. I have to get her to stop. I'm getting a headache. "It could be my dreams that are causing me to feel this way, right?" I take a long sip of my tea through my metal straw, which is beginning to heat up, and wishing I could dive into my mug and not resurface.

"One of the most common side effects of Chantix includes sleep problems like vivid, unusual or strange dreams." She looks up at me with motherly concern, again. "I think you should stop taking it. You could try a nicotine patch instead."

"I tried the patch before." I hug my knees to my chest and balance my tea on one knee. "It didn't work."

"Give Chantix a week's rest and then try to the patch, again." Dr. Hall scribbles in my file and finally reaches for her tea and sips. "I'm going to have to call the FDA and report your side effects from Chantix. They will want to know."

"My problem with smoking has actually moved to the bottom of my personal 'fix it' list, right now."

Dr. Hall sips and looks at me from across the top of her tea mug.

"Nile doesn't know I started smoking in California and while I don't intend to start again, I don't want him to know of my former vice. I figure without prescription help, I could relapse due to what I am going through now."

"Wouldn't he understand?"

I nod. He would, but I don't want to tell him of my nasty coping vice that I picked up to deal with my separation anxieties from him, my grandmother, my mother, my other life, Tino.

"I brought home another souvenir from last night's nightmare sponsored by Chantix."

My doctor doesn't laugh at my joke, but it makes me smile for a fraction of a second. I put my tea down on the end table and pull up my boot-leg jeans to show Dr. Hall bloody scratches across both shins.

Dr. Hall gets up from her desk and steps closer to inspect my latest battle wounds from another distant trip. "It looks like a scrape from barbed wire." She straightens and places both palms against her lower back and stretches backwards a bit.

Once again, she's dressed in a springtime business suit and skirt, the color of honeydew with no wrinkles and no stains. I could never get away wearing such a light color. For me, it is nothing but dark colors, especially dark jeans or anything with a busy pattern due to my innate nature of being born a slob. Maybe that's why I don't mind the piles and clutter on every surface at my grandma's house.

"Chantix can also cause you to act aggressively, become angry or violent, perhaps even against yourself."

"But you said it looks like cuts from a barbed wire fence." I let my feet drop back to her taupe-colored rug.

Dr. Hall leans against her desk. "I didn't say 'fence'."

"It was a fence that I walked into because I didn't see it in the dark."

Dr. Hall walks around to her office chair. "Let's get your leg cleaned up." She reaches for her phone and dials. "Hello? Ellen?"

I pull my boots back on along with my coat.

"Dr. Hall here. I'm going to send down one of my patients right now. She'll need tetanus shot…"

Great, more needles. I take my empty mug with me as I exit. On the other side of the closed door, I can hear Dr. Hall saying, "Please do a thorough examination. I want to know if and where she came into contact with rusty barbed wire. Run whatever tests are needed. In fact, run a new panel of blood work. I have to know what else she's ingesting outside my prescriptions."

As I pass by Sally's desk in my usual fog, she reaches for my mug and intercepts it.

[Morse code message: DANGER]

Today, the twenty-third day of the year feels like spring, the first, semi-warm day so far. I can tell without even going outside to confirm this weather tidbit. Warmer weather just seeps into my bones and announces its presence just like cold weather does for my grandmother. We both dread it; she, the cold, and me the return of hot days and nights.

Nile has talked one of his best buddies out of his car with the promise of a buff-and-shine car wash and a full tank of gas upon its return. Now he is jumping up and down on my bed because of our opportunity to be outside all day today in the sun. In anticipation of springtime in its full glory, he runs to the window to test the outdoor temperature. He peels the gray duct tape off my windows and slides one open. "Hi Mrs. Nelson! Spring is finally here!"

"Hello, Nile. Yes, I do believe you're right, but it very late this year." The voice of my next-door neighbor comes up to me as well.

Nile attempts a happy dance across my hardwood floor, but ends up just stomping a lot.

My grandmother bangs her floor with the broom's handle to match his dance.

I pull the blanket back over my head. While he's ecstatic, I feel a bit blue. If I could have it my way, the year would be all winter and July. I couldn't miss the Fourth of July and all its festivities including the fireworks, but the other dog days of summer could be used up for more sweater and scarf days.

"Ha! Maybe it will snow again!" I yell from beneath my pretend snow cave.

Nile stops his dance. "What did you say?"

He charges the bed and dives on top of me.

I'm beginning to think that Dr. Reid could have been right. I get my bruises from my overzealous, puppy-like boyfriend. "Ouch." I emerge from my blanket holdout and cradle my forearm where his head hit.

Nile kisses my invisible bruise and then continues up my arm to my neck and finds my lips. He pulls away to see my sad face. "You can still wear your winter sweaters all spring if you like!"

"And I will." I pull on my jeans from yesterday including my sweater and motion for Nile to follow. "Breakfast time. We do have a road trip today."

Nile sits upright at the mention of food. "Will you make me an omelet with green peppers, ham, onion, and Monterey Jack cheese?"

"Your Denver omelet will be ready in twenty."

"I'll collect your grandmother." Nile buttons his denim shirt that I occasionally borrow from him.

"She might want to eat in bed."

"What?" He jumps into his jeans. "And forego my company?"

In the time my grandmother brushes her hair and listens to Nile's wild stories about who knows about what, I'm ready for them. Their plates with their delicious breakfast of Denver omelets are waiting for them in the warm oven.

I glance across the tiny kitchen table at Nile, who chows down his omelet. He has to fold his legs underneath and looks like an adult, who's sitting at the kid's table at Christmas time. My grandmother also watches him but with a different admiration as she witnesses such a healthy appetite. With her fight against cancer over the last two years, her appetite has been fading.

"Is there more orange juice?" Nile wipes his mouth with the edge of the red cocktail napkin that reads: "The Kitchen Is Closed Due to Illness. I Am Sick of Cooking."

My feminist grandmother is one to collect all things kitsch, especially cocktail napkins. One summer, she arranged a dozen pink flamingos in the flower garden. One by one, their pink heads do pop up out of the snow with the advent of warmer days.

There is also her assortment of fifty-plus gnomes purchased or received as gifts over the years. They too, do materialize after all the snow is absorbed into her perennial flower garden since most of them are very short.

"Tess? Juice?"

I point to the refrigerator. "I think."

Nile rummages through the lower shelves. A small white statue of Virgin Mary stares at him from behind a gallon of milk.

"Hi Mary." Nile always talks to the woman in the refrigerator. "No. Looks like we're out."

My grandmother takes a small bite of her blueberry-jellied toast and washes it down with her English breakfast tea. *Yerba maté* is only for after lunch, she once informed me. Besides, it tastes yucky with sweets, she also told me.

"Look in the freezer." She says without looking up from her breakfast.

We both look at her.

How does she know the inventory of the kitchen when she lives most of her days upstairs and hasn't gone grocery shopping in two years?

She pours herself another cup of black tea from the English teapot covered in delicate purple pansies.

"What? I asked Rosalyn to pick up some frozen orange juice in case I wanted some. Whenever I wanted some."

She dumps two sugar cubes in next and stirs, clinking the side of the teacup.

Nile peels the upper door open of the ancient icebox. "You keep Mary in here, too?" He holds up a six-inch, plastic statue of Virgin Mary who wears a pearly pink, hooded gown.

"Tess bought her for me at the flea market and since I put her in the icebox, my appetite is returning. A bit."

"Yeah. Like your appetite for frozen foods." Nile smiles.

"Yes. I like frozen foods." She bites into her second slice of toast. "They're always available no matter whatever time you have a craving." She smiles into her cup of tea.

"Next time, can you two invite me to your sundae social?" I down my glass of orange juice.

"It was 12:30 in the morning." My grandmother pats my hand. "We didn't want to wake you. You were finally sleeping soundly. None of this thrashing around that I can always hear."

"Trust me. Wake me next time. You'll cut my nightmares short and I'll thank you."

My grandmother gives me a serious look. I know what she's thinking and this time I wish I didn't. But I have to keep going into my dreams; I have to meet up with this woman that the little girl keeps leading me to if she is really my mom.

Nile stirs the concentrated blob of orange juice in a blue glass pitcher, making our breakfast drink look green. He pours a glass for each of us, but uses a 'To-Go' mug for his taller portion. "Let's go! You wanted to be on the top of Lookout Mountain by noon to stare at your precious snow that might be still on the other mountains west of us."

I take another bite of toast.

"Quick! The snow is melting as you sit there eating!"

My grandmother giggles.

She knows my undying love of snow and all things winter.

Nile grins to hide his smile.

I trade glances between both of them and am glad that I can be the butt of their jokes.

Rosalyn enters the kitchen through the back door with an armful of library books and magazines for my grandmother's day.

"Perfect timing, Rosalyn." Nile helps her with the slippery stack of magazines.

I wave to Rosalyn even though she's standing right beside me.

"I always come on Saturdays at ten." She smiles at everyone. "I don't want to be waking anybody up sooner than they would be up."

I kiss my grandmother goodbye on the top of her thick hair.

She grabs my wrist with unusual strength. "Take a picnic blanket and those two sandwiches on the lower shelf in the refrigerator."

"Your grandmother had me make them for you last night." Rosalyn holds up two bundles wrapped in blue bandanas. "She said she had a premonition that you two would be going on a picnic soon."

"What if it snowed today?" I hold onto the back of her chair.

"I see all." My grandmother points to the crowded counter next to the sink. "Take that bottle of wine, too. Over there, behind the stack of newspapers."

"Grandma, we're driving."

"So stay a few hours longer, the sunshine will do you both good."

Nile leans against the kitchen's door. "I do like the way things work around here."

Rosalyn packs up a wicker picnic basket with our goodies and adds two good wine glasses that she carefully wraps separately in embroidered dishtowels.

Nile tosses in a bag of salt-and-peppered, potato chips. "Yum. Spicy."

"Oh, now you like spicy?" Rosalyn nods. "I should cook my world-famous, masterpiece of spicy for all of you and soon."

"No, but thanks Rosalyn. My mouth can't even begin to compute what your level of spiciness would be. I definitely can't go there, again."

She grins at his honest remark.

My grandmother pushes herself upright and away from the table. "Just remember to bring me another Mary statue if they still sell them."

Nile joins me on her other side. "They sell stuff at a mountain? I thought it was just a mountain."

"Wait until you see, Nile." Rosalyn steers my grandmother down the hall toward the living room for their morning session of reading.

"Bye! Have fun!" My grandmother yells.

"Oh, it's a mountain and so much more." I dash out the door to the borrowed, blue VW, waiting in the back alley for us.

Nile follows like a packhorse loaded with the picnic basket, blanket, and a thick book.

What is he thinking? Like he'll have time to read? I have other plans for his attention this afternoon.

He races me across the barren lawn still brown under foot. With his extra-long stride, he easily wins and piles our picnic supplies into the back seat of the VW.

I slide into the driver's seat.

We flipped a penny to decide who will drive even though I'm already sitting behind the wheel. Nile drives like he is one-hundred-years old.

I win. I get to drive.

"Are you sure you don't want to sleep?"

Nile is not too thrilled with the toss of the coin. He studies it to make sure it's not one of those same-sided ones that my grandfather kept around the house.

In my opinion, fast is the only way to go no matter what way the road dips and turns. He runs back into the house to get Dramamine. Since I seem to usually win this little 'driving toss' game of ours, he knows where our motion sickness stash is kept without asking.

I rev the engine.

Rosalyn and my grandmother stand together in front of her second-story window and wave to me.

They must have decided to read upstairs, today.

I toot the horn.

Nile tucks himself into the small passenger seat of the VW. "I went as fast as I could."

"I was just honking 'bye' to them." I point up to our audience.

Nile waves to them like he's five years old. "Hey, what's that on your roof above your grandmother's bedroom?"

I pull away from the house without looking back. "Oh that? That's Mary, the protector of our abode."

"Is she doing her job?" Nile rolls down the passenger's window to keep waving.

"She works better than an owl to keep the cooing pigeons off the roof."

Nile is still waving good-bye even though we have turned the corner of the alley and merged down the side street of our block. The age range this guy exhibits in the course of a day makes my head spin, although in a good way. I love him for his juvenile antics as well as his wise wisdom that anchors me whenever I go "bonkers" on him. That's what he calls it.

I'm sure Dr. Hall has another, more technical description for my behavior like: "She's completely nuts".

No, that's what my grandmother would say, and lately I am beginning to think they're all correct. Their collective answer of "insanity" would be easier than trying to interpret my dreams, anyhow.

I rush us through the quaint neighborhood and down the narrow streets lined with arts and craft cottages towards the stately brick buildings of our campus and then through the expanding plots of suburbia, saturating this part of America.

I wave good-bye to the half-million dollar, cookie-cutter houses, and drive down the four lanes of traffic-filled streets, dodging the speeding cars with housewives and their families going shopping, our country's new pastime and entertainment. I know this because you can't see in their back windows due to the sheer amount of purchases just acquired. Is it Christmas, again?

We blast out of my college town and into the greening fields that lie south and are already littered with tall spikey, blue larkspur blossoms and endless meadows of mule ears that look like yellow daisies jacked up on the Miracle Growth. I would have to use that garden enhancer if I ever tried to grow anything. Thank God for Rosalyn's green thumb.

For about fifteen miles, lies expansive open space to the south and east as we motor parallel to my beautiful, snow-capped mountains. These magnificent landmasses stretch up to ten thousand feet and higher, one of my favorite views in the world—or at least this reality.

Nile laughs at me whenever I refer to the Rockies as "my mountains", but that's just how passionate I am about them. I love to hike, ski, and bike them, breathe in their fresh air, and admire the vistas they usually offer for free when you make the effort to summit by your own volition.

Sun-bleached, red barns and their matching houses are tucked farther back from the two-lane road that we follow toward Lookout Mountain. Three-wire fences parcel off these high mountain meadows where several dozen, dairy cows munch on bales of hay on one side while coppery-colored, Scottish Highland cattle stare at them from the other. These long-haired cows with their nonthreatening horns that turn up like a smile above their eyebrows move their big heads to watch us pass by with equal fascination. These fuzzy animals are one of the regular sightings on our road trips. In their tawny, long-haired coats, they look as if they're dressed for a formal affair when standing adjacent to the black-and-white cows, who I call, "the waiters". Of course, I look around too much while driving at such high speeds.

"Hi, waiters!" Nile waves to the dairy cows. "Have you come up with a nickname for the Scottish Highland cattle yet?"

"Look! A fox!"

The golden fox dances across the remaining patches of snow barely leaving his imprint on its white surface.

"Is that a barn owl?" I point to the big-eyed bird nesting in a cottonwood snag.

"The road, Tess! The road, please."

"Oh look! New snow!" Last night's snowfall at this higher elevation has dusted the enormous, rolled bales of hay, which are scattered across the empty fields and to me look like the frosted, shredded wheat cereal made for a giant.

I fly us up and down this country road like we're on a rollercoaster ride. I toss a quick glance to check-in on Nile. He looks rather green, so I slow and pull off onto the shoulder of the narrow road to let him drive.

After we run around the car five times before getting into our new seats, his coloring has improved. A farmer and his barking dog drive by in a rusty, pick-up truck and look at us curiously, wondering what the heck we are doing, but not with enough interest to actually stop and ask or wait to see what we will do next.

If Nile is already car sick on this relatively straight shot of a road minus the ups and downs where I can sometimes get the car airborne for a few inches, he'll never make it as my passenger up the tight switchbacks to the very top of Lookout Mountain.

"Thanks. The little yellow pill wasn't working yet."

"I think it takes twenty minutes for the medicine to get into your system and stabilize your unstable inner ear."

"Quit picking on my inner ear. It's sensitive."

"You can say that again."

Nile starts to say it again, but I slap my hand over his mouth. He licks my palm.

"Yuck!" I wipe his spit on his shoulder. "Ahhh, I shouldn't have done that. That is where I usually rest my head." I attempt to dry his shirt with the arm of my jacket. I give up and blast the heater's vent at his right shoulder.

Nile just looks at me like I am losing it and maybe I am.

Five months of living days and nights in two lives, one where I'm a college student and semi-awake stumbling around to my classes and the other, in some foreign city following a small girl around without answers to why I am there—the only easy answer is to why this is happening is: I'm insane.

"Don't worry. Lookout Mountain will have your answers." Nile reaches over to hold my hand as if he knew what I was thinking.

Is he reading my mind like I do with everyone else?

Or just reading my face? He knows the real reason why I wanted to drive up this big mountain today. I need to see for myself in daylight what I might be seeing in my dreams or not. After last night's dream and fruitless hours spent at the doctors' offices, I've decide to embark on my own research to put this nighttime puzzle together.

[Morse code message: REASONS]

.--. .-. --- --- ..-.

I had to go to Lookout Mountain to differentiate whether I was indeed time traveling to Rio de Janeiro and *Corcovado* Mountain or just dreaming about the time my mother took me on a drive up to see the statue of Jesus at the Mother Cabrini Shrine high above Golden, Colorado. If I did go with her here, I must have been tiny…maybe three years old.

So, here I am again, but this time with Nile. He parks the VW in the small parking lot that's crammed with other vehicles, shoulders our picnic basket, blanket, and grabs his thick book about volcanoes.

I pick up the pillow that I bought from my bed.

"A pillow?" Nile looks around to make sure no other tourists see what his girlfriend thinks is necessary at all picnics.

"What if I want to stare at Jesus while I'm lying on the ground? This way my neck won't hurt."

"Where's my pillow?" He takes off walking already knowing my answer.

"I'm your pillow."

He looks over his shoulder and sends an air kiss in my direction.

I can't but help love this big guy and run at him to bounce off of him from behind with my pillow, although I do feel guilty for having memories of Tino and not being able to distinguish between what is fantasy and what is reality in my heart and in my head.

Together, we climb pass the Stations of the Cross and up the three hundred and seventy-three steps. I know there are that many stairs because my Google brain just told me and of course, right on step number seventy-three, so now I know there are three hundred more steps to go and it's straight up with a dog-leg turn up one third of the way, which does not allow you to see the very top from the bottom step or even from the seventy-third step.

Today's weather is a cool, sixty degrees up here at more than seven thousand feet and with a slight breeze to keep me happy and any brand new flying bugs at bay. Grass is starting to sprout alongside the path and so are the naked bushes now with a mossy green coloring on their tips.

I forgot Sunday is not the day to visit the Mother Cabrini Shrine for solitude and solace. There are crowds everywhere as the Catholic Mass is over. The good people of the world are streaming out the double doors, across the parking lot and scampering up the hillside; some using the cement steps and others running up the hillside where the dangerous snakes live.

Nile points out the small sign staked into the earth that reads: "Danger: Snakes" and mimics man in the painting by Edvard Munch, *The Scream*.

Nile likes snakes as much as I do. We don't. He tries to warn some of the little kids playing on the hillside next to the steps. English is not their first language, so they might not be aware of the hidden dangers in the new grass. They scream and run up the hillside. Maybe they saw a snake or were afraid of Nile at his great height.

Some of the three hundred and twenty-three steps are half steps, which makes the maneuvering upward difficult for the smallest of the small children and many of the older people that are visiting here today, too. They teeter and totter like they are about to fall backwards, yet somehow managed to regain their balance at the last moment.

On our right, the stone-inlayed mosaics depicting the steps that Jesus took on this particular journey are beautiful, yet sad. Along the Stations of the Cross are cement benches for resting, on which one Nile is now occupying.

"I'm tired. Can we sit here a minute?"

I look behind me to confirm the short distance we climbed so far. I hope he is just kidding. We'll never get to the top at this rate. "I thought you were a world-class athlete."

"Just a world-class water polo player and this is not the water. Gravity is a lot tougher." He pulls me onto his lap and kisses me, a long kiss that only stops when he feels people watching us as they pass by.

"Oops." Nile smiles. "I guess this is kind of a sacred spot. Let's go over that next hill." He stands and dumps me off his lap onto the bench.

I follow and run up the steps after him, passing him. "We are on a mission here and that mission starts at the very top of this mountain."

"Then, can we go off alone to the Rosary Garden next to the Grotto?"

I look back at my boyfriend with a "maybe" in my smile.

He smiles at me, but lingers back to give me time to figure out whatever I need to figure out here at Lookout Mountain.

I jog to the top by myself.

Luckily, today is not a smoggy day in Denver and at the top of Lookout Mountain, I can see forever. The sky is a brilliant blue that only Colorado knows how to deliver—a perfect solid stretch of pure, one-hundred percent azure without a single cloud between heaven and me. As I look east, the plains of Kansas stretch to Missouri with only Interstate 70 dissecting the expansive fields of wheat.

There is no massive body of water, anywhere.

The bells toll from the chapel far below.

I hug my pillow across my chest and step up to the tall statue of Jesus.

His shadow falls over me, so I can see up into his face without squinting. I ask for answers:

Why did my mother bring me here?

Or were we on *Corcovado* Mountain in Brazil?

Were we waiting for someone?

Nothing.

Nile slowly walks to stand beside me. He's silent for as long as he can be, which is about only ten seconds.

"He's a tall guy." He nods up to Jesus.

I grin. "According to my internal research and because you commented, he's twenty-two feet tall, stands on a base that's eleven feet, which was constructed in 1954—"

Nile kisses me, again to stop the stream of information.

The family that passed us on the steps minutes ago, steers their young daughter away from "the sex fiends". I heard her mother say it to herself.

I smile at the little girl and then look at Nile in hopes to convey that public affection is definitely okay. Look at her parents. They haven't touched in years and what a tragic way to live. She smiles back and then shyly looks at Nile, all of him.

"Is she checking me out?" Nile grabs my pillow and hugs it over his belt.

"I told her it was okay to look."

"What? No. I'll get arrested."

I lead him by his hand out of their line of sight.

To the west of the rounded neighboring hillsides, Nile claims to spy a herd of elk. At first, I doubt him, with us being so close to human populations, but he's right. There they are, ignoring us staring at them, yet they're a very deep ravine and steep hillside away from the masses and probably know they're safe.

I spin one-hundred-and -eighty degrees and stop on the high rises in downtown Denver, which looks like a mini version of the city of Oz. I turn west, passing the immediate greening hills to find any of my beloved snow, and there it

157

is on the distance mountain range: thick and white. It never leaves the tops of those mountains and I'm so glad.

Nile moans as if he can hear what I am thinking, but it just might be the massive smile on my face that gives my thoughts away.

"Melt snow!" He chants. "Melt!"

"Hey, not nice!"

"Is this Mother Cabrini?"

Behind a wrought iron and glass-plated door is a black marble statue of Mother Cabrini. Somehow, people have squeezed coins and dollar bills into her sacred area.

"Yup, that's her."

"Can we go to the Grotto, now?"

We run like little kids down all of the steps and head over to a grassy knoll. We set up our picnic and take turns feeding each other the salt-and-peppered chips in between bites of our ham and Swiss cheese sandwiches loaded with Dijon mustard.

"Yum." I feed Nile another, big crunchy chip.

After each spicy chip, Nile has to take a sip of wine. I wonder how he's ever going to survive another of Rosalyn's hot and spicy dinner that she promised to make us.

"Any answers yet?" He lies back to stare at the cloudless sky.

"Yes. I just have to double check one more fact." I join him and share the pillow, our heads touching. "I think I was here with Rosalyn and my mother."

"Now that would make sense. Brilliant, Tess. You're just brilliant."

I knew that I loved him for many reasons—besides his hair—he's always full of compliments reserved for me.

[Morse code message: PROOF]

158

.--- --- ..- .-. -. . -.--

Professor Wilson spies me from across the campus mall and motions me to him from in between the skinny trunks of the aspen trees.

I grab Nile's hand, not wanting to go at this alone, and drag him across the lawn with me. Professor Wilson is walking very fast, so we have to jog to cut him off at the top of the plaza. He must be in a hurry to his next class, so maybe his explanation about my vial of sand will be a quick discourse, but then again this man is into rocks and probably sand, too. He is Nile's favorite professor. Maybe I shouldn't bring Nile. They might talk forever.

"Hi Professor Wilson—" I try to start with formalities, but he's on a mission obviously.

"When I was a child, I begin to notice differences in sand. What I collected from beaches, river beds, sand dunes, mountain river beds, deserts, and sandpits and quarries was all so different." My professor slows his gait a bit as he remembers his previous and numerous digs.

I look to Nile to see if he has any idea how to cut this lecture short, but he looks intrigued. This could be a very long monologue.

"Sand, as you know, Nile, is when the grain's diameter is between 0.05 millimeter and two millimeters and when it's larger, it's gravel. Below 0.05 millimeter, it's silt or clay. So, Tess, what you brought me, I can see its grain with a naked eye—"

"So it's sand!" Nile raises his hand like he's in class.

"Is it from seashells, then?" Nile has just taken Professor Wilson deeper into his passion by asking such a question—I can tell by the way our teacher's face shines.

159

"Sand could be from skeletal fragments liked sponges or the nicely-colored needles from urchins, other marine organisms. Or from the erosion of coral reefs."

"But where is this sand from?" I'm afraid of the answer, but have to confirm with someone where I think I go every night in my dreams.

"Mostly, this kind of sand is of local origin. Unless a very strong ocean current transports the material way out of the original spot, which can happen." Professor Wilson pulls my vial of sand from his coat pocket and holds it up in the sunlight.

"But we're in a landlocked state." I have to increase the length of my stride to keep up with the tall men.

"More often, however, the source of the sand is way up in the mountains and is being transported by rivers, sometimes for thousands of miles."

"I'm confused." I stop walking.

They don't.

I hurry to catch up with them. "Is my sand from rivers up on the mountain? Or the beach?"

"You'll find the sand from the source of a river much different from the sand found miles and miles farther down along the riverbanks as each grain is subject to abrasion and impact on its way to beach. Or to a lake."

"It's from a lake or you're not clear of its origin?" I'm getting desperate for a real geographic location, not speculation.

Nile's getting anxious now, too and pops the question to hurry along Professor Wilson's answer. "Maybe a beach then?"

My professor pockets my vial. "Rivers will add different materials, so the composition gradually changes…"

"It's from a river, then?" I hold tight to the belief that these grains are the only way to find an answer about my travels.

He pulls the vial out of his pocket, again, rocking it like an ocean wave. "Sand from the beach usually has rather smooth, clear grains due to the constant wash of the waves."

I hold out my palm to receive the vial.

Instead Professor Wilson opens the glass vial and shakes grains into my right hand and places the fragile container in my other.

I look closely and have to agree, the grains are clear.

"Dune sands, on the contrary, are sandblasted by the wind and so, after a long time, the grains get a round and dull appearance, which can also be the case with the grains of desert sands having been blown over miles."

Nile jumps into the question game with me. "What about our sand dunes over there at the San Juan Mountains? Could this sand be from there?"

"Or like sand dunes on a beach." I point out this other possible landmass option to help Professor Wilson place my sand's origin, but he just starts his sand lecture, again.

"Oxygen and silicon are the most frequently occurring elements in our earth's crust, thus quartz is very abundant in our rocks."

He's talking like he's standing in front of the classroom.

"You'll often find an overdose of quartz in most of the sands as well. Quartz is also comparatively hard. No wonder it can survive long journeys where other minerals cannot." He smiles like a proud father over the grains of sand that I hold in the palm of my hand.

This is why I sleep through most of his classes and while he does know his stuff, he simply does not know how to teach it in an engaging manner. Or maybe it's just my lack of interest. I look to Nile. No, his interest is fading, too. He's playing with the zipper on his jacket.

"Nevertheless, it's lightweight and thus easily blown away by the wind to form dunes."

"At the beach? Can you tell what beach?" Nile adds to the list of our ever-growing questions. I've given up and sat down on one of the many benches lining the plaza. My sudden movement encourages my professor to sit beside me.

"Last year, when I walking around nose downwards, of course, on a beach in Brazil and it is indeed true what composer André Filho captured in his song, *Cidade Maravilhosa*, Rio de Janeiro is a marvelous city…"

I blink hard. He said it. He said the city where I think I'm visiting in my night travels.

"I discovered a dark spot between the large pebbles. Everybody would think it was dirt, or oil, but it was caused by heavy minerals. I thought maybe magnetite, ilmenite, or garnet, which is sorted out by the sea waves and is absolutely beautiful under the microscope!" He smiles.

He must be so fun on vacation.

"This heavy mineral sand is only in special places in the world where strong northwest winds deposit these grains near the dunes, though it's not easy to find as it's usually covered by quartz and other lighter material, but you found it, Tess."

I drink in every word he said and study the small glass bottle holding my answer.

"When were you in Rio?" my professor asks.

On the beach with Tino, I think to myself, but don't say out loud.

Nile saves me from answering my teacher's question, which would have only opened up more questions. "How do you know all about sand, Professor Wilson?"

"I'm a long-standing member of the ISCS. That's the International Sand Collectors Society."

"Really? There's an association for everybody, isn't there?" I toss in my two cents to stop my mouth from saying things out loud about my trips south of the equator and saying Tino's name.

"Are they chapters here in Colorado?"

Nile wants to join. I can see it in his eyes and, of course, I heard him say it to himself inside his head.

"They're based in Connecticut, but there's an active group here." He stands. "We, sand collectors are called "arenophiles" or "psammofiles." Awful words, aren't they?"

"Why not belong to the fossil society or the petrified forest organization instead?" Nile has joined both of these societies recently and reads to me from their journals each month. It definitely puts me to sleep, so I let him read pages and pages.

"I like the study and collection of sand. It makes me aware of the infinity of time in a spiritual sense and in a very possible realm."

I'm impressed with Professor Wilson's answer and take this as the close of his lecture. I stand and shake his hand. "Thank you very much, Professor Wilson. I must get home to take care of my grandmother."

"Yes, of course. Good luck with your sand collection."

I hurry down the sidewalk to think about what my professor just said.

Nile skips up beside my hurried feet. "Why does everyone I know collect something? My parents with their frog and binocular collection, your grandmother and all of her collections, and now you with your first vial of sand and your origami paper cranes—if you're anything like your grandmother, you're going to need a bigger house."

He takes the vial and tips it to one end, watching the sand rush to the bottom. "We should make a sand dial, clock thingy with this."

"It's called an hourglass and I think we'll need more sand." I reach out for his hand, but he stuffs his hands into his coat pocket.

I slow to see if I really did see what I thought I saw and felt.

He had stiffened his posture and moved away from me, not the normal Nile, I know.

"You go to the beach enough, just bring back more each time." He now walks faster ahead of me.

His words confirmed what I saw and felt. He's still miffed about something. Was it something I did?

"Hey, can you help me hang my paper cranes today?"

He shrugs and keeps walking.

"I thought they would look nice hanging from the ceiling in front of the living room windows...Nile?"

Or maybe it was something that slipped out of my mouth when I was talking in my sleep.

[Morse code message: JOURNEY]

…. --- .--. .

    I don't feel like studying nor do I need to with my upcoming exams, so I follow Rosalyn around the kitchen like a toddler under foot, trying to determine what feast she's create tonight.

    "Kung Pao chicken? With red chilies? Nile will love it!"

    She just smiles. "That's Chinese."

    "Moo Shu pork? Can you make it spicy instead of sweet or both?"

    She shakes her head.

    "How about sushi?"

    Rosalyn steers me to the kitchen table so she can prep dinner. "I want dinner to be my surprise for you."

    "Tell me about your family, Rosalyn. I hardly know anything."

    "My father was from a farm in Japan, but my mother was from Connecticut."

    "What? How did that happen?"

    I dip a piece of flatbread into the mango salsa that she just created from scratch—both the flatbread and the salsa.

    "My mother came over to Japan with her church. She was very pretty." Rosalyn pauses for a moment before returning to chopping.

    "Your dad didn't have a chance, did he?"

    "No, he did not. They were married for a long time. They were living in Brazil when I was born."

    "Why did I think you were born in Japan?" The chopped red onions give the salsa a spicy bite, which will send Nile over the moon.

    "No, I grew up in Rio, however, after my father died, my mother returned to Connecticut. I came to the states to take care of my mother." Rosalyn crosses herself and says a silent prayer to the ceiling. "I didn't go out much."

"I'm so sorry. I didn't know she passed."

"Ten years ago." She nods her head, accepting my apology. "After some time, I wanted to see your country's tall, beautiful mountains and I did. And that's where I met your mother, up on Lookout Mountain. You were so very tiny."

I think back to the road trip up to Lookout Mountain with Nile last weekend. We had fallen asleep in the warm sun in the Rosary Garden and now we both sport a weird tan on one side of our faces. When we awoke, the gift shop was closed. I felt terrible that we didn't go there first.

"I've known you that long?"

"Yes. And I knew your grandparents in Rio. Did you get a Virgin Mary statue for your grandmother?"

"No. We had to get her something else."

Rosalyn looks up from her chopping and raises an eyebrow.

"Nile searched the church grounds until he found Father Ortega, who had kindly opened the gift shop for us."

Nile does have a charming smile, so it's no wonder that he can get me to do anything.

"We looked around the small gift shop, but there were no statutes of the Virgin Mary. The priest had suggested a bottle of holy water."

He had unlocked the glass cabinet where the glass bottles for holy water were kept. I selected a small glass bottle with a painted image of Mother Cabrini. In this tiny portrait, she looked determined in her black habit.

Father filled the two-ounce container with holy water and accepted our money.

"My grandmother was thrilled with the gift of holy water, but a bit surprised at our red-beet faces due to our sun nap."

Rosalyn laughed. "Nile's funny suntan stops half way up his arm."

"Yeah, she lectured us about the sun being much more intense at seven thousand feet even in the springtime than at sea level."

"You two should know that."

"It was the wine that made us forget."

"I bought your grandmother a gift, today." Rosalyn pushes a small box across the counter to me. Through its plastic window, I can see a ceramic statue of the Virgin Mary dressed in a long gown of the color of lilacs.

"It has been you who's adding to my grandmother's collection of Virgin Marys in my absence!"

"Maybe." She smiles. "Maybe not."

"My grandmother couldn't put up all those Marys in the nooks of the trees. On the fence. Or on the roof of the garage or on the top of the house!"

She laughs. "Come back in one hour for dinner. You are just in my way, child."

I feign hurt feelings and head down the hallway to my bedroom. Since Nile was coming over to study, on a rare burst of energy, I made up my bed like an ad out of an interior design magazine and piled it with a dozen pillows. I fall back onto the pillows and feel safe for a moment.

My journal is on the nightstand. I sketch a bit while waiting for Nile and then hear the front door slam.

Nile has let himself into the house and knows where to find me. He thunders down the hallway, through my open bedroom door, charging the bed and belly flops next to me. My pen skips across the blue lined page. I give him a dirty look that I don't mean. Two pillows bounce off the bed.

He curls up beside me.

I'm amazed his large body can get so small, but it's his gentle nature that I love. I hand him the notes that I had typed up earlier in the day and snuggle against his warm body. "You know I can write without looking at the page."

"It is legible?"

"Of course. I have very neat handwriting like an architect's. Not like a doctor's or yours."

He flips through the typed pages. "Why don't you take the notes in class then?"

"You're the volcanology student-in-training and like their foreign words. Not me."

"I can write without looking at the page, too." Nile places the notes on his flat stomach.

"You can? I thought it was one of my special talents."

"Nope. I got it, too."

It's a good thing that Nile's a very good, note taker because the university actually pays him for his class notes, but he's a lefty with bad handwriting. Since he's a faster writer than I, we have a deal. He takes notes in his chicken-scratch handwriting and I type them up for the university and for us. I don't know if the athletes need them or if they're for other students, but the cool, two hundred bucks paid every semester is a nice windfall for us. We're going to celebrate by going out to an expensive place that we normally would only peer in the windows and wish we could dine there.

My grandmother said she would go with us.

Rosalyn said, "Maybe."

Another bonus for me in our deal is that I make him read them back to me aloud in bed whenever he stays the night. It's sexy to hear his voice describe volcanic rock, sedimentary layers of the earth, and whatever else he wants to whisper to me about the creation of the world.

I used to wish I could time travel back to the earth's days before humans arrived to see the newness of the world, but with my recent showing of whacked-out dreams in my own private theater of the mind, I've cancelled all requests for such trips.

With the Flatirons rising up behind my college town and the acres of farmland stretching toward Kansas' state line, I did once feel safer here than when I lived in Santa Cruz that the surfer's paradise perched on the edge of the high cliffs over the Pacific. I know it's the unknowns I experience at night, which I should be worried about and wonder what I can do to stop this short film before it turns into a feature movie. Every night, the picture show playing inside my head seems to replay back a bit and then goes deeper into the unexpected, the next unwelcome realm of my unconsciousness madness.

Nile jumps off the bed. "Do you want to go fly over the erupting *Eyjafjallajökull* volcano with me?"

"It's always cold there. I'll go."

"Yeah—you could wear your sweaters every day. My parents said they would fly me to whatever volcano I want to see once I graduate." He digs in his jacket for something.

"Don't you need your master's degree to do whatever you will be doing?"

"Yes." He pulls out his ChapStick out of his jacket pocket, but looks disappointed after figuring out the length of time that's between now and his very distant graduation date.

"Maybe for your birthday then?"

He brightens. "Great idea! I need to print some photos to show my mom. She thinks I'm making up the *Eyjafjallajökull* name." Nile sits at my desk and types on my laptop.

"It does sound like you are just mashing vowels and a few soft constants together."

He searches for the best, four-color images of spewing lava and smoke. His smile grows bigger with each 'click' to print another photo, which to me is just a new angle on the same volcano.

I move over closer to Nile and sit up on the floor with my legs bent into the shape of a pretzel.

"Ouch" is all my grandmother says when she sees me like this and usually Rosalyn echoes her sentiments.

I like the floor and can't fall from here. Recently, I have been getting bouts of vertigo, so this is the safest place to be for me. I close my eyes and can see the reverse impression of the woman, the one that I met at the statue of *Cristo Redentor*. She is holding the little girl's hand. This image is burnt as a silhouette across the underside of my eyelids. I wonder if she's my young mother and the little girl, is she me—at age three or four?

Or is she my grandmother's sister, my aunt, with my mother as a little girl? "Hey Nile?"

"Yes, my Cinnamon Girl." He swivels around in my desk chair. "Are you stuck down there?"

"I think I saw my mom in my dreams, but she was kind of ghost-like like she was almost transparent."

"Maybe you're seeing her soul." He rests his elbows on his knees. "I'm sorry. That sounded bad, didn't it?"

"No, she was real. A three-dimensional person."

"How do you know?" He hits the 'print' command for the fifth time as another color photo comes out of the printer.

"Just because I could kind of see through her doesn't mean she wasn't real."

"You just might be seeing an apparition. Sorry, that sounded bad, too." He sits beside me on the floor. "Touch her next time, Tess. To be sure she's real." He touches my arm.

If he doesn't believe me, then I can't tell him about taking his jacket every time I go traveling at night. Maybe it's meant to be my protective cloak of sorts, but protection from what?

Nile jumps on the bed, clears his throat, and begins to read the class notes that I typed for us.

I need to pay attention to him, especially after last night, and crawl up beside him. The "garble inside the head" that's what Nile calls my incessant nightmares are turning me into a bad girlfriend. Last night, he told me that I called him "Tino".

[Morse code message: HOPE]

.- -. ... .-- . .-. ...

The sizzle of Rosalyn's barbeque dinner still lingers in the air, a smoky sweet aroma that enticed Nile to stay again, although it is his seventh night in a row. Rosalyn and Nile are in a food battle. Nile's trying to act as if 'hot and spicy' isn't a big deal and Rosalyn's kicking it up in every dish to make him shout, "Uncle!"

Tonight, however, she surprised Nile and made her normally, fiery masterpiece a bit sweeter to accommodate the lower level of hotness, one his tongue can handle. After his first bite, he looked very relieved

Rosalyn just smiled her way through dinner. The ringing of my grandmother's landline, probably the only one left in the state, interrupts our dinner, so in order not to be annoyed by its drone of seven rings before her answering machine picks up, I race out of the kitchen and down the hallway to answer it.

Without a proper hello, a raspy male voice launches into his monologue. It's Dr. Vendall, who I talked with earlier in the week and emailed a lot prior to us speaking. He must think we're best buddies now, so he skips the formalities of a basic "Hello" and assumes it's me who has answered.

"What you were referring to is the theory of genetic memory. This feeling of knowing where you are is correct because you are seeing through your mother's eyes or grandmother's eyes—whoever knows this particular house on the beach, knows her way around the *favelas* and the alleys where you end up in your dreams."

I lean against the wall of the foyer since my grandmother doesn't have a phone in the house that isn't attached to a wall. I can only stretch the cord so far so not to be heard by Nile, my grandmother, or Rosalyn. "Is that

172

why I knew where to run? To run home to my grandparents' house?"

After racking my brain about this very real possibility of living out two lives at once, one here in Boulder with Nile and my grandmother, the other in Rio, I had to talk to an unbiased source, someone who doesn't know me or anything about my life in any capacity.

I had found a physicist, Dr. Vendall at MIT, online and read his theories on parallel universes, and left a lot of questions on his voice mail and also emailed him. To my surprise, he called back—the same day. Now after just a few minutes of his answers, I'm beginning to see how all of this might work for real, not just in my dreams, but in my lives.

"Perhaps that is how you did know where to go to safety."

"Tess! Call them back!" My grandmother's loud voice travels through the wall and down the hall to me. "We're in the middle of dinner."

"You understand that if you would have stayed in Rio with your mom that reality would have been your future or your demise, right? Instead of what you're living now."

"I'm starting to see it…but—"

"Parallel lives exist all at the same time, which causes havoc in the universe if you step out of one and into another with any regularity like you're doing."

I think back to what my grandmother told me, "Stop going into these dreams. It is dangerous."

"Be careful." Dr. Vendall clears his throat. "You could die in one reality and be alive in another."

"I'm eating your BBQ ribs! Yum!" Nile tries to get me back to the table, but I fire off more questions for the physicist.

"How I can be alive now at nineteen in Colorado and possible dead at nineteen in South America? Is my mother living two or more lives, too? Is she dead in my reality of her in the states, but still alive in Rio? Is this why I can't stop going back to her?"

"I would advise to stop all medications. They seem to be enabling you to travel with greater indiscretions than before."

Dr. Vendall stops my questions, which is fine because I didn't really want to know the answers. I just wanted my mother to come home.

"You, your doctors, and even the FDA don't know how the side effects affect everyone, especially because everyone's body and brain chemistry is so vastly different."

"Really? Stop taking all of my prescriptions?"

"I don't know your body's ability to assimilate the medication, however, due to what you told me, I'm worried for you.

Now he sounds like my grandmother.

"This cocktail of prescription pills could be very dangerous with their combined effects."

"Thank you." I walk back to the small table in the hall where the phone lives. "I appreciate your concern."

"I have to go, Tess. The producer wants to start filming, again. You can watch my show on A&E later this week. I'll be discussing parallel universes in an hour-long session, however, that's not nearly enough time to explain all of it, but it's a start. To open up people's minds to such realities."

As I hang up and walk down the hallway, back to my cold dinner, his words and answers ring in my ear.

[Morse code message: ANSWERS]

--. --- -... .- -.-. -.-

I sit on my second, most favorite couch in the world, Dr. Hall's. My grandma's purple one at home still rules supreme.

I pick up my gourd of hot *yerba maté* that Dr. Hall and I now regularly drink during my visits. I call them "visits" because it makes me feel less sick than calling them what they truly are "psychological evaluations".

"Okay, back to your bridge dream." Dr. Hall places her gourd of *yerba maté* down and holds paper and pen ready to take a transcript of my crazy life. She thinks they're hallucinations. I just heard her say "hallucinations" to herself inside her head.

Before I divulge the unnerving memory of my bridge dream, which hasn't ended yet because I keep waking up before its conclusion, I know it will not end well and hesitate to start the rewind process in my head. I take a long sip from my medicinal tea and hope its tincture can heal both a damaged mind—as my doctor believes—and the hole in my heart for my missing mother—as my grandmother believes.

"I stood on a very long bridge, the far end of it seemed to be bent with the curvature of the earth—but perhaps my eyes betrayed me."

I close my eyes to see and feel what I experienced that night. It's too easy to do these days, to flip back and forth between my parallel worlds. "I feel dizzy."

My heart is jumping into overdrive, again. My breathing tightens into short, rapid gasps. I think, 'What's wrong with me?' I won't be run over. There are no cars. There are lanes for many though, and another route runs down the middle for the street trolley.

I realize that I have stopped talking to my doctor, so I tell her what's around me. "I can see overhead electric rails."

"Was anyone with you this time? Your little friend?"

I don't like the way she says "your little friend". I can call her that or Nile, but no else.

"No, there was no one else on the bridge. It's an ornate cement bridge. With designs stamped into its walls. The black, wrought iron lampposts are swaying."

In the breeze? Due to the intensifying white caps below? I don't dare look down over the thick ledge of the bridge because my heart's already in the red zone. I feel as if I'm standing on the bridge and yet at the same time, I know I am sitting on my doctor's couch. My eyes remain closed.

"I step into the center of the traffic lane and am confused as to which way to go, but can hear Nile's voice from faraway."

"Nile yells, "Tess! Come here! Come to me!""

My doctor scribbles quickly in her tablet.

I look one way. No one. I look the other way, down the long expansion. I think I can see Nile in the crowd.

"It's night again and everything is in black, except for showers of light falling from the lampposts that line the sides of the bridge."

"Nile yells, again. "Tess! Yes! Come this way!""

As I try to lift my feet to walk toward him, nothing happens. My feet seem as if they're glued to the ground. I don't tell Dr. Hall this, I just remember the sensation again or maybe I'm feeling it again.

"I look up and see that Nile is even farther away— as if the bridge stretched."

I am really beginning to not like my dreams. They're so frustrating, especially when I feel like I'm stuck to a spot on some dangerous bridge in who knows what city. Well, I know it's Rio, but I haven't been on this side of the city before.

"I can't walk. I crumble to the ground and hug my knees. I can no longer hear Nile. The mute button in my dream is turned 'on' again. I can't even hear the slapping of water against the pylons or the wind over my ears. It's weird how my senses just shut off. Am I operating on a self-preservation mode, Dr. Hall?"

She doesn't answer me.

I kick off my boots and pull my legs up in front of me, placing my forehead on top of my knees in defeat.

Dr. Hall patiently waits for me to continue.

I do continue thinking, but in my mind, not out loud. Will these psychedelic adventures ever end? I'm as baffled as much as my shrink to what starts and keeps triggering such vivid dreams. Or maybe they're hallucinations and then there's my recent bout of paranoia with almost everyone, except Dr. Hall, Nile, and my grandmother. I'm not going to classes now because I think everyone is after me. My shrink added Ativan to help my anxiety prescription of Lexapro. It's a new add-on treatment. I never heard of such a thing, more drugs to help other drugs.

I can hear Nile's voice, again, distant and muffled. His words slowly come into my world. "Tess? Are you okay? Why are you over there?"

I open my eyes.

Nile lies on his stomach at the end of my bed.

I'm no longer sitting in the middle of the expansive bridge—or in Dr. Hall's office. I'm back in my bedroom. It's nighttime. "How long have I been on the floor?"

"You were with me for the first half of the night. I do remember kissing you good night, but after that…" He shrugs.

My realities are blurring. I can't keep up with what life I'm supposed to be living full time since they both are so real and yet so fleeing. My mind has a free ticket to go wherever and whenever it wants and I'm forced to follow.

"Weird." I check my arms and legs for any new souvenirs from my night travels, nothing, except a string of "dah-di-dit-dit" sounds playing inside my head that seems like a warning.

I crawl across the round rug with its multi-colored braided rags that dig into my knees and up and into Nile's arms. "I like when I can stay in bed and when my dreams don't require me to physically relocate."

Nile pulls me back under the blankets. "I got cold. That's how I knew you migrated to your cozy corner on the bare floor."

I nestle my chilled body against his.

Nile recoils from my full-body touch. "You're an ice cube!" He reaches for the extra blanket at the end of the bed and tucks it around me like I'm in a cocoon.

"Now, I look like a caterpillar."

"No. A beautiful butterfly—ready to fly."

I hide under the blankets. "I don't want to fly away, anymore."

"Good point. Let me think of another analogy since you didn't like that one."

I pull the blankets over my head and wait for his witty response. Under the blankets, my body heat and breath is finally making me feel warm. I wait for my intelligent boyfriend to give another pretty comparison. It doesn't have to be an insect. He's thinking too hard…I lean closer to his mouth and hear him snoring. I guess he's going to sleep on it and tell me in the morning. I hold on tight to him, my arm stretched across his wide chest and try to sleep, in this bed, in this room, and in this world for the rest of the night.

[Morse code message: GOBACK]

... - --- .--.

My grandmother shuffles into my bedroom. It's barely daybreak and my room is full of ground fog like someone has flipped on the switch on a fog machine as a joke.

I wish it was Nile playing a joke on me.

I sit up, surprised to see her here, but I guess Nile was right. She moves around when it's convenient for her and doesn't always wait for one of us to help her.

Nile hasn't been coming around ever since our fight about this "Tino character" as he calls him.

My grandmother wants to know why he's a "no show" at the last couple of our dinners, but doesn't ask.

I squint at her.

"Are you all right, dear?" She sits on my bed and pulls one of the extra blankets at the foot of my bed around her shoulders.

"There's a dense fog I can't see through, Grandma. Like now."

My grandmother pats my hand like I'm a little kid, again. "You know, you can stop your dreams."

I shift up to sit against my headboard. Whether I'm dreaming or not these days, I can always hear and feel the presence of someone near me like someone's trying to tell me something. And there's this infrequent beeping still happening. Do I dare ask her if she hears it?

I pick up my journal off my nightstand and hold it open to show my grandmother what I tried to transcribe. "Do you ever hear this sound? It's something like "dah-di-dit-dit". Or maybe it's more like a beep-beep-beep sound."

My grandmother's face goes ashen like before.

"Dr. Hall thinks I'm hearing Morse code. See? This here is the word or Morse code for hotel—or that's what Dr. Hall translated."

Maybe my grandmother might actually know something or say something that will make sense verses what I've not been hearing from my doctors.

"Grandma, at first these Morse code words were benign like 'family' and 'fate', but Dr. Hall has decoded messages like 'return to me' 'escape' 'find me' 'lost'."

She leans in closer to look at the dots and dashes and the words Dr. Hall has written under each random pattern.

"I feel like there is no escape from my dreams. Who is this 'her'? Am I missing some of the words in translation? Or are they just one- and two-word messages?"

Before she speaks, she looks at the brightness streaming in the window, in from the life outside. It contrasts against the gray dim world that we sit in right now and I wonder if there is any light left in her life or in mine…

She clears her throat and returns her attention to me. "Your mother and grandfather used Morse code to communicate to each other when they ferried people to safety. That's where she was taking you and Tino—to the airport—the night they pushed the Range Rover off the road into *Baía da Guanabara. Guanabara* Bay. Morse code is an antiquated way to talk, so they thought no one would figure it out."

My grandmother pulls her bathrobe closer to her chin even though it's stuffy in my room. "But the cartel did figure out what they were saying and they will figure out what we're saying now, your mother and I. So you have to stop."

"What? She alive?"

"You have to stop it. Stop going into these dreams. It's not safe for you, or for her, or even for Tino."

I close my journal and stuff it into my nightstand drawer. "I can't."

"You can't? Or you won't?"

"Grandma, is this woman, is my mother?"

"Yes, and she's in much danger. If you go, you might not come back—nor will she."

I fall back against my pillows with my hand on my forehead. She said it. She is my mother. She is alive. I look up to my grandmother for more answers.

As quickly as she appeared in my bedroom, she's gone.

[Morse code message: STOP]

-- ..- ... - ... - .- -.--

A thread of daylight, the color of orange sherbet underlines the bottom of my fabric window shade…another morning is here, again and so fast. Where my grandmother bought these old-fashioned window shades, I have no idea, but maybe they came with the house. As I watch the fabric-covered pull ring blow against the wall below the windowsill, I feel safe at least for the moment, hidden inside here at my grandmother's house.

I look across the bed to find Nile is not here. He's still a bit peeved I keep saying, "Tino" instead of "Nile" at very crucial points late in the evening. I tell him it's nothing and what kind of name is that, anyhow? I ask if he's sure that I'm not saying, "Tina"?

He gets a really weird look on his face like I might be saying I prefer girls and he doesn't like that answer, either. Nile told me that he checked the college registry's database of enrolled students to find a "Tino" and found nothing. "If he's an old man, like out of college, then fine, he can have you."

Did he really mean that? What happened to "You're the one for me" like my grandmother predicted, like he had parroted?

I sit up and pull a blanket around my shoulders. His running shoes are still at my bedroom door. Maybe he's not that mad. Maybe my tossing and turning sent him to the couch, although Dr. Hall said I rarely moved at all the night that she studied me the very first time in the sleep lab. I'm due to go back again this week.

This time, she suggested that we create an atmosphere similar to what I am used to, so I get to bring Nile. I haven't told him yet, but I hope he will agree. He'll just be bummed that we can't play like we usually do or maybe he will think that we can and will eagerly oblige. I guess I won't tell him we can't until he agrees to go to the sleep lab. He probably won't go since we aren't really on good talking terms or loving terms, right now.

I rub my eyes and the moment of darkness behind my eyelids flashes me back into the middle of my dream even though I know now that I'm awake. How can my brain transport me while I'm conscious? This is truly a different sensation from my previous night trips. I feel like someone's trying to tell me something. There's a message deep within all of this mystery—its dark places and half of the answers in Portuguese, words written by my hand each week in my journal, but not understood by me.

The pull of my dream is powerful. I'm carried by the rush of the air that rises over me like a thunderous, steely wave. I feel myself being picked up by its crescendo and I crash onto the dark sand.

I'm back on the beach, at its water edge, much farther away from the driftwood lean-to shack than the last time that I visited. I'm wearing the same waterlogged, silver evening dress, knee length. Thank God, it's not floor length.

My wet hair curls against my neck as the wind pelts me with tiny bits of sand. I pull a salty strand from the corner of my mouth and creep across the packed surface and up and over a dune in the cloak of night. Again, I don't feel as if I am alone, but I cannot see another person anywhere on this dune section of the beach. However, there is a presence either pushing me forward or pulling me toward him, or her, I can't tell which way the momentum is coming from, but I am definitely powerless within its strength.

A cottony cloud that had completely covered the full moon before has slipped off and now illuminates the long stretch of sand, showing me the way to the beach shack. My crouching shadow beside me is a solid black figure on the snow-white sand. I feel exposed, so I jump into the darkness offered by the tall grasses of the dunes.

Just like the sensation that I experienced on the endless city bridge, my forward movement through the deep sand of the dunes is not taking me any closer to the shack. Panic climbs from my stomach into my throat. I turn and spit into the strong nighttime wind. I keep moving toward my destination, an illusion of safety. I stand and stride down the side of the dune, running, and leap across scattered pieces of sunbaked driftwood, rocks polished smooth by the constant marine currents, and catch my toe on dried seaweed left behind from an old tide. I tumble down the rest of the dune like a ragdoll.

That must be why there's sand in my bed. I'm a klutz. I sit but just for a half of a second before I surge forward and reach out toward the makeshift door, lifting its latch, but stopping to breathe and think—before opening the door to the unknown. A stiff wind blows off the top of the dunes, showering me again in a shroud of sand and pushes the door open for me.

I hesitate, but enter, scanning the small room. In front of me sit a woman on the ground. She looks to be my grandmother's age. She's bent over something in her lap, but looks up as soon as the door clunks shut against its rough frame. Behind the door is my little tour guide, who keeps appearing in most of my dreams. This is the first time I've seen her at the beach away from the slums of Rio.

Do they know each other?

The woman sits with her legs crossed and pats the folded blanket beside her.

I'm surprised at how well the small campfire before her lights up the shack. I thought I had smelled a fire, but hadn't realized it was so close. There are no windows in this small shelter. It's shaped like a yurt and only has slits up high where the walls meet the awkward circle of the ceiling and lets the smoke escapes into the night.

Funny, I don't remember smelling a fire in my previous visits to the beach, but this time, I can make out the essence of orange in the wood burning before us. It's the same smell I remember from my childhood when my grandpa used to make bonfires on the beach. What beach was that? Was it here? Was that when it was safe for all of us?

I approach her with caution and sit where I have been directed. The little girl takes a seat on the other side of the woman and leans against her, but still watches me, the gringo who's back. On the far wall, leans a tarnished mirror and I can see my reflection. With my wet hair, I look like a lot like her, just aged progressed thirteen years into the future.

Initially, I thought the woman looked at a book, but now I can see what she holds in her lap. It's a tarnished silver frame with a dated photo of my grandmother when she was a young, my age.

I look closer at the woman sitting beside me. Is this woman my grandmother's sister? My great aunt?

Finally, she looks up to me and speaks in slow English, "Please tell her I cannot come. And I am sorry."

In my mind, I can see the pages of my recent journals, again and the words that Dr. Hall had translated from all of the beeps and taps I heard inside my head. Some of the messages scared me:

SAVE HER
KEEP HER SAFE
HIDE HER

I want to ask my great aunt why she lets her niece run the alleys of Rio. And am I the "her" the Morse code messages are about? Is this little girl trying to show me the life I could have had lived if my mother had kept me in Rio with her?

The little girl crawls into the woman's lap, hugging her tight.

My mind swirls more questions that it can't possibly answer. Is this little girl really me as a little girl? Is this possible?

While Dr. Hall kind of believed that someone was trying to communicate with me, however, she couldn't answer my questions of "who?" and "from where?" Now I think I know…

The vision of the two females in front of me fades like the reverse development of a Polaroid picture. I realize that I have opened my eyes and can see the fuzzy image of Nile outlined by the break of day in front of me.

"Hey, Cinnamon Girl? You okay?" He slumps onto the corner of the bed, trying to see into my head through my dazed eyes like so many medical people have been doing lately.

"You forgot the can of whipped cream."

"You're among the living, again, demanding food. That's a good sign." Nile pulls up beside me and takes me into this his arms. "Your grandmother was in the kitchen, again in the middle of night. I couldn't get it."

"What?" I bolt upright onto my knees, searching under the quilts and comforter for my bathrobe to toss over my skimpy negligee. "Is she okay? Did she fall?"

"Relax. She said she was hungry."

"But Rosalyn made all of us that great feast last night—"

"You can call it "great". I think "fiery" is a better word. She's out to get me." Nile pulls me back to him, wrapping the top comforter over us. "Your grandmother said she had a craving for ice cream."

"How did she get down the stairs?"

"Sheer willpower. And don't worry, she made it back to bed in one piece, but only after we created the world's best banana splits!"

"Did you bring one back up for me?"

"For breakfast? You know it's nine in the morning, right? Not the middle of the night, anymore."

"Of course." I lied. I never know what time it is anymore without looking at a watch. "But who knows when my last meal will be? And I think a banana split sundae would be worthy of such an honor."

"Don't talk like that Tess." Nile leans his head close to mine and wraps me in the nook of his elbow. "But the answer is, "No." We ate the last two bananas."

"I can't believe my grandmother went the whole way downstairs."

"She told me she's only bedridden when it's convenient like when you're home or Rosalyn's here." He lies back against the pillow, letting go of me. "Otherwise, she gets too bored playing a stiff."

"I can't believe it." I climb on top of him to look into his eyes to see if he's just kidding. He's a lousy liar and his eyes give him away every time.

"Believe it. She's pigheaded like you." Nile tosses me and the comforter off and slides his sweater over his head. "I think you just say you have nightmares to guilt me into staying the night."

"What?" I launch a fat pillow at his back. "You beg me to stay every night."

Nile dive bombs back onto my bed. "I know!"

"You're not mad at me, anymore?"

"Let's just say if I find him, the mysterious Tino, he's a goner, but if he only exists in your dreams, then he's safe."

[Morse code message: MUSTSTAY]

-.. .- -- .- --. . ...

Nile screams at me from the far end of the bridge, but no words make it from his open mouth to my ears. The sun has disappeared over the end of the wide river as night's shadows cover me, again. I'm frozen in this spot in the middle of the bridge, unable to move. Next to me are torched cars. The street trolley has burst into a hot, sizzling flume. People run passed me as if I'm not there. In front of me, an explosion rocks the four-lane bridge, although I can't hear it. My dream is on mute, again and everything plays out before me in a funky silence.

This place looks like where the world will end.

I find the energy to move my feet forward, toward Nile's arms that he holds high above the row of police in their BOTE's uniforms—or Brazil's version of America's SWAT, my Google brain feels the need to inform me.

The heat from the infernos makes me dodge left and then right around traumatized mothers and children and smoldering piles of what once were vehicles. People race pass me to the safe side of the bridge, marked by the armed men in black uniforms. Sniper bullets fly above my head at the retreating arsons, terrorists, or is it the cartel that is firing the guns?

Nile tries to get to me, however, the line of police officers hold him back. "The structure isn't safe! Get off now!" He screams.

Now, I can hear Nile and everything exploding once again, and everyone around me, screaming.

The chief of police echoes Nile's message through a bullhorn, but in Portuguese.

I feel invisible and invincible as I move around danger untouched, thinking or knowing that my dream will somehow protect me that is—until I see her.

My tiny friend is cowering against a rolled over car and tucked up in its wheel well. She shivers and waves me over to her hiding spot. I question its perceived safety, yet go anyhow. She doesn't flinch when I move in close to her. I remove my sweater and pull it over her head. It fits her like a dress.

She tries to smile a thank you, but is visibly frightened by the war happening in front of her. Through her teary eyes, I see the terror that I should feel, but don't. Out of sheer gut instinct, I swoop her up into my arms and run.

She wraps her legs around my waist like a toddler. Her fingernail scratches the left side of my face as she tries to wrap her arms around my neck. We dash as one through the thickening smoke. I can't see Nile, but can hear his voice. Thank God that my sense of hearing is back on, again. "Tess! You gotta get off the bridge, now! Hurry!"

I rush toward him and leap over a pool of gasoline on fire. My clinging passenger screams, but we emerge unscathed. She loosens her grip and points at one of her glittery red Mary Jane shoe that has slipped off her foot and landed just inches from the fire.

As a westerly wind pushes the smoke off the right side of the bridge, I can see Nile again, waving his arms at me and willing me to move toward him. I stop and look back at the shoe.

Nile yells, "Noooooo!"

I turn and hurry back to pick up the shoe by its broken strap. At that very moment, another bomb explosion makes the bridge shutter and crack in two in front of me. The support beneath the bridge is destroyed and loses its battle to stay parallel to the choppy water one-hundred-and-fifty feet below.

The little girl and I cling to each other in pure horror and slide along with the debris off the bridge, down into darkness.

I stop my long monologue to breathe and calm my racing heart.

Dr. Hall stops writing in her tablet.

I pull myself off the couch and move to pace back and forth in front of Dr. Hall's seventh story window. Once I notice how high up I am, I back away from the window and circle her room mindlessly.

Where one phobia starts, her fear of heights, another obsessive, compulsive behavior begins, mindless pacing…this is what I hear my doctor saying inside her head as she makes a new note about her patient, me.

I think to myself, isn't all pacing mindless? Isn't that the point of it? But I don't voice it, instead I tell my psychoanalyst, "I don't like bridges."

Today, she's wearing an all-yellow business suit like the color of whipped butter. She told me she was hoping summer was just hiding around one of the corners on campus.

I'm content to stay in the beautiful months of winter and in all of my gorgeous ski sweaters, however, since my insomnia is making me feel cold all of the time, I'll probably still be wearing my sweaters into late July. I probably won't mind the heat so much this year—usually any degree over seventy-two sends me to cold water like at a lake, a river, or even to my blue, inflatable wading pool my mother had bought for my sixth birthday just before she vanished. Every summer for years afterwards, my grandmother would shake her head whenever saw my grandfather blowing up my blue pool, again. She knew it would live on the front porch until Labor Day.

My doctor leans toward me. "I think you suffer from gephyrophobia."

I stop wandering. "I don't need another phobia."

"It's fairly common, this fear of crossing bridges, and treatable with a behavioral therapy such as reciting street names or counting words that begin with an 'T' every time the radio host says one—"

I wish she hadn't mentioned that new brain game because now I know I will be listening to the radio with a new intent. "I wasn't in a car. There was no radio."

Dr. Hall sits back in her chair. "The new medication that I prescribed should be working to ease your anxiety about your fears. Are you taking your Ativan?"

Inside my mind, I yell at Dr. Hall, but this is happening in a dream, right? Not my reality! Besides, there are no bridges in my flat town before the mountain's foothills! There are no major bodies of water to cross!

"We'll have to watch to see if I should increase your dosage of Lexapro with this add-on treatment of Ativan." She flips through my pages of prescription drugs to see what other prescription might be adversely affected. Can she really know? Does anyone know how these medicines work when all put together in one person's body? Dr. Vendall is right. I should just stop swallowing the pills, all of them.

I put myself back in my usual position on her couch: prone. I think my shrink is wrong on this new assumption and to stop my mouth from spitting out angry words, which she will just write down in my file and prescribe more medications, I look around for a distraction.

Her high heel shoes match her suit perfectly, again. How does she maneuver around the ever-present mud puddles in those heights?

It's not working. I never cared about or for fashion and I can't let go of my fear about this bridge, real or imaginary, so I blurt out: "This possible plunge to the waters below, the swaying motion of the bridge, its endless expanse—it all seems quite unstable and real."

"Tess, you know many engineers put much time, thought, and money into building these passageways, right?" Dr. Hall grins.

Her cheerfulness generally helps to squelch my rising anxiety, however, my mind keeps flashing back as it replays the moment of my terror, not anxiety, due to my inability to move out of the way of danger plus someone was blowing up the bridge. Bet the engineers didn't build their bridges with bombs in mind.

I fold my arms over my chest and continue to try and convince her that I'm not crazy. "The more steps I took, the farther I seem to be from the safe end of the bridge. In fact, when I looked back to see where I came from, it was even farther away and I swore I hadn't taken a step backwards, yet somehow I was still stuck in the middle."

I sit up and pull on my jacket. "I never did make it to the end, either."

"That's curious." My doctor studies her notes, flipping her tablet back a page and then skims back about twelve more pages. She now knows my history better than I do now. "When you were thrown overboard from the yacht, the water didn't scare you—"

"Actually, it did, but I was more afraid of why and who threw me over—."

"Can you remember what he looked like?"

"No...I do remember my dress because I keep wearing it in my dreams...it was pretty, but rough to the touch since there was a metallic silver thread sewn throughout the black and white smoother threads. My dress was heavy to wear even before it got wet..."

Dr. Hall stands and walks over to examine both sides of my neck near my hairline. "What's this red mark on your neck?"

"Is it that damn rash, again?" I lift my long hair up off my shoulders. "I broke out in a skin rash back at my old college when these dreams had just started. It was why I went to see Dr. Reid."

"It's actually a red scratch on your left cheek. It looks like someone was hanging on for dear life, by your neck."

I reach up to touch my latest souvenir. "She was…"

[Morse code message: DAMAGES]

···· · ·-·· ·--·

Tino pushes the two-story, metal door open with his whole body and eventually it slides easier once the momentum of its sheer weight gets moving. He slides it open entirely, which makes me nervous even though the night outside is completely black except for the faraway, flashing white, runway lights lining the tarmac.

Inside, it's equally as dark. No one will see us—or us them, which is why I'm nervous about entering.

Tino nods to me to do so.

I enter, but only take two steps inside.

He grabs me around my waist and hugs me tight as if to say, "It's okay, trust me". He pulls me along by my hand in the dark like he can see where he's headed. Up a narrow staircase of metal steps, he jingles a set of keys out of his jacket's pocket. I cringe at its loud echo and quickly look around to make sure we have not summon any demons; that's what I call them now, the unseen presence of men that want me to go away—out of Rio permanently or want me…dead.

I think Tino is on their list, too since he has been with me every time something goes haywire: in the Range Rover, in the bay of black water—only the beach appears to be a safe haven for us. I wish we were back on the beach instead of inside this deserted airplane hangar. He pushes the solid office door open and pulls me inside.

Tino must have heard my wish and pushes against the wall to kiss me slow and long on my lips. The heat from his body always makes me feel safe for the moment despite the fact that I have no idea why we're here or where we're going or who we're waiting for.

"We'll have time for more of this soon." He smiles with his eyes.

We enter the small rectangular room lined with computers. Tino deposits me in a well-worn office chair. He takes a seat beside me.

I spin side to side to calm my worries and watch Tino turn on the monitors. The green hue from these ancient computers brightens the room a bit to reveal another antiquated device on the far end of the table. I get up and touch the dusty machine that kind of looks like a two-hole punch, but upon close inspection, it's a Morse code device.

Is this where my mother is sending messages to my grandmother and to me? Could it be she that we are waiting for? Or are we waiting for my grandfather? I get instant chills in anticipation of what I've always wished would come true. I still have 321 more paper cranes to make and since I believe in superstitions now along with my other mind games, I don't feel it is she who will be arriving this evening…my math brain starts to calculate, if I make three origami cranes a day that will be 107 days! More than three months? I double the amount of crane output per day and it will still take me 54 days…I need to crank it up to a dozen birds every day—

"Okay. Now, we wait. We could be waiting a long time…" Tino opens his arms to me. "…so come here, beautiful."

While I'm intrigued by the old-fashion, communication machine, I can put my curiosity on hold and pay attention to Tino. I nestle into his lap and it's a good thing that he chosen the larger of the old office chairs and one that doesn't spin.

He reaches for my face with both hands and pulls me close to him until first our noses touch and then our lips. The way he kisses me is as if he is trying to memorize all of me and as if it might be the very last time he kisses me.

I feel a bittersweet bubble of emotion filter up from my heart, but I swallow it, so not to ruin the moment with the sad thought that this could be our last time together. This fragile world that I keep being pulled into has no time line, no promises, and worst of all, no answers, so I just follow my body's wish for tonight.

Tino moves his hands from behind my neck down my back, holding onto my hips to lift me up and over him so that I am straddling his lap. He wraps his arms around me and pulls me very tight again to make us one in the night. His lips move to my neck and find their way down my throat to my breast. My shirt is buttoned shut at the top of my cleavage. With his teeth, he unbuttons the next button. I can feel his smile against my skin; he's proud of himself that he was able to do this without his hands and without resorting to biting off the button instead. I'm braless, which makes it easy for Tino to kiss me everywhere. I lean my head back away from him to give him room. With one hand centered on my back, he uses the other to hike up my skirt and unbuckle his jeans. He moves slowly, making me ache, and without ever breaking contact with me. Tino returns to kissing me as he lifts me and enters. Together, we rock in the noisy chair, but there is no one there, so for once I don't mind the noise, which goes on for a long time rotating between fast and slow, and then fast again. When we finish, I stay on top of him to block the sad feeling from returning that this could be the very last time we can be together. I hope I am very wrong and hug him tight around his shoulders.

Static from the radio that I hadn't notice before crackles and interrupts our silence.

Tino kisses me hard and separates from me, moving over to another chair in front of the computer and radio while reassembling himself.

On the radio, Tino is talking in what sounds like gibberish at first to me, but my Google brain translates for me. He's directing a plane onto the tarmac. I look at this man, who I really do not know at all. He's an aviator, too? The confidence beaming from his words and his intense stare at his computer monitor answers my question.

I quickly make myself presentable to who we might be greeting tonight.

Tino points to a bathroom door at the end of the long room. I duck inside.

In front of the mirror, I appear to be younger, maybe only sixteen. I splash water on my face, dry it, and try to fix my hair. Next, I wash up the best I can with the paper towel. There is a bottle of hand lotion that has a mellow fragrance like cucumbers and green tea. I rub the lotion all over my arms and legs. When I exit, Tino is still on the radio and motions for me to sit beside him. I can hear the drum of an airplane engine above us before I see its lights brighten the runway. "Who is it?"

He just smiles and then pulls me out of the room, down the stairs, and outside to watch the plane's arrival.

The small plane putters to a stop about fifty yards away from us. Tino moves toward it.

I hesitate. I cannot see the pilot inside the cockpit. I jog after Tino, who's already opening the airplane's door and helping a tall man, who ducks a bit due to the number of years he has carried around with him in his long years on this planet. He steps onto the tarmac and walks towards me—my grandfather! I must be seeing the man, who died just after I turned sixteen and when my grandmother told him not to return to the old country. Were Tino and I to be his last rescue mission to the states? But I don't ever remember Tino in the states.

"Theresa! Come here!" My grandfather yells at me.

"Grandpa!" I run to the man who I have missed so much.

"Theresa!" He bear hugs me easily as he's a foot-plus taller than me even when he stoops.

I never liked my true name, Theresa, and commanded everyone to call me just, "Tess", but to hear my grandfather, who I thought had perished, call me by my given name, I'm heart wrenched with both a deep love and the rush of pain from missing him. "I missed you so much, Grandpa!"

"Me, too. Soon all this craziness will be over and we'll be together again."

"Grandma misses you, a lot."

"I know…how are our mosaic tables holding up in the snow?"

"Great. We built them tough."

Tino stands there, happy to witness such a reunion.

"Thanks, Tino." My grandpa turns to face Tino, but leaves his arm over my shoulders. "My eyesight is not what it used to be, so it was great to have your verbal guidance to get me here safely."

"Always here to help. Ready for dinner, now?"

"Yes, of course, dinner. I'm starved."

Tino takes my grandfather's black satchel and my hand. "I made a reservation."

I love the fact that all of the men in my worlds can cook or at least make dinner reservations.

We all pile into a black Jeep—the kind that doesn't have a roof. Tino bounces us down a dirt road to a desolate spot on the beach. The full moon lights up this thin stretch of sand to a bright white; we're only a short distance from the airstrip, although it feels like we're on the other side of the continent.

"Where's the restaurant?" I look back into the palms and undergrowth to see if maybe Tino passed it by mistake.

Tino jumps out of the Jeep and runs around to the back of the vehicle. "It's in here, Tess."

My grandfather laughs. He helps Tino lug a big cooler from the back and carries it over to the fallen log fashioned to be our seat for the night. While my grandfather strikes a match to start our fire, Tino unloads the ingredients for our dinner.

"We'll be feasting on oysters on the half shell, next, corn on the cob, and then buttery pastry tarts filled with shrimp, and we'll finish with grilled prawns." He concludes the announcement of his menu by knocking off the top of a coconut with a meat cleaver, adds a straw, and serves the beverage of the evening. "And only fresh coconut water."

"Wow, impressive." I accept and sip.

"Yes, I know." Tino hits a second coconut with the cleaver.

My grandfather accepts his coconut water, too. "I taught him how to do that—works wonders on the women."

"Grandma?"

"Ask her sometime." He seems to be happy to be out of the sky for the moment and on the ground and holds onto the log with one hand either to steady himself or make sure that he is really here.

We watch as the fire first climbs higher and higher while slurping raw oysters.

I can see that Tino's meat cleaver has many purposes as he expertly opens one oyster after another for us. My grandfather pokes at the corn still wrapped in its husks, rolling them around to make sure all sides are cooked equally. We work on the corn on the cob as we wait for the shrimp tarts to cook. I want to ask my grandfather a million questions, but I don't know what chapter of my life this is and where he fits into all of this confusion in my head. I do begin to remember all of our previous beach dinners. They're rolling back through my memory like an endless wave. I wish there had been more. I think this is the same log where I sit now with Tino and my grandfather tucked between them is the same log from my earlier childhood bonfire dinners…

"Tino, Tess, I think we should fly out tonight."

"Yes, sir." Tino stands to remove the tarts from the fire for us. He had wrapped them in foil to keep them together as a pie as they heated up and now slides one per plate for each of us.

"Get as far away from Rio as my gas tank can take us with, of course, a half hour to spare." My grandfather looks to the dark heaven above us. "Never like to take it to the limit."

We're going home to the states? Great, but Grandpa's plane can hold four passengers, so who will be our fourth? Can I push this dream and wish for my mother? Even without having made the one thousand paper cranes as the Japanese folklore says I need to do to get my wish? I've been carefully trying to fold an origami crane out of a piece of my gum's foil wrapper since we arrived on the beach. It's kind of hard to do with such a tiny piece of paper, but I keep folding to make a tiny origami crane.

"My brothers are getting the plane ready now. Gas is topped off. Engine and propellers checked. Everything is ready to go." Tino sniffs at the air to confirm my shrimp tart is done and slides it onto a plate for me. "No worries for us tonight."

I take the plate and use its flat metal surface to make the last cease to make the crane's wings.

"What are you making there Theresa?"

"Oh, just a wish." I hold up the tiny silver bird that shines in the night.

"Very good." My grandfather nods. "I always knew you had artistic abilities."

"Now I only need to make another 320."

"And I always knew you were ambitious, too."

I slide the tiny bird into the pocket on my shirt. But if my mother was coming with us tonight, wouldn't she be here with us now? Maybe Grandpa is to bring back Grandma's sister, although when I met her at the beach shack, she seemed pretty insistent on staying in Rio.

As Tino reaches into the fire to remove my grandfather's dinner, a sonic boom makes the sky above the palms turn the color of platinum for a moment and then makes the sand tremble. My grandfather and Tino are already sprinting to the Jeep. Tino still has the meat cleaver in his hand. I race as fast as I can and jump in the back seat as Tino makes the Jeep fly off the packed sand to the dirt road much faster than before.

I sit, grasping the roll bars, repeating to myself: Let Tino's brothers be alive. Please let Tino's brothers be alive. Let Paulo and Márcio live. I can now remember his brothers and can picture two young men, who are the shorter, but older versions of Tino.

Red flames jump high into the night sky and a heavy black smoke engulfs the airplane hangar. Tino careens the Jeep onto the tarmac as my grandpa's plane is also swallowed in flames. Why is this happening? And why now? How can my grandmother say, the future is good?

Before the Jeep comes to a complete stop, my grandpa jumps out with a revolver drawn and circles the plane.

Tino pulls another handgun out of the glove compartment and runs to a body on the tarmac. As he nears the quiet outline of a man, the man slowly sits up and holds his head.

"Márcio, are you all right?" Tino kneels beside his brother and scans for blood or other serious damage.

"I got thrown as I was filling the gas tank. Just landed on my head. I think I'm okay."

"Where's Paulo?" Tino holds his brother by his shoulders.

Márcio points to the hanger.

Tino and my grandpa run to the building.

I bend to Márcio. "Let me get you into the Jeep."

[Morse code message: HELP]

--. --- -. .

Today is my grandmother's birthday.

My head is still spinning from last night's dream, however, Nile wants to cook my grandmother a gourmet meal to help pull me out of my daze. He's off to the store to collect her only request for our celebration, but I'm banished by my grandmother to the kitchen table to finish my homework. She thinks I'm slacking these days because she never sees my studying and she's right, I don't crack the books; I don't need to.

To appease her, I sit and write my critical analysis on my final, industrial design project, drawing the product and creating a three-dimensional prototype was the easy part, but I'm finding that writing the consumer specifications is taking some time.

My practical coffeepot is guaranteed to keep the coffee truly hot, looks stylish on any counter, and doesn't have irritating flashing blue or green lights on its console. I'm proud of its unique design borrowed from the fifties with its blue-and-white enamel surface similar to my grandfather's camping coffeepot just like the metal plates that we had dined on last night or whenever I had my last meals with my grandfather.

I don't know about Tino…will I see him again or was that our last meal, too?

To bring myself back into this world, I study the illustration that I drew in black ink and then painted with acrylics to make my coffeepot more contemporary with a sleek look, adding a stainless steel trim around its lid, handle, and the bottom edge of the pot.

I also specified glass only, no plastic parts to come apart with daily use. In the product specifications, the enamel will be also available in red, black, and at my grandmother's suggestions: canary yellow, cantaloupe, and honeydew—the colors of her former world. She also recommended a larger-sized type for the operating buttons and its clock. She's right. I bumped up the font size, so the brewing and timer options can be read from across the kitchen without having to reach for glasses.

I tap my pen against my notebook, trying to think of what else to add to make it real and to keep me here—physically—in this world.

My grandmother divides her time between the stove and the refrigerator, making a hearty soup that she's craving and knows I will love—and she tells me, "You'll love my birthday wish soup!"

I'm still hearing people's thoughts before they speak. She calls this pot of every vegetable from the refrigerator her "birthday wish soup". She had all the ingredients needed to create her masterpiece, but also wanted ice cream, her only request for a birthday present.

Nile knew what to get and ran out the door.

I quit trying to help her about an hour ago. She insisted on making it herself.

Nile has promised her another fabulous dessert. Maybe this time, I too can indulge and be included in their secret, ice cream meetings usually held in the middle of the night. Her renewed energy is good sign.

I shudder to think of living here without her and watch her whack the potatoes into thick, chunky squares with a meat cleaver, which brings back a flood of memories from last night's dream once again. I can't seem to stop staring at the meat cleaver, which just makes my eyes well up with tears from what I believed I lost, once again.

I hesitate to tell her what just happened because today is her day. She'll just be mad that I went back into my dreams, my other world again, so I say nothing and blink my tears back into my eyes.

As I watch this wisp of a woman cook with sheer determination, I realize she does what she wants—in life and with recipes. In this culinary case though when a recipe says, "finely chop", she just cuts the roots and the tops of the green scallions off and dumps them into the pot. When it says, "pinwheels", she peels the carrot, but just drops the whole stick into the bubbling stock. Any celebrity TV chef would cringe, but Nile eats anything put in front of him and offer many verbal accolades for his personal cooks. No wonder he's a frequent and welcomed guest at our table. The trick I learned to make any meal tastier is to just let everything simmer for a long time.

I move to my laptop's screen. My spec sheet has a place for a suggested retail price. I start to use my Google search engine in my brain, but thought it might be fun to actually use the real thing and give my fingers something to do, so I type in the key words: 'premium coffeepot suggested retail prices' and wait. Before Google can respond, I receive a pop-up notification: "You got email!"

I didn't know my system could send this notice, but Nile has been using my laptop. He likes all the gadgets, reminders, and electronic calendars and has tried to convert me.

I refuse to have a computer tell me what to do. I like my paper calendars. Actually with the way my mind processes and stores information these days, I really don't even need paper. I can remember everything without jotting it down and recently, my dreams are becoming clearer and more complete, too as in starting and finishing in sequential order rather than just jumping all around inside the theater in my head.

I click on my email account and find a message from Kali, my old college roommate, who I know is now studying abroad. She had left Santa Cruz about the same time I did to cruise the world and study on a big ship, but my memory is sketchy of what ports of calls she told me she was headed to and which way around the earth she was going. There's no message, just a link.

Nile bounces in the kitchen door with this frozen dessert held in front of him like a prized possession. He has gift wrapped it in the brown paper bag and placed a red bow on the rectangular carton of ice cream.

"Is it my favorite?" My grandmother leaves her post at the stove. "Pistachio?"

Nile holds the ice cream high above his head, so she can't ruin her surprise. He hands her a bunch of bananas and tucks the ice cream into the back of the freezer. "Happy Birthday! But you have to wait until after dinner to open your present." He blows on his fingertips to warm them.

"It better be pistachio. Otherwise, you need to march back to the grocery store this instant."

Nile smiles at my grandmother and takes the seat next to me, scooting the wooden chair with its cushions closer to me. "Hey there. Shell shocked from too much studying?" He plants a kiss on top of my head.

"She's been working hard all afternoon and hasn't been much help to her dear old grandma." My grandmother stirs her soup and smiles.

"Grandma, I tried several times to slice, chop, and stir. You kept taking the utensils from me."

"I'm just kidding." My grandmother turns her back to us and sniffs the steam rising from the large pot on the stove. "Plus you're a hazard with a knife."

I hear her laughing at her own joke and smile.

Nile digs out his thick textbook all about rocks.

I click on the link in the email message and stare at the story on the screen in disbelief.

"What's the matter? Bad news from the other world? A love email from mystery man?" Nile chuckles at his own bad jokes.

I point at the screen and whisper. "This has to be a mistake."

On the computer screen is a close up of the Rio de Janeiro's daily newspaper's masthead, *O Dia*, today's date and its front page story.

The headline reads: Body Found Believed to an American. The photo shows a BOTA team outside *Hotel Praia Ipanema* and emergency responders carrying a black body bag to an ambulance.

"Tess, really?"

"She's a good girl, Nile. Just let her do her homework. Didn't you bring your textbooks, too?"

I look over to make sure she isn't coming over to the kitchen table. She has her back to us and is in the refrigerator again, looking for another vegetable to add to her soup.

I click back to the message. The subject line screams at me in all caps: TESS! TELL ME YOU ARE ALIVE!

Nile grasps my hand. His fingertips are still cold from carrying the ice cream home twenty blocks or maybe it's from this shock. "You should email your friend Kali back right away. Isn't she in South America?"

"She did a semester at sea. I think Rio was one of her stops."

"Tess, we need to go." He whispers, "Dr. Hall's. Now."

"No, no. My birthday dinner's almost done. What's the matter, Tess? Don't you feel well? " My grandmother moves toward me. I close my laptop before she makes it to the table. "I just need to pick up a prescription, so I can sleep soundly tonight."

Nile grabs my hand and the car keys. "We'll be right back."

"Hurry! Or I'll eat my ice cream without you! Plus we get to make a wish tonight—each one of us!"

I can't or couldn't have died on my grandmother's birthday. Life can't be that cruel, can it? Why does Kali assume I was in the bag? I can't call it what it truly is.

She was at the restaurant in Santa Cruz with me when I was spoke with the waiter and then with chef in fluent Portuguese. I told them a bit about my family or at least what I knew, which wasn't much.

Niles runs to the curb where my grandmother's Oldsmobile sits. I walk to the passenger door in a daze. Her car doesn't run very well anymore, but we only use it to go to the neighborhood's grocery store or the library to pick up more books for my grandmother. Glued on the dash is new plastic statue of Virgin Mary. This one is in a baby blue gown and robe. From some reason, her presence comforts me even though she's barely three inches tall.

Nile looks at me as to ask, when did this arrive?

Mary wasn't here the last time we took the car to the store. I shrug, but I'm glad to have her with us tonight. "Nile, this can't be happening…"

"There were probably many Americans in Rio today, yesterday, whenever."

"Rio is only five hours ahead of us…and in the same day."

Nile squeezes my hand before he starts the car's engine.

A miniature Virgin Mary swings on the key chain.

Nile looks at the keys. "Where did your grandmother find a key chain like that?"

I'm trying to hold it together about the very real fact I could be dead in another dimension. "When I was gone at college in Northern California…

I can hear my voice softly giving Nile an answer, but don't feel as if I'm talking out loud. "Rosalyn had to drive my grandmother to chemo. I think my grandmother attached it to the keys then."

207

Deep inside my head, I'm running through the "What if?" scenarios, yet I keep talking…

"Rosalyn never did take a driving lesson here in the states…I still don't know if she has her license."

"That explains all of the dents in your grandmother's car."

"Nile, does this mean I'll die in five hours?"

"That's why we're going to see Dr. Hall right now." He guns the massive car out of the spot where it has been parked too long.

[Morse code message: GONE]

.-. ..- -.

"The wind up clock on the nightstand reads 12:03 am. Next to it, a black rotary phone is vibrating as it rings. I adjust my eyes to the darkness of the room to confirm what I see and hear. Weird. Nobody knows I'm here."

"You're in a dream." I hear a muffled voice that I recognize as Dr. Hall's.

"Oh. Right. This place has fabric window shades just like my grandmother's. I wish I was in my bedroom and not in this dream or in this other world again."

Nile had driven me over to my doctor's house off campus, so quickly that I didn't have time to protest about bothering her after hours. He reminded me that she said I could contact her at any time of the day or night.

I really want to call Dr. Vendall.

Nile also reminded me it's after dinnertime back on the East Coast on a Saturday night and I only have his office number. I had tried to get my Google mind to operate as a phone directory, but I can't find his name in the long list of last names that begin with 'V'. Who knew there were so many people at this end of the alphabet?

Now, I lie on Dr. Hall's modern couch in her darkened living room. Nile sits on the other end of the couch and holds my feet in his lap. My head doctor perches in a chair under the beam of a brass floor lamp and leans towards me.

"Go on. Then, what happened?"

I hesitate because Nile is here and while he has heard some of my wild tales, this one is still making my legs shake despite the fact that I'm lying prone.

He reaches out to stop my knees from shaking and from knocking into each other.

"So…I picked up the receiver and heard a man's voice. It was kind of distant as if we had a lousy connection. I had to press my ear against the receiver to hear him."

"Good evening," he said. "This is the front desk, calling to make sure everything is up to your expectations."

"Yes, of course. My suite is quite lovely. Thank you, but why are you calling me in the middle of the night?"

"We just want to make sure we can—"

I hold my forehead as I repeat what I remember as my head is starting to pound out a wicked headache for me. "Static interrupted his sentence."

"—your expectations."

"He sounded as if he was using a cellphone, not a landline to call me.

"Will you need a wake-up call, *Theresa Cunha de Almeida Santos Abreu?*"

"Yes, that would be—"

Now I'm covering my eyes as I speak. How did he know my name, my full name, my birthright name that no one is supposed to know? His inflection was disturbing...

"I think you rang the wrong room." I told him. I remembered standing up, ready to drop the phone and flee the room because something in my gut is telling me to get out, so why don't I move?

Next, heavy footsteps thundered down the carpeted hallway on the other side of the wall, the sounds stopped outside my room.

"No, actually Theresa. We have the right room."

"His voice comes through the phone that I still hold in my hand."

"Someone's trying to pick the lock." I tell Dr. Hall. "I slammed the receiver and attempted to push the four-drawer dresser in front of the door only to find that it bolted to the wall. With trembling hands, I slid the security chain into place across the door. I ran back to the nightstand to find my cellphone. The battery was dead. I pick up the hotel phone again to dial for help."

"It will be over very soon."

He's still on the line.

I can hear a ring of keys jangling together outside my door with the hush of male voices arguing.

I dropped the phone, again and heaved the mattress and box spring of the queen-sized bed up against the door. In front of the mattress pile, I pulled the nightstand against it and added all of the pillows and blankets to slow up whoever is trying to unlock the door. I balanced a glass vase of purple Irises on the corner of the nightstand.

Now, someone is working on the deadbolt and now I'm not longer talking to Dr. Hall. I'm back in my dream.

I run into the large bathroom and lock the door behind me. I stuff the thick Turkish towels under the door to jam it from opening. I search the room for an escape only to find the tiny rectangular windows above the toilet are too small to climb through and out of this nightmare.

The vase crashes to the marble floor in the other room.

They're inside now.

My heart tells me to act as if this danger is indeed real, especially since I already read about my demise early today.

The diameter of the square air condition vent is also too narrow to accommodate the safe passage of an adult woman…a fire sprinkler suspended from the white, pressed tin ceiling tiles. I dig through my purse left on the sink's counter and locate a little box of restaurant stick matches. I climb up on the toilet and onto the sink's counter, light the match and hold the flame to the sprinkler's sensor.

With a shriek, a shower of water bursts from the ceiling's fire sprinkler, dousing my match and me immediately.

In the distant, I can hear fire engine sirens pierce the night air. Not too far away, I hope, I pray silently afraid to speak. Hurry! Hurry! Please hurry!

I can hear swearing in Portuguese and yelling exchanged between two men. They're outside the bathroom door. Inside the bathroom closet, there's a fire extinguisher attached to the wall. It's the best weapon that I can find to defend myself. I pull the pin and duck into the bathroom's closet. The sprinkler keeps raining, splashing a deluge of more water onto the small puddles already collecting on the marble tiled floor. I try to curtail my panicked breath, fearing if I breathe too loudly, I'll lead my perpetrators directly to my hiding place, but where else would I be? They know there is no escaping.

Then…there is silence outside the bathroom, except for the indoor rain, the spray of water hitting the pools of water now forming between the marble tomb of a tub and the vanity area.

"Are they gone?"

I don't move from my hiding spot. I don't release my death grip on the impromptu gun that will only spray chemicals instead of bullets.

"Am I alive?" I am clutching an imaginary, fire extinguisher between my hands over my chest. I'm back on Dr. Hall's couch at her house.

"Tess, you're still here with us." Dr. Hall scratches a new prescription for heavy-duty, sleeping pills on a tablet. I could hear her talk to herself inside her head as she wrote these words: *Tess desperately needs sleep.*

What? Sleeping is what I'm trying to avoid now. I don't like where I keep going. I want to stay here in this world above the equator—

Dr. Hall stands and hands a prescription to Nile. "The pharmacy on campus is open twenty-four hours."

[Morse code message: RUN]

--. .. ..-. -

Through the speakers tucked up high with the spider webs in the ceiling's corners, broken lyrics spit out and wake me up from another afternoon *siesta*. Either the wiring to these ancient speakers is bad or the radio airwaves are crossed because I think I hear two songs playing at once. I hope I can't be tapping into radio waves now, too. I don't think anything else can fit into my overloaded brain at this time.

Across the ceiling, the recessed lights burns their beams down upon my head, making my brain hurt. Can I be dreaming in broad daylight? I had hoped that I immunized to such traveling when the sun was up and out.

Why I am sunk in a chocolate brown leather chair, waiting, I am not sure.

Did Dr. Hall order new furniture? In a new color and texture?

I run my hand over the arm. I do like it. It's smooth to the touch. As I try to look around, I find I can't turn my head, again.

Am I still in that horrid hotel, but now in their posh lobby? What happened to my pursuers?

Then I remember reading the email and the photo of the black body bag flashes into my mind's eye. I take my hands and deliberately turn my head to look out the large window to determine where I sit.

Outside, the closed buds have split into the color of Kelly green, making the aspen trees heavy. The canopy of the neighboring cottonwoods is leafed out in a softer green across the sleepy afternoon sky. This doesn't look like the tropics, so I can't be dreaming and I can't be in that dreaded hotel.

Two college students wrapped in lightweight scarves and sweaters are connected to each by their linked elbows. They hustle down the sidewalk deep in secret girl talk, something I have never experienced, yet witness frequently on campus.

Suspicion confirmed.

I'm back in my college town.

The thick aroma of roasted coffee beans permeates the air of this tiny place. Even after I leave the coffeehouse and go home, I still smell like a cup of coffee for hours. Nile says my hair, too smells like the roasted beans and knows where I've been hiding for most of the day, so I reason I must be in my favorite coffeehouse.

Why am I losing the ability to recognize my world?

What is my real world, now?

On my right wrist, my mother's gold watch might tell me why I was hiding in a bathroom closet in a Rio de Janeiro's hotel one minute, or however long I was there, and now am seated back in reality—if this is my true reality. Maybe my night travels are my true reality and this, right now, is just a dream. I wish someone, anyone, would answer my questions.

The crystal-face of the petite watch says: 5:03 am. What? I shake my wrist. Did I break my mother's watch on my latest nighttime trip?

That time isn't right here, in Mountain Time Zone. Besides, it would be dark and I doubt if this coffeehouse would be open. College students go home at 5 am to sleep after studying all night or being out at the bars, not get up at this hour.

A five-hour difference would put me again in Rio…at 12:03 am, the same time those thugs broke into my hotel room. My body reacts to this thought and goes rigid again with terror. Frantically, I search for something outside to distract my mind, but can't latch onto any one thing to hold my mind still. People are moving too quickly again in their own busy lives, racing pass me—

Nile runs up to the window and plasters his body against its pane like he walked into it without realizing it was there.

I laugh.

It feels good to laugh and push away all of this unsettling anxiety pulsing through my body.

He grins and pulls himself off the window.

The manager looks annoyed at the large handprints left behind on the glass.

I seem to step back and forth over this very thin line that separates my reality from fantasy and what's most disturbing is that it is becoming increasingly more difficult to distinguish which life is true. I fear I'm losing my grip on my reality, not knowing where I am and feel as if I'm succumbing to its control over me…until I see Nile enter the coffeehouse.

He beelines to me and wedges himself into my wide chair. His physical presence is helping me lose some of my anxiety.

I fake a smile.

He cups his hand under my chin and knows. "Do you want me to take you to Dr. Hall's?"

"She doesn't have hours now."

"You know she said you could call her anytime. Or do you want to Dr. Reid instead? Bet he would be happy to tie you up with more electrodes and run some more tests that involve needles."

"Just hold me and make me stay here. I'll be okay." I lie and lean against his body.

Nile wraps both arms around me and kisses my head.

The store manage is outside the window with a bottle of Windex and a handful of paper towels. He looks annoyed. I know because I can hear him say, "What do these kids think this is? A hotel?"

The word, "hotel" triggers the dream, again and my body shudders. I look to Nile to stop my mind from pushing me back into the dark bathroom closet.

Nile's kiss upon my lips makes me smile mid-kiss. I'm safe, at least for now.

He makes the decision for us to go home and study there and that way we can be around for my grandmother since Rosalyn is leaving early, today.

I agree and let him tuck me into my sweater and wrap my lightweight scarf around my neck and head. I laugh and have to unwrap my *burqa* a bit to breathe. I follow my tall guide down the wet sidewalk, stepping in his safe footprints that he leaves behind. Somebody is already watering the slumbering shrubbery and trees to encourage summer to show up sooner.

Nile glances over his shoulder to make sure that I'm close to him and not lost in my thoughts.

To prove to him that I'm here in this world with him, I hug him behind and almost knock over both of us.

He pulls me around to walk beside him, hand in hand. "So cheffie, what are you making me for dinner?"

"Do you want all-Americana, *Italiano*, or Mexican?"

"Yes." He replies. "All of them."

"You're that hungry?"

"Always. Water polo practice was brutal. We treaded water for three hours like a bunch of egg beaters."

"Three hours, really?" I'm glad we went grocery shopping this weekend. "So tonight will be an international feast."

Nile and I climb the steps to my grandmother's arts and craft cottage, my home, too. Her white Christmas lights twinkle in the flower garden despite the fact the holidays have been over for months. A tall statue of Virgin Mary, which is in the constant shadows of a Blue Spruce my grandfather and planted years ago, looks as if she's wearing a bridal veil. A cold early rain had dusted her this morning in a shawl of fragile snow.

"It's kind of creepy where Mary shows up at your grandma's."

"Please don't say that in front of my grandmother. She might pop you. She's very protective of Mary and vice versa."

"Sorry. I thought Mary was just a collectible doll for her." Nile turns the brass doorknob on the front door, which is sticking as usual. "You know, like my attorney mom collects ceramic frogs and my doctor dad has a thing for binoculars and now has added all different sizes of magnifying glasses to his collection. Between the two of them, we could almost open a museum at our house."

We stand in the foyer and kick off our shoes.

"You would think it would be the other way around, your doctor dad with frogs and dissections and your eagle-eye lawyer mom with a thing for scrutinizing."

"Good point. Never thought of it that way, but you're right. I'll suggest that they switch collections." Nile unwraps me from my scarf. "What happened to your neck?" He touches the spot where the little girl, the younger me, hung on for dear life. "Did I suck on your neck last night? What an animal."

"No. Maybe. I don't know."

"Okay that was a solid answer." He brushed my hair away from my face. "Why does your grandmother have so many Marys?"

"When my grandmother first moved to the states, she brought a few Marys with her to protect her in her new world." I sit down on the bench to pull off my cowboy boots since my attempt to kick them off wasn't really working. "Since her cancer diagnosis, she has added new Marys for her health with Rosalyn's help."

"See? It wasn't me. I didn't put Mary up on the fence and the rooftops!"

"I know now, I just didn't think Rosalyn was so agile or game to appease my grandmother. Anyhow, her friends keep adding to her obsession and bring Mary as "Get Well" gifts when they come to visit. It makes for an easy present to find and buy."

"She must have a lot of friends." Nile hangs our coats up on the wooden pegs above the bench inside the door.

"She does, but not too many of them speak English very well."

He looks at my grandmother's fur-trimmed coat hanging next to his green-and-blue plaid, flannel shirt on the foyer's coat rack. "Your grandmother brought a fur coat with her?"

"She bought it here after she arrived. She was freezing all of the time."

"She needs to add a Mary here at the entrance of your home."

I point above the front door where a gold frame holds a portrait of Mary. "She's one step ahead of you."

"Hey, I have to go home after dinner tonight—"

I pretend to cry, but Nile hugs me hard and it feels more like a headlock. "You know that I can't stay here every single night. You won't appreciate me if I do."

"I always appreciate you." I squirm to get out of his hold, unsuccessfully.

"Promise?"

I yell a muffled, "Yes".

"Okay, you better." Nile releases me and races up the stairs to say, "Hello" first to my grandmother like he always does. He's such a good guy, how could I not always appreciate him?

"I'm the best!" Nile yells over the railing to me.

He's a good guy, however, not too modest.

[Morse code message: GIFT]

-. --- .- -. ... .-- . .-. ...

I did survive the night without Nile nearby and without heading deep into any other new dreams or trips to my parallel reality.

After classes today, I run up the steps to my grandmother's house with a renewed energy—or maybe it was the cup of coffee I wasn't supposed to drink.

Last night, I slept pretty soundly. Nile's presence was missed, but maybe he's right. His tossing and stealing the blankets might be a distraction that wakes me up unconsciously and rolls me into the other world. Either way, I don't sleep as well or as much when he's with me. Today, I did doze in my classes, so I'll be refreshed for tonight—whatever that may bring: Nile or another crazy dream.

Earlier this morning, the warming temperature of the day promised the arrival of the next season and even motivated me to exchange my beloved ski sweaters for one of my bright hoodies.

My grandmother will be happy that warmer days are on their way to our town. I hope she's awake. There's something that I need to ask her. All of these unanswered questions need to be answered. After talking to my geology professor and after my extended conversations with quantum physicist, Dr. Vendall, I know some the answers are right here with my grandmother.

I rush through the front door, leaving it open because this house that I've called home for most of my childhood feels stuffy, confining, and heavy. Each time I enter, its invisible weight surrounds me and makes me tired and lethargic. Sometimes, I think that there are just too many sad memories stacked up in here. The past is holding down any promises for the future.

The fresh air follows me inside. I pause to kick off my running shoes and feel blue as I realize my boot wearing days are probably over for months. I dash up the stairs and without knocking, I throw my grandmother's bedroom door open to see a neatly made bed with a multitude of pillows perfectly aligned against the headboard.

Bile fills my throat since the first thought I have is, "Oh no! She died!" but then I hear Rosalyn's muffled voice filtering up through the floor from the kitchen. I thunder down the stairs, slipping on the plastic runners in my socks down the hallway, and into the kitchen.

"Slow down, Tess." Rosalyn stops stirring the homemade applesauce on the stove. The rich, sweet cinnamon scent is wafting around the square room. She points out the window with her wooden spoon.

"Your grandma wanted to take in some vitamin D. She's been reading your healthy magazines. Lordy. What's next? Drinking your Vitamin E? She just needs more of my good cooking."

"I know she'll want some of your applesauce. Save some for me, too please."

I run outside to my grandmother, who has raised her face to the sunbeams that are filtering through the branches of our maple tree. She's going to get a funny tan line if she continues to sit there like that, I think to myself, but hold my opinion. Our summertime backyard is returning to us and I can't believe it—all of her flowers are in full bloom.

"The crocuses are popping up everywhere, too." My grandmother nods toward the sunny side of the house. She must have been reading both the emotions of astonishment and mourning of winter racing across my face.

"It can't be over already." Defeated by the insistency of the warmer weather, I sink beside her on the love seat made from old skis that Grandpa and I crafted years ago.

"Everything ends. Eventually. Even your beloved winter. But don't worry, I heard it is planning a comeback."

"You're funny, Grandma." Rosalyn has loaded the bench with pillows and a blanket to make it a cushy sanctuary. I pat the fat pillow beside me and surround myself with others on both sides of my legs. "Comfy out here?"

"I've perfected the art of sleeping anywhere, anymore."

"And I thought you were just bored by my monologues about my illness and its possible causes…"

"No, I just find it easy to doze."

The afternoon sun has just slipped behind the neighbor's detached garage, casting a soft gray shadow over us, the usual state of my world, the constant grayness in my mind and felt throughout my body.

"Grandma, I just don't understand why Mom just couldn't come back whenever she wanted. Granted, the flight between Rio and Boulder isn't a short jaunt, but still."

"Tea?" My grandmother is already pouring me a cup of her favorite.

The thermos sits on my mother's birthday table— another sharp memory of what I don't have. I wiggle around on the wide bench and lodge a small pillow behind my head between my neck and the back of the chair. "But Grandma, I need to know what happened or what's happening to me."

She steadily hands me the teacup, which is more like a small bowl due to its lack of a handle. I found this teacup set at the local flea market. The vendor told us these ceramic cups were handcrafted in Japan and would hold the heat from the tea until the last drop. Of course, I bought them for my grandmother, who hates cold tea. She hates sweet, cold tea even more.

"You need to stay here with me now, Tess. No more gallivanting around the world in your dreams."

"Why? I think I might have some answers from the little girl, who I follow at night."

She sips before she answers me as if she's searching for the right answer or an answer that I would accept. "Everyone has his or her reasons for what they do." She sips, again.

What? That's it? I hold my cup until my fingers inherit its warmth. "You're talking in present tense. Does that mean she's still alive?"

Rosalyn hurries down the back steps into the yard. "Now, you two are going to be frozen to that ski bench if you sit in the shadows any longer." She collects my grandmother and waves at me to pick up the tea tray, pillows, and blankets.

"Grandma?" I stand, wearing the blanket like a cape.

Rosalyn holds my grandmother by her elbow and guides her down the narrow, cracked cement sidewalk toward the back door.

My grandmother stops and turns to me, "The future is good."

I pull the blanket up over my head to create a hood and sink back down into the mound of pillows. Between my lack of sleep and the pills that I ingest daily to counter my insomnia, anxiety, phobias, and depression, and to stop my smoking habit from resurfacing, it's really no wonder I have some crazy ass nightmares and anxiety, phobias, and of course, depression, too.

I still don't know what to call the condition I have. Nor do my doctors.

I pull the blanket over my face and snuggle against the thickness of the wall of pillows. I sigh, tiring of trying to find an answer to, what's wrong with me? I feel a presence in front of me and peek out of my cave: a pair of black, high-top sneakers.

"Hi buddy," I mumble from beneath the blanket.

"Can I come in?'

"Sure, but I don't know where you'll fit." I sit up and open the blanket.

"We always find a way." Nile sits very close to me and holds my hand. "You're an ice bucket. Surprise, surprise."

"I like it this way."

Nile takes both of my hands in his. "Sit tight, Tess."

"Not moving as usual. You know, sitting around in my usual stupor."

"I have big news."

"Should I take notes?"

"Funny girl. In my last class, I read all of your prescription inserts that no one ever reads and now I know why—boring! However it all makes sense now!"

"Good. Because I'm tapped out at any logical answers and my grandma isn't talking, or at least not in coherent sentences, just her own koans. I need some solid answers."

Nile pulls a folded piece of notebook paper from his jean's pocket. "Check this out!" He shakes open the paper and reveals a handwritten chart.

Down the left side, he has listed my drugs of choice or maybe I should say drugs of default: Ambien, Valium, Lexapro, Lunesta, Ativan.

"Did you know, according to the manufacturer of the drug, Lunesta, it may not work if you suffer from depression?" He gives me the evil eye as if I'm supposed to know this.

I just shrug.

Nile continues reading the tiny notes that he has written down on the right side of the chart. "It also states that high-fat meals may slow your absorption of the drug and make it less effective. I gotta talk to Rosalyn about our menus." He gets to a half stance before I pull him back on the bench with me.

Nile jabs at next side effect on the paper as he reads: "Stopping the drug suddenly may cause symptoms of withdrawal such as anxiety and unusual dreams." He underlines the words 'anxiety' and 'unusual dreams' with his finger to make sure that I both hear and saw these words.

"You're still on Lunesta, right? Or on Ambien? Or are you on both? Can you take both?"

"Just Ambien now and I'm taking Lexapro and Ativan for my panic disorders. Dr. Hall calls them my "anxiety problems" and "social phobias" like being afraid of crossing bridges and taking elevators."

Nile looks across the backyard to the front street, which is barely visible between the narrow passage between my grandmother's house and neighbor's. "Good thing we don't have any long scary bridges in our town."

"Exactly, so these bridges must be in my mother's city. In Rio."

Nile's research, which is making a lot of sense is also making me heat up. I feel flush and shake off the blanket.

Nile hogs the blanket. "I should be a doctor. I'm good at piecing this puzzle together. Oh wait, that's what my dad wants me to be."

"Well, maybe your dad's right and maybe you're right, too."

"Shhhh. Your doctor-in-training is thinking. You're keeping a journal for Dr. Hall, right?"

I nod without looking at him. I'm annoyed at myself for not figuring out the connections between my symptoms and the side effects of my prescription drugs.

"Let's go back through your diary and highlight in neon yellow when these ailments cropped up and then we can check the dates on your prescription bottles to see if there are any correlations." He pauses and stares at the sky. "God, I'm brilliant."

"And so modest." I drain the last of the tea from the thermos. "You love your highlighter, don't you?"

"Only neon yellow, baby—and you."

"I don't have the bottles, anymore. I hate plastic. I put the pills in glass jars on my dresser."

"How do you know what pills are what and when to take which one?

"There's a white one I take three times a day and a blue one two times a day and—"

"Tess, you have to be serious about your medicine."

"At this point and without any noted improvement, I would rather just forget about my medicine."

"Hear this!" Nile is reading the inserts, again whether I want him to or not. "Lexapro, which is for your anxiety, only has a success rate between ninety and ninety-three percent. I am amazed. Why did I think all drugs worked one-hundred percent of the time?"

I'm not sure if he's talking to himself or including me in this rant. "Well, Ativan is an add-on treatment and maybe it increases the chance of working to one-hundred percent?"

"What? How can that be? You need more pills on top of pills? I am definitely going to be a scientist that studies landmasses, not humans. Humans are a complicated mess."

"Thanks for your support." I pull away from him.

"I'm here for you." Nile fills in the gap I made on the bench, touching his thigh against mine. I can feel the heat from his leg next to mine. "Anyhow, the insert for Lexapro said to get emergency medical help if any signs of an allergic reaction like a skin rash. Ha. See? It's your drugs, not what you eat in your dreams."

"How can you be sure?"

"I'm not, but the drug companies are, I think. This is a very long list of side effects for all of your drugs. Maybe you're right getting off of them. They seem to be compounding your situation, although they might be your answers as well as what are causing your symptoms."

"Like what?" I prop my legs across his lap, knowing this report could take a while.

"You complained of blurred vision, the visual snow, "floaters" as Dr. Hall calls them, well, Lexapro, that nasty little pill, can also cause blurred vision."

"Is that the same as visual snow?" I'm confused about what constitutes visual snow and blurred vision. Is it the one in the same thing or two separate and unrelated eyeball issues?

"Just ask Dr. Hall or your ENT doctor, Tess."

"Check. Will do."

Nile holds his own personal diagnosis up in front of my face. "Also, ask about cold hands. Because it says here on your inserts that it's another common side effect of this beta-blocker."

"How can they call side effects "common"? Those words should not be allowed to live beside each other. And do I dare ask…are there any other, possible side effects?"

"Yes, but the only common side effects for all of your medication surfacing on your radar and the various, pharmaceutical companies' radars repeatedly are…nightmares."

"Really? My prescription drugs could be responsible for my scary, nighttime travels?"

"Yes, but they don't say anything about going to Rio." Nile holds the inserts up close to his face.

"Funny, real funny, Nile. Just when I thought you were on my side."

"I'm always on your side." He scoots even closer, almost knocking me off the bench. "See? Literally and figuratively."

"You need to add Chantix to your chart."

"You smoke?" He looks stunned as if I had announced that I had a STD.

"I got a $30 dollar coupon off their website."

"You can get coupons for drugs?"

"Relax. It's working. I don't smoke, anymore."

"I knew that Tino was a bad influence."

With that last statement, I decide it's time to go inside and surround us with other people and their thought and words. I need Nile, but not for this. I stand and pull him up with me.

Nile holds out his arms as I pile the pillows and then the blanket up to his eyeballs. I thought this type of discovery was what my doctors were for, so why can't they make these connections for me?

[Morse code message: NOANSWERS]

......- .-. .-. . -. -.. . .-.

"Can you wake up?"

Recessed lighting trims the perimeter of the square of a room. I stare at a ceiling that I don't recognize. It's not my favorite coffeehouse's ceiling. My hand touches a crisp white sheet folded over a wool blanket near my face. I'm definitely not at home. We do not iron our sheets like Nile's mom does. I almost don't have the energy to guess where I am now—

"Tess? You can wake up now." I can hear Dr. Hall's voice coming into the sterile room through the speakers. "Tess? Did you sleep, okay?"

Actually, I did sleep well with only one recurring dream—the one where I'm in the ocean. I can't tell if I spoke that aloud or just said it to myself.

"You didn't move around much except for the flailing of your arms at one point like you were swimming."

The weight of the university-issued, wool blankets holds me prisoner to the bed. I can barely move my head from side to side as I try to respond to Dr. Hall.

"Tess? Can you hear me?"

I can't move almost as if a paralysis has taken over my limbs.

"Tess?" Her voice rises with concern I can hear despite its travel into the room through speakers.

"I'll go to her, Dr. Hall."

It's Sally. I smile with my eyes shut or at least I think I'm smiling. My muscles on my face also seem to be frozen. Footsteps come down the linoleum hallway followed by a pause and then the click of a door opening. I hear the continuing sound of a few more footsteps until I sense her standing over me.

"Tess? Open your eyes." Sally rubs my shoulder. "You're kind of scaring me. Do something, please. Move your fingers. Smile. Burp?"

I laugh, but no sound comes out of my mouth. From Sally's heavy sigh, I detect I didn't move or burp, either.

"Dr. Hall! Her blood pressure's falling! Rapidly!

As Sally leans over to me to detect if I'm still breathing, her hair touches my cheek. It tickles. I laugh.

"Breathe!" She yells at me.

I thought I had laughed, which would have meant that I was breathing.

Sally shakes me by my shoulders.

I am, breathing, barely. Actually, I feel like I'm drowning.

"Her respiration is shallow. Call the medics! Now!"

More doors open and slam, followed by a herd of thunderous shoes headed right at me, and then all I can hear is solid silence all around me, which feels thick like humidity.

When I do wake five minutes, or five hours later, I don't know. My eyes open to a brightness that makes my whole body hurt. I squint to make out the identity of the person that hovers over me.

"Tess, you gave us quite a scare…can you hear me?"

I nod, but shield my eyes from the intensity of light coming through the window and reflecting off the curtains that circles half of my bed. I'm no longer at the sleep lab.

This other, sterile environment must be a hospital room. There's machinery around my bed with various wires attached to me, confirming this is where I lie.

"Can you pull the shades?" The constant beeping of the machine to my left isn't helping to lessen the harsh severity of the room's ambiance. "Or turn off the lights?"

"Yes, of course." A young nurse, who I finally can see at the foot of the bed, dims the brightness of the room's overhead lights to where I can remove my hand from above my eyes. She moves across the small room to close the blinds, too.

"Thanks. That's better." I try to sink back into comfort, but only find a thin stack of stiff pillows. The mattress has a plastic wrap over it. I can feel it under the sheet.

Dr. Hall clicks into my room in another, new pair of high heel shoes, a pale purple this time to match her suit. "Hello, Tess. I'm glad you're back with us. Can you remember what happened?"

"I was in the black ocean…and before that sipping beer on the beach…around a campfire … and then I heard your voice, Dr. Hall, inside my head telling me to wake up, but I couldn't."

"You went into hypovolemic shock, but we were able to stabilize you." Dr. Hall looks down at the chart in her hand. "What's peculiar is that you didn't suffer massive blood loss, but the lab findings state you were severely dehydrated."

"That's because I was treading water for hours."

Dr. Hall does not look at me.

Dr. Reid and Sally enter.

Sally smiles at me. "You scared me."

"I scared me, too. It's getting scarier in my other reality."

Dr. Hall hands a metal clipboard over my feet to Dr. Reid. "Check line number five. I find it peculiar."

Dr. Hall is always describing my case as "curious" and "interesting," not using medical terms I expect her to say. I didn't mind when she called the floaters that skew my vision "visual snow", but when she told me they can point to a large variety of focal neurological or perhaps an ophthalmic disorder, I knew her suspicions were all wrong.

My mental research did support that I was dehydrated, probably from all that time I spent bobbing in the sea, and which caused the floaters to appear before my eyes and I told her this, at the time.

She ignored my explanation and booked an appointment with an optometrist.

Luckily, the vision tests agreed with my suspicions.

My vision was fine. "Exceptional" actually as my ophthalmologist reported.

So now, what does she think I have?

Nile reasoned Dr. Hall probably did this because she didn't know what to call what I had. Maybe I should see his dad, again. He's now in charge of diagnostic medicine at the hospital, but travels all over the world most of the time handing out international grant money for collaborative research.

"Tess, do you take any recreational drugs?" Dr. Reid is rubbing his forehead, which is leaving red marks behind.

I scoff, but realize he's serious. "No. Of course not. Why?"

"Another possible cause of this visual snow you keep complaining about is what we call "hallucinogen persisting perception disorder" or HPPD, following the ingestion of LSD, MDMA or on the street known as "ecstasy" and any other hallucinogenic, psychedelic drugs. Users have described this visual impairment as "aeropsia" or "seeing the air".

I feel trapped in more ways than one and try to kick the sheets that are tucked tightly around my legs looser. No luck, housekeeping here at the hospital is better than most hotels. I realize the doctors are waiting for me to respond.

"No. I don't take drugs and even though I was out in California, I wasn't anywhere near Haight Ashbury and I didn't trip back in time to the sixties in my dream, either."

They don't laugh at my attempt at humor.

Dr. Reid passes the clipboard with my file back to Dr. Hall. "HPPD can occur after a single dose of a psychedelic drug and with a considerable latency between last drug intake and onset of persistent perception disorder, so taking a thorough, lifetime drug history is mandatory in the diagnostic work-up of visual snow. In many cases, the neurological action for HPPD is not known and the majority of evidence surrounding it's anecdotal and difficult to isolate."

I look confused because I am.

He looks to Dr. Hall to provide the explanation in English.

"After you collapsed, we ran a new blood panel and found you had ingested a recreational drug. On the streets, it is called, "Good night, Cinderella". It's a powerful sleeping pill."

Dr. Reid pats my foot. "We think that's what caused havoc when you tried to wake up, but couldn't. Your blood pressure plummeted, too."

Sally looks between my doctors and then to me. "Tess, you slept for two days."

"No wonder I feel so much better." I smile at my doctors, but don't get any smiles in return except a sympathetic one from Sally.

They can't be serious about me popping pills for fun—I have already taken too many pills this year and my stomach flinches in protest every time I open another bottle. "Look, I didn't go out to the bars or drink before I came to the sleep lab. Or any time this week. It's my crazy dreams that are affecting me in real time."

"Tess, you have to be honest with us or we won't be able to help you." Dr. Reid leans over me.

"Honest? I tell you what happens and no one believes me! Maybe someone slipped me something on the beach. In my beer." I look back and forth between my doctors trying to read their thoughts. For some reason, I can't hear either of them saying anything and then I realize they aren't.

Dr. Hall picks up my chart, again. "Your tests don't show any signs of drinking alcohol."

"I think I only drank half of one beer before I found myself flailing in a strange ocean. Or maybe I had a few over a period of time. You, and I, don't know how long these trips last in real time. Maybe I was gone for days, and here, it was only a few hours?"

Dr. Reid takes a seat across the room in a chair against the wall, arms crossed. His body language says it all. He's unconvinced that this time traveling with bodily, side effects could actually happen.

Dr. Hall seems to share his same sentiments. She drops my file back into the plastic bin attached to the end of my bed and tucks her pen into her jacket's pocket.

That's it. I'm out of here if no one is going to believe what I'm saying. I'll figure this out on my own. I'm the one with the Google brain. I try to toss off the blankets only to find my wrists anchored to the bed with straps long enough to let me touch my face, but when I move my feet I feel my ankles tied to the bed, too. "What is this? Let me go!"

Dr. Reid rubs his eyes. "Tess, both Dr. Hall and I think you might be suffering from schizophrenia, and sometimes, the illness makes it hard for people to do certain things like think clearly to keep themselves safe, not know the difference between what's real and what is not real."

I am mortified. From beneath the sheets, I work on wrestling myself free from one of the wrist straps. "I suffer from chronic insomnia."

"Isn't that due to the dreams and nightmares she experiences?" Sally tries to help me, but from the look on the doctors' faces, she, another student, is not going to win this argument against the professionals.

"Schizophrenia is treatable now, but we need to keep you here." Dr. Reid tells me.

Dr. Hall steps over to where Dr. Reid sits. "People with this disease sometimes think they hear or see things that are not there."

Now I know I'm in trouble.

"I do believe I hear and see things that are there—"

Dr. Hall continues, although I thought I was talking. "They may feel as if they are being watched."

"But I am and I'm being pursued. And guided." Under the sheet, I push at my right ankle strap with my other foot, hoping my doctors haven't noticed slipped out of it.

"They may develop an extreme focus on religion or the occult."

How does she know about my grandmother's collection of Virgin Marys? And how does that make me schizophrenic?

Dr. Hall holds onto the rail at the foot of my bed. "We visited your grandmother yesterday."

Oh, that's how they know about the Marys. I start working on the strap around my left ankle with my toes.

Dr. Reid stands up beside Dr. Hall, "We believe you're a danger to yourself, and your grandmother can't help you if you hurt yourself, so we asked to keep you here for observation. She agreed."

"What? No." I twist back and forth in the bed, which has now become my prison. "She can't. I'm not a minor. Let me out of here! Where's Nile? Call Nile."

Dr. Reid nods to a nurse at my elbow. She turns up the dial on the IV drip that leads to my arm.

"Besides, Tess, you need some rest. Your body system is shot from lack of sleep." Dr. Hall picks up her briefcase and heads toward the door.

"I thought you just said I slept for forty-eight hours! I don't need any more shut eye— Sally! Help me! Call Nile for me!"

I feel the heavy blanket of sleep overcoming my body and can't fight its deadening sensation.

Sally slips out of the room.

I fade into darkness and silence except for my distant voice inside my head yelling: Nile! Nile! Nile!

[Morse code message: SURRENDER]

When I open my eyes again, I'm home at my grandmother's house.

Nile is not here. I found out later he did save me from the university's hospital and convinced my doctors that his parents would be personally responsible for my care. It didn't hurt that Nile's father is the Chief of Medicine at the hospital, who materialized moments after his son phoned him. I vaguely remember seeing Nile's face and his father's face hovering above me as he spoke to the other doctors about my release.

Half a day later, I'm camped on the purple-paisley purple couch, which I helped my grandmother pick out when I was only seven. She had liked it too instantly and said, "It will be perfect in our house."

She went on to tell me a story about how she is still mad at a pushy salesclerk, who insisted a white couch would blend with her new household so much better than the red velvet one she wanted as a new bride. My grandmother did buy the boring, white couch, believing the experienced salesclerk was right and then watched it get filthy over the years no matter how much she scrubbed its arms and ottoman, and washed its cushions.

Now, with our infamous couch front and center in our living room, I know my grandmother would have been right to purchase her red velvet couch.

My grandmother tells me she still loves this purple couch, although I question her sincerity if not her eyesight. I don't like the color purple anymore, but everything I commandeered my grandmother to buy me when I was little was purple whether it was rain boots, a winter coat, sheets for my bed, or groovy bellbottom pants. I liked any variation of purple, especially those found in fruits and vegetables like the color of grapes or eggplants or any flowers that bloomed in hues of periwinkle and lavender. My grandmother did keep a wonderful garden and perhaps this is where my inspiration and persistence to buy all things purple originated.

After learning about my grandmother's diagnosis of cancer, I bought her magical pillows, or at least that's what the salesclerk told me. As I touch them now, they feel as if they could have been made from clouds, so soft to the touch and no button on them. Whoever thought of that dumb design? Buttons on pillows? Anyhow, I thought the living room couch with her new, dreamy pillows would be her new stakeout whenever she got tired of hanging out in her bed, but I'm the one now found here more often.

As my thoughts return to last night's vivid dream, I hug the purple, velvet couch pillow to my chest. This dream is the one that I'm happy to replay even though it's at nighttime, again. It was a safe dream because I came home without any body damage.

I dreamed about my mother, and this time, I remember all of it.

In this excursion, I feel comfortable, encased in maternal love similar to what I think the lucky ones have with complete nuclear families and what they experience at the holidays despite the constant noise and usual disagreements. My eyes water at this thought of not having such regular, family get-togethers, but these tears today are tears of happiness, not sadness. My mother has been gone for all of my Christmases that I can remember, but last night, her appearance in my dream made up for much lost time.

Once again in this dream and as I lie here recalling the details, my tiny guide leads me pass palaces left behind from the reign of Portuguese royalty, in front of colonial churches, and expansive, neoclassical buildings that now house the politicians of the city. I only know all of this because my Google brain told me like a museum's audio player, turning on and off whenever a patron passes a masterpiece painting or a sculpture—or in this case, whenever I pass a landmark in my dream.

I trail the little girl, who's wearing a clean and ironed, button-downed blouse tucked into a pair of red shorts. She has on her glittery red, Mary Jane shoes. The broken strap is now fixed. My body shudders at the memory of falling off the bridge while holding her. I remember grabbing her shoe and holding onto to it and her as we plunged into the cold night water…somehow and by someone, we were rescued.

Where did she get a clean, ironed shirt? Maybe someone's taking of her, washing her clothes, buying her food. Maybe she doesn't always live on the streets of the *favelas*. The thought of this tiny person living on a piece of cardboard with a dozen other kids in an alley makes my stomach turn, but I know there is this societal problem in Rio, so why wouldn't it be a prevalent portion in my dreams? But why her? Or why me?

While experiencing this dream once again, I try to focus on some of the details of the city where I walk. In my Google brain, I conduct a photographic search of these areas matching what I saw through my eyes to what my brain could find in the world's archive of photos. Now, I am sure of where I go in my trips: Rio de Janeiro. Articles about the area where I visited also popped up beside the images in my head, so I read: "The walls have become a symbol of the inequality between the notoriously violent *favelas* and the people who live below on "the asphalt," as Rio's wealthy beachside neighborhoods are known."

Through the spiraling, back alleyways and alongside tall, tenement buildings that keep these people contained in the slums, I continue to follow her in the shadows without question.

In this particular jaunt, this dream from last night, I'm far away from the pristine beaches of my childhood. I

238

round the mounds of garbage and pass a small, street grill tended to by two older boys. They crouch and cook chicken kebabs over short flames—at least I think it's chicken, but there are too many feral cats and stray dogs roaming the filthy streets to be sure what it is.

Gray smoke puffs up to my nose. I hold my breath not wanting to know its aroma. Hungry street children and a skinny dog bunch nearby.

Again, I wear one of Nile's jackets, which is sizes too big for me and in his pocket, there's a small bag of unopened jellybeans. I toss the candy to the tallest boy, who keeps a tight watch over my little guide. He doles out three candies per child.

Why does he look so familiar? Could he be Tino at a younger age?

Is this little girl really me at age seven? Were we forced to hide on the streets due to what our parents did? Fight the cartel.

I can't be me and her, now both at the same time, can I?

Up the steep, narrow dirt street, I clamor after her. Where she gets her energy, I'll never know. She now accepts food from me. Each time I reach into my pockets, there's a chocolate candy bar or a packet of peanut butter cookies. She has come to expect my sweet treats, however, one time when I reached into my windbreaker jacket, which turned out to be Nile's again, I could only offer her a beef jerky.

He told me he quit that stuff. I guess not, at least he has the common courtesy to brush his teeth before he plants one on my lips.

My little friend had accepted the savory meat product. She chewed it a lot slower than with my previous gifts, making a sour face at its taste, yet finished her mini meal.

I wish I could give her more.

We traipse around more vertical apartments clinging to the mountainside and then moved down a side alley. Its dirt path is hardened like cement and is deep in garbage along its edges. We wind up its trail to where the grime falls behind us and the air is quiet. On the other side of the bay, clouds circle the distant mountaintop.

My little friend hurries me out of the dank corridor of the apartment buildings and into the fringe of fading daylight. Graffiti covers most of the walls in angry words and again I wish I couldn't read Portuguese. Some artist has drawn a huge marijuana leaf over the vile profanity.

On top of the knoll, the little girl stops and plops down on the only plot of grass, making her brunette loose curls bounce. She is tiny enough to sit in the shadow of a palm tree. My little friend scans the hilltop as if she was expecting someone. Her face holds the look of eager anticipation for someone, who she believes wouldn't break their promise or her little heart. I, too hope this person comes along and soon.

I sit beside her and watch the horizon turn a brilliant crimson color laced with uneven ribbons of lilac and butterscotch just for a moment before the sky sinks into another black night. We are high above the dark aquamarine bay that sparkles and reflects the city's lights.

My guide watches the dirt path, not the sunset and approaching twilight like I do.

She sits up taller.

First, a head of a person appears, then shoulders, and the waist as the person climbs up the steep path and into our view.

I can detect that the person is a woman by her slight frame and when then a slight breeze blows her long hair flows back off her shoulders. The streetlights flicker on and catch her large, silver hoop earrings in a beam of light. They sparkle against the darkness.

As she emerges into the space before us, she grows taller, much taller than I. She wears a white dress with small, red poppies embroidered around its square neckline and hem. Her bare arms and legs are very tan. Her red sandals flap on the hard-packed, dirt path.

My little friend points at the approaching lady in case I didn't see her. What does she mean? Should I know this woman? All I do know is that I feel surrounded by a sense of peace, something I've been missing in my dreams, and in my real life for a long time…so, maybe I do know her.

[Morse code message: FOUND]

... .- ..-. .

While Dr. Hall and Dr. Reid believe I should be under constant supervision at the university's hospital, they did agree to let me stay at my grandmother's with the understanding I would make my daily psychological appointments. I know this route so well by now that I could walk to the mental health building with my eyes closed. I try it, but veer off the edge of the sidewalk and into a puddle of mud. I open my eyes to find a small girl stomping her right boot into the same thick mud just a foot away. With her head cocked to one side, she studies how the substance is reluctant to release her. She does it two, three, four more times.

Her mother looks down on her daughter's impromptu science experiment.

"Wow—that stuff is really sticky, huh, Alba?"

Alba ignores her mother's question and repeats the process.

"We should get going, honey." Mom shifts her brown paper bag of groceries from one hip to the other and offers her hand to her daughter.

The toddler bends to pull a large stone sticking out of the mud and holds it up like a prize.

"I bet that's a great rock under all that mud. If you want, you can take it home."

Alba sticks the muddy stone into her pocket and accepts her mom's clean hand with her mud-caked one.

They toddle down the empty sidewalk.

I wonder about my instant draw to children.

Dr. Hall repeatedly points to my abandonment by my mother at such a young age, the ages these little girls are. I don't like the word 'abandonment'. It sounds like my mother didn't want me. However, my mother is still missing and that isn't the same thing as being deserted.

Something pulls at my reasoning, questioning if what I was told was true? Is she dead? Or unable to come home? Is this why I keep looking for my mother in order not to believe the possibility that she is gone forever? Do I look at other mothers and their daughters to try and remember her? Try to remember us?

There are no pictures of me as a little girl around my grandmother's house, only ones of the older me and long after my mom disappeared. I need to scour my grandmother's photo albums, again to see if I can find out what we looked like as mother and daughter way back then.

I realize I'm still standing in the center of the mud pool after other students walk by and look back at me. I unstick my running shoes from the mud, slide across the grass to get the muck off the soles and walk into the medical buildings on campus. After my recent visit to *Cristo Redento*r or Christ the Redeemer in my dream and my visit to Lookout Mountain with Nile, I wanted to talk to Dr. Hall about this, but with what just transpired; I hesitate to tell her anything anymore. Nile's father had reassured me she would not have me committed and to speak freely with Dr. Hall.

"She's here to help you." He reminded me when I gave him the 'you must be crazy look'. I'm here again and make my way up the many steps, accept a cup of tea from Sally, and enter the usual domain.

"Can déjà vu can be explained by seeing through my grandfather's or mother's eyes?" I plop on her couch.

Dr. Hall stands before her expansive windows and looks out across the green mall of campus, trying to come up with an answer to what I just asked her.

No response, so I ask her again, rewording my question a bit. "Can I see through my grandfather's or mother's eyes because I inherited their memories in my DNA, too?"

She tries to wipe a smudge off the window's glass with her fingertip. I can't hear her thoughts today. Maybe the litany of medications did temporarily improve my auditory abilities and now that I have stopped ingesting some of the little pills, I'm losing my talent to eavesdrop.

"How else can I explain how I knew where to run that night and ended up at my grandparent's house on the beach?" I continue to press my shrink.

"Tess, I had Sally do some digging. You were born here at the Lucent University Hospital. Here in Colorado."

I roll over on the couch with my back to my doctor to take in what she just told me. Too many questions percolate to the top of my head and the internal pressure makes it hurt.

Why hasn't my grandmother told me?

Perhaps no one was supposed to know I was there, at one time, living in Rio on the streets…and that included me.

"Maybe you visited your grandparent's house a long time ago and remember that memory?" Dr. Hall sits at my feet.

I lived there, at my grandparents' house with my mother, I wanted to yell, but I can't prove it except with my dreams. She looks at me with concern in her eyes like a mother would, not a doctor.

I sit up and fold my legs in front of me. "Dr. Hall, is it possible to feel the presence of another person long after they left a spot? Can their spirit linger on forever or imprint on the environment?"

"What do you mean? A spirit like a ghost or their soul?"

I pull my journal out of my courier bag. "In addition to the little girl in my dreams directing or pulling me along to where she thinks I need to go, I have a feeling, a confirmation in a sense of where I need to go." I page back through my newest journal and read to my doctor: "I know where and when my mother has been. Maybe this is why I felt her pull for me to go to Lookout Mountain with Nile."

"You did draw the statue of *Cristo Redentor* in your childhood journal."

"I remember going to see a statue when I was a little girl with my mother."

"To the Mother Cabrini Shrine on Lookout Mountain?"

"I think it was to the statue of Christ the Redeemer in the *Parque Nacional da Tijuca*." I didn't mean to speak in Portuguese, but still don't translate it out loud to my shrink. She should know by now what I mean from reading my memories on paper that go back so many years—in pictures drawn by the younger me. "Or maybe I have been at both."

I hand Dr. Hall an old journal that I found in my grandmother's room, one she hasn't seen before. "I felt safe there. Maybe my mother did, too."

I page to the passage where I write and draw about meeting Rosalyn up there at the Mother Cabrini Statue when I was three. She was a neutral third party and my safe passage to the states. Dr. Hall looks at my juvenile drawing, yet it is obvious the locale is here in the states, especially with the snow I added to the mountains all around.

I reach over her and turn the journal back a few pages to my sketches of *Cristo Redentor*. There is a beach and boats below this statue.

"But you never left the states."

"Right, after I arrived here from Rio when I was six. I've stayed at least in this reality most of the time."

Dr. Hall sits back against the couch. "You think you're time traveling between North and South America? Now?"

"Yes, in my dreams."

She sighs.

"But it's much safer for me here."

"Do you mind if I call this Dr. Vendall you mentioned in your journal?" Dr. Hall picks up the journal and turns to the page where I wrote and underlined his name each time he had said something I suspected to be true. His name is written more than twenty-five times. This man knows his science. I listened to him and finally believed what could be possible.

Dr. Hall is already at her desk, phone in hand. I rattle off his phone number easily since I've called him too many times, but he invited me to and because I see numbers as numbers inside my head, usually in a neon color like electric green against a black background— making it kind of hard to ignore. The upside to this new talent is that I don't have to memorize anything anymore. I just can read it to recall it for whatever purpose, class or doctor sessions. My mind is like the Library of Congress now, jammed full of so much necessary and perhaps unnecessary information…

"To be honest, Tess, my understanding of quantum physics is very limited." She must be 'on hold' to some bad country music—that's what his lab likes. Go figure. I thought it would be classical music for sure since the mainstream thinking now is that listening to Bach or Beethoven will make babies, and probably adults, smarter. But whining, crying, heartbreaking country music, really Dr. Vendall?

I nod a response to Dr. Hall's unusual confession and stretch out on the couch, hoping to eavesdrop and that Dr. Vendall will support my theory, my thinking.

[Morse code message: SAFE]

.- .-.. .. ...- .

The only cool spot in the entire house is on our shaded front porch. Most people that live in this latitude and in older houses don't have air conditioning. This luxury wasn't a necessity until the growing and real threat of climate change showed up in the last decade. Summers in the mountains just did not get hot, until recently.

"Now, I miss my cold feet and hands!" I say out loud to no one. I think it must have been my meds causing this side effect because now with no pills in my system, my problem of cold feet and cold hands has gone away as well.

On the hot nights of summer, which is almost every night, I sleep here with the hope my dreams won't follow me, but they do.

Luckily, so does Nile. We barely fit on the daybed. Each morning, the songbirds wake us up, which is much better than the air brakes on the weekly route of the garbage truck. But what I want to know is why do these birds start singing before the sun awakens? My Google brain is silent. Maybe my pills made more of my brain work, too.

Sometimes, when I am awakened in the middle of the night by another runaway nightmare, I find Nile asleep on the round braided carpet. I must have thrashed around too much for him to stay by my side. Since the days have warmed, my grandmother instructed me to stash the summer-weight, handmade quilts she bought at the church bazaars in the white wicker chest on the porch.

I'm glad I did. Nile found the blankets before nodding off to sleep, again. He looks like a puppy with his body wrapped in a circle underneath the quilts. He's gorgeous with his eyes closed, too. Usually, he looks so comfortable that I leave my soft spot to crawl onto the floor with him until he wakes. I stare out between the slats of the porch and play the game, "I spy" my grandmother taught me a long time ago.

From the porch, we would search her front yard garden for the plastic pink flamingos and the gnomes too, but they're much shorter and not painted as brightly, so they were more difficult to find—plus I was only seven.

This morning when I awoke alone on the porch's floor, I knew where Nile was. After dinner last night, he had said that he wanted to talk more with Professor Wilson about my sand dilemma, which is becoming his problem, too. The other night, he woke up with a rash across his back from the excessive amount of grains in our sheets. The sand keeps appearing in my bed.

Nile used the handheld vacuum to suck up the sand. It didn't work. We ended up shaking the sheets out the bedroom window at three in the morning. After all of this nighttime racket, I know my grandmother thinks I'm the one inflicting my own body regularly with bruises and cuts.

Nile thinks Professor Wilson should know about my dreams, too, to see if he can make sense of what's happening to me every night. I'm open to anyone giving their opinion at this time, yet would rather have Nile tell my story. I'm tired of watching people roll their eyes.

I stretch my entire body like a cat.

My grandmother stands outside the front door on the porch.

I jump up and move to ease her into the wicker chair. Either, she's intent on telling me something or she does possesses sheer willpower and will do what she pleases regardless of what the doctors limit her to do. By the look on her face, her motivation to come to me on the porch is a combination of both. She does not like to be a prisoner in her own body. She's mad at its sudden betrayal of becoming older, slower, and now sick.

"Can I get you something to drink or eat, Grandma?" I perch on the edge of my daybed. I'm surprised she made it downstairs with a thick book under arm and without any aid.

She pages through the large art book. It's the one that she had asked me to check out from my college's extensive collection.

"Do you like the art book?" I slip on my sandals to go into the kitchen and make us breakfast despite the fact she didn't answer.

My grandmother smiles at my pink, flip-flops with the plastic flower on top, knowing I hated packing up my boots.

I look over her shoulder at the book opened in her lap. "Mary looks so young in that artist's portrayal."

She turns the book to the next page to reveal a color illustration of the Virgin Mary, wearing a red robe sitting against a background painted in a golden patina. "The Bible says she was around the age of fourteen when she became a mother."

"Really? She was that young and a mother? Yikes. But why then in other paintings of Mary, she looks old and tired?"

"Perhaps the artist just wanted to her to look realistic and to look like most new moms."

"Was my mom like that?"

"No. Your mom had a vitality to her, a purpose, which did not allow her to tire or rest ever…" My grandmother closes the book.

I sit on the front steps that still hold the coolness of this early morning hour. "Can my mother choose to come to the states? To be with me? With us?" I lean back against the pillar of the porch, not really wanting to know the answer if it isn't what I want to hear.

"Your grandfather and I tried to protect you, your heart." She rubs the smoothness of the worn wicker on the chair's arm. "Your mother came and went all of the time when you were little, but then her visits became less frequent and you would cry and cry, and not eat, just sleep all of the time. I never heard of childhood depression, but you were a case study for the hospital here. That's how you came to know Nile's family. His father was instrumental in setting up a team of doctors to help you when you were only seven."

"Did they?" I pull my knees tight on my chest.

"They suggested the best way and perhaps the only way to handle the situation would be to tell you your mother had died. Based on what she was doing, it would only be a matter of time…the cartel doesn't take kindly to anyone meddling in their business."

I just stared hard at the air in front of me. The visual snow is back. This time, I see the floaters as spider web strands weaving erratically in front of my eyeballs and I can't see my grandmother clearly now. She's blurry to me. Maybe it's not floaters, but tears of hope? Of joy? Of despair? "You never said, 'died'."

"I know. I couldn't. She is your mother and she is my daughter, too. I know the power of words, so we simply let you believe she disappeared, that she went missing, and then there could still be hope."

"Tell me that she's alive, Grandma."

"You know that Tess. You met her the last time you traveled to Rio. On the mountaintop."

"But she was my younger mother, probably only thirty."

"She is still your mother." My grandmother looks uncomfortable in her chair.

I know I'm uncomfortable with where this conversation is going, yet I'm tinged with excitement. I had an inkling of this possibility.

"When you go, you're seeing your life as it would have been if your mother kept you in Rio. That's who that little girl is—the one that keeps showing up, to guide you, to show you the life that you didn't have to live. You are her and she is you. You both exist here and there."

"Even with the different time zones, years, and ages?" My head is swimming with questions.

"You're seeing your alternative reality."

"And my mother?" I turn with hope that my grandmother will tell me what I want, what I need to hear—my mother will come back to me, to us.

"Your mother is only living in that alternative reality, trying to get out, but not until she makes her last two rescues: my sister and Tino." She taps the book in her lap, the decoy to come see me and tell me what I need to know. But how does she know all of this? And why tell me now? She could have saved a bundle of money on prescription drugs and therapy.

Then I remember with both pure joy and sudden grief what the woman in the beach shack told me to tell my grandmother. I find the courage to say it now: "Grandma, your sister told me to tell you she cannot come here. And she is very sorry."

"I know my sister can't come. And I'm sorry, too. If she leaves Rio, you, your other self at the age of seven, will perish. There will be no one except Tino, who's the same age to watch over you."

"But when I meet Tino, he's nineteen, my age now."

"Right, it just depends on where and when you meet up with him in Rio in the other world."

I'm both moved and grateful for her sister's sacrifice that she's willing to keep the other me safe and stay behind in the turmoil. My mind races ahead of our conversation—realizing that if her sister chooses not to leave, all my mother has to do is get Tino out of the country and then she can be here with Grandma and me.

Tino…what to do with Tino? What to tell Nile? What to do with both of them? If I wasn't around, they would probably be good buddies, yet if I'm around, this could be a mess. Maybe Tino will stay in Florida with his relatives. My grandmother once told me anyone from her country that left Brazil first stopped in Miami and then many of them did not leave. Florida was cold enough for them in the winter months and they couldn't image living in the Colorado Rockies like my grandmother and grandfather had elected to do.

My grandmother looks to the porch's low ceiling as if she can see through the roof and into the heavens.

Does she also travel in her dreams? Does she communicate regularly with my mother or it my mother who is making the attempt? Is that what all that beeping is about?

But the short messages that Dr. Hall translated for me are not telling me anything, so I ask, risking her fragile state. "Will my mother choose to come to the states? Soon?"

"Let's only hope."

[Morse code message: ALIVE]

... . -.-. .-. . -

There is the sound of creaking on the staircase...someone going up or down...

I can't tell. Next to me lies Nile, asleep, so it's not he, who is sneaking into the kitchen for another midnight, ice cream sundae rendezvous with my grandmother and without me, again. I should wake up my huge boyfriend, his presence would scare away any intruder, but I feel no danger.

"This time, it was one of yours." My grandmother's voice whispers inside my head.

I bolt straight up in bed, slide out from under the covers, and creep down the hall toward the foyer.

My grandmother is lighting a white tall candle, not her usual votive and this means only one thing. She has seen something in the mirror and it is not good news. My grandma lights a candle each time she knows the cartel has killed one of ours. She honors the newly deceased with this action and helps them make it to their maker by lighting the way, or this is what she told me the last time that I found here kneeling on the hard floor before her Virgin Mary altar. All she said was "Uncle Regis..." her sister's husband, a prosecuting attorney and a very successful one with many enemies. He was gone, too.

Now to see her in this fragile state, lowered on the unkind surface, crossing her chest in the sign of the cross...I don't want to ask.

Hesitantly, I move toward the altar, stepping on all the spots that I know don't creak, so not to disturb her, her prayers.

She kneads her rosary through her fingertips at lightning speed. For someone the doctors pronounced is living on "limited time," she's moving pretty fast.

I wait behind her, away from her in the shadows of the house at this hour, watching, wanting to know "Who?" but also dreading her answer. Maybe I don't know who has perished, however, I am afraid, very afraid that I do indeed know who it was.

She raises her head and looks into the mirror—it shows a reflection of Tino's face.

"Noooooo!" I scream the word of pain that I thought I had only said inside my head. My thoughts rush at me, the memories of Tino at the parade with me, the first night at the beach alone with him, and just recently at the airport hangar upstairs in the office…emotions of loving and losing him in this world or the other world is very hard to comprehend right now, so I cry, softly at first.

My grandmother struggles to stand.

I am frozen with the impact of grief hitting me in the chest with such a force that it physically hurts. I'm unable to make myself move to help her up, but I finally do and grasp her elbow and wrap my arm around her waist.

Her eyes are teary, "Tess, I am so sorry, I thought they were done with these senseless killings."

"Grandma!" I bellow like a baby and unsuccessfully try to hold back the tears. I bury my head against her small frame and sink to the floor at her feet holding her knees. Can life end so rapidly and before it begins? He's only as old as I am and…I was just with him and Grandpa.

She pats the top of my head, which only makes me sob harder.

I remember all of our moments together almost as if it was my life flashing before me and perhaps part of my life has died, too. I can see Tino as a small boy. He is taller than me standing beside me with his protective arm around me. Behind us are the impoverished children, our friends, who we lived with in the makeshift shanties under the city's bridges and in the alleys. We were seen as a problem like dirt—instead of like soil in a garden. We were the *"menino de rua"* or the street kids who begged, shined shoes, or did odd jobs to make money for food, but the older kids graduated to pick pocketing and stealing to survive. We saw people murdered, young girls pushed into prostitution, and those who couldn't cope, inhaling glue or paint stripper to be numbed to their reality.

Another memory creeps into my head: an older Tino sits beside me, holding my hand as one of the medics wraps a wool blanket over my shoulders. Tino had ended up in the black water bay with me and my mother. Was she trying to take both of us to the airport to fly north? I do remember seeing the headlights of our car swipe across the roadside sign that read: *Aeroporot 4 km.*

I only wished now she had succeeded in getting all of us to safety in the states or wherever she had planned. I know that the driver was my mother due to the perfume that lingered in the front seat between us; it's the same light citrus fragrance my grandmother keeps on her dresser as if she's keeping hope bottled up, so her daughter, my mother, will return to us.

My entire body shudders at the thought of Tino gone. Our recent rendezvous seemed like a dream, but now I know it was not. I have stepped in and out of these parallel lives all of my life. It all makes sense now between the words and drawings inside my childhood journals and what I have been experiencing at night.

Now, another part of me is gone. I groan and fall to the floor, slapping it with my open palm to hurt myself and to stop the hurt. Nothing works. My grandmother is murmuring comforting words that I cannot hear.

Nile speeds down the stairs and across the hallway to collect me off the cold floor.

I wail and cannot control my emotions right now, which is so out of character for me. I'm crying, sobbing, and neither my grandmother nor Nile knows what to do.

Nile tucks his head against mine as he carries me to my bed. He knows the news my grandmother received from the mirror is not good.

Inside my room, he buries me under a mound of blankets and touches my tear-stained cheek before he heads out to assist my grandmother back up the stairs to her room.

I can hear him asking her, "What's wrong with Tess?"

I'm sure my secret is safe with her—and from him. It will be up to me to tell Nile.

[Morse code message: SECRET]

.... --- -- .

Daylight streams into my grandmother's tall windows that frame the living room walls. I'm happy to just be here and watch the dust particles slide down the sunbeam to the polished wood floor.

Nile has strung two hundred of my origami paper cranes on five lines that he has borrowed from my grandfather's old fishing reel. The invisible vertical lines of the cranes are packed so tightly together that they look like Hawaiian leis. He must have dragged the painter's ladder inside before I arrived home from the hospital and filled the space in front of the living room window with my paper art. Everyone knew that this was where I was going to be camped out other than my bedroom, especially since that was where he and I last fought. Nile knows I don't want to be sad or upset anymore and this room is where I feel a bit more cheery if that mood is possible, considering my altered state of mind and altered state of being in this world and the other world.

He still hasn't returned to me, though.

I've been here all day—afraid to move, afraid to fall asleep, afraid of falling into my other dark world even though I'm lying here in broad daylight and on the world's most comfortable couch; the one I knew was great when I was only seven. Luckily, my grandmother agreed and here it is: the purple centerpiece of our house, worn on the arms and seat cushion edges much like a favorite sweater.

My head is pounding—despite the fact my happy space did make me smile…for a few seconds about a minute, ago. Before my vision, I see little white, squiggly lines as if I have foreign particles swimming around my eyeballs, the visual snow is back, again and I can't blink or rub them away. When I close my eyes to rid of them,

257

they're there, too on the inside of my eyelids. I let them swim around and try to ignore the microscopic amoebas.

Dr. Reid called them "floaters" in her "layperson's medical speak."

I do think they look like snow.

Nile thinks I'm just bonkers about all things winter.

At this point, I think I'm just plain crazy.

The heat of the late afternoon fills the room and surrounds my body like a warm wet blanket pulled from the dryer too soon. I can feel it all over me.

Today is somewhere in June and that date puts me much too far away from my favorite season and preferred temperatures. I try to lose myself in thoughts and memories of winter, but even this attempt is too weak to make me happy.

I should sit in front of the coffee table on the floor and make another paper crane. I only have three more to make, although the thought of exerting any energy makes me tired. Besides, making cranes out of paper didn't work for Sadako Sasaki, the little Japanese girl, who became ill with leukemia after the atomic bomb dropped on her city of Hiroshima. She was only twelve when she died.

I don't want to die and not see my mother, again. I reach for the cellophane package of floral patterned-paper that Rosalyn had bought for me. She had slid the package of the square-cut papers under my bedroom door yesterday when I returned from the hospital, knowing I needed a new motivator to finish what I had started.

The grand velvet curtains, the color of aubergine, trim the tall windows and hang motionless in spite of the fact all of the windows are wide open. My paper cranes don't fly, but are just suspended like I feel most of time. Motionless, but present for what reason, I still do not know…

No breeze enters to cool me. I wish it would snow, again like it did that one summer so long ago.

I am getting faster at folding and creating a bird out of a flat sheet of pretty paper. I grin and place my art in line next to the others. Since arriving home, my goal was to make the final twenty cranes, the last one, number one thousand, and to increase the possibility of having my wish, my dream, come true. There is room only for two more before the end of the table is reached. Next, I choose a pink piece of paper covered with white swirls and rapidly fold and fold.

Summer has landed in full force with its scorching sun and accompanying heat. My lack of sleep last night and for the last several months has zapped me, taking away all of my physical, creative, and emotional energy. I still do get ideas of how to improve some of my grandmother's dishware accoutrements like her gravy boat. Initially, I thought about adding two spouts, one on each end. The wider spout would serve those well who like to bury their turkey, stuffing, and mashed potatoes in gravy. At the other end, a tapered, smaller spout would be perfect for anyone like me, who prefers just a few drips—nine to be exact— and similar to the vessels created by the Greeks.

I roll over and curl up into a ball, hoping the humidity would land on less of my bare skin. My mind drifts back to a field trip when my industrial design teacher took us to a traveling exhibition filled with such early dishware at the capital's museum. She was completely mesmerized by the inventions of the Greeks and Romans, but especially enamored with the fifth Duke of Argyll, who despised how his gravy usually arrived stone cold from the kitchen of his Scottish castle. He had decided to do something about this issue.

With the vessels that contained his sauces, meat gravies and juices, he was supposedly awarded the credit for creating the double jacket allowing the glorified liquids to maintain their heated temperatures, and that of being served hot. With a separate compartment at the gravy boat's base, hot water could be poured into the silver or Sheffield plate container, solving the dilemma of ingesting congealed gravy on top of a perfectly good slab of prime rib.

My grandmother made a face when I had told her this story. "I can't stand the look of a thick chunk of meat on my plate."

When I had talked this idea out with my grandmother, she only mumbled that people had servants and then in later centuries, maids to trouble with such nonsense of filling the gravy boats with hot water to keep the juices and sauces warm. Besides, she mused, "Americans eat fast enough these days that their food, and their gravy, doesn't have time to cool, so it doesn't matter, anyhow."

I still made her one for Mother's Day in my ceramics class.

She used it as flower pot.

I guess I had forgotten that we never made gravy.

Her candid statement should have given me a clue she would have no use for a "sauce boat" or gravy boat as Nile's family calls it and now uses it since I re-gifted it and after I made her a ceramic flower vase.

I had always admired the everyday amphora that the Romans made to transport their wine and olive oil. And the fact that no matter what material they decided to use: glass, metal, or ceramic, the design was technically sound and possessed an aesthetic sophistication unlike the plastic junk being hawked today at the super stores as "pitchers".

One day for class when I was sketching a modern-day amphora at my favorite coffeehouse, Nile had suggested I make a double-handled coffee cup for the Americans that like to down their daily intake of caffeine from buckets.

I looked up to see if he was kidding.

He wasn't.

I watched in awe as he poured a *"Trenta"*
cappuccino down his throat, which means in Italian "thirty"
however, in modified, Starbucks-American English is
actually thirty-one ounces.

I, however today, did not possess any ambition to
take this start of a sketch forming inside my head and put it
to paper.

Nile used to laugh at how excited I got when I
thought of a new idea. "You're such a dreamer. You walk
around with your head in the clouds."

"It's a good place to live." I would nudge him in the
gut with my elbow. "Admit it. You know I'll be sitting on
several patents very soon now and I'll be rich."

"Then I'll marry you." He laughs, again and kisses
me.

I probably am sitting on several, million-dollar
ideas, but when my health is comprised, this matter of
getting better becomes my number one priority. Now, I can
begin to understand how my grandmother is feeling with
her battle against cancer.

Nile is particularly concerned about my loss of
emotions, especially the love part. I'm just too tried to feel,
care, or do I dare say it, too tired to love?

It pains me to see his face when I reject his
advances, his touch, and his kind words. I need to reserve
any energy that I still have to breathe, get dressed, and walk
to the bathroom. Little things like brushing my teeth that I
never included on my daily 'To Do' lists now must be
planned for with each step calculated plus a rest period
factored in before and after the exertion.

Of course, my grandmother is worried. I'm in a far
worse state than she and I'm forty-seven years younger
than she. I shouldn't have such health inflictions. I'm too
young to be this old.

The soft padding of footsteps comes down the
hallway toward me. Rosalyn enters the living room where I

lie like a queen. She clucks her concerns and approaches with a tall frosted glass of frozen limeade, knowing my preference for anything citrus and tart on the tongue.

I force a weak smile and suck on the swirly pink straw she kindly thought to add, which allows me to sip while remaining prone.

"Is Sir Nile stopping by tonight for dinner?" Rosalyn bestowed this title upon his head the other night after he bemoaned the fact his parents weren't too terribly thrilled that he had chosen not to be a doctor. He said they were all hung up on titles. Rosalyn solved his dilemma by providing a substitute one, at least for one night.

She moves to prop open the front door to let any possible breeze circulate across the foyer to me.

I shake my head and wipe the condensation off the glass with my fingertip and place it in the center of my forehead, which does not make the heat in my head subside. Maybe Dr. Hall and Dr. Reid are right. I might suffer from migraines and that would explain the floaters.

"I miss our boy." She climbs the stairs to collect my grandmother for dinner.

"Me, too, Rosalyn. Me, too."

Nile has not been over to the house since our fight on Friday, which made for an empty weekend and a very long week since I have nothing, except my illness and dreams to occupy my days and nights. Not really what I had in mind for my summer break.

My mind replays our conversation from last month. "Who the hell is Tino? What is a 'Tino", Tess?" He sat up in bed and shifted his body away from me.

"What are you talking about?" I rolled closer to him only to have him inch away, again.

"Are you with me now—or far away, again on one of your erotic adventures? Now, I think I know why there's always sand in our bed!"

"You're scaring me, Nile." He never gets mad. "I really don't know what you're talking about." I pulled the comfort up to hide my teary eyes.

He got out of my bed and paced back and forth in front of it. I had never seen him so agitated. What did I say in the middle of our love session? Did I call him "Tino"? Of course I did…and then, I remember him again, the man on the beach in the white, button-down shirt and dark jeans, the man I followed to see the parade with, the man in the ocean with me and on the rescue boat, my *noivo*, at the airplane hangar, but could I possibly say to Nile?

So I told Nile the truth.

My confession did not go over very well and caused him to storm out in the middle of the night. Maybe I should have just stopped my story at our kissing, but I can't lie to Nile.

I can hear Rosalyn maneuvering around my grandmother's room upstairs. The floorboards creak as Rosalyn goes back and forth to my grandmother's closet to present possible outfits for tonight's dinner. My grandmother is funny in that regard. She doesn't dress out of her nightgown all day, but for our evening meal together, she does her hair, adding a hairpiece, dangling earrings, and one of her many heavy necklaces with a gold medallion or crystal pendant. I swear it's the weight of her necklaces, which make her stoop, but she doesn't seem to mind and absentmindedly toys with it throughout dinner. If I admire her chosen necklace, she fumbles with the clasp until it releases and places it in my palm, saying, "You take it. You keep it."

I've stopped complimenting her jewelry. She doesn't have a lot to hold onto at this point in her life. Few things matter in her days besides fighting her disease and there seems to be less and less to bring her joy—or maybe that's me speaking for her.

My grandmother did say, "The future was good" and if her sister can't come to her, then Tino…none of that is good news…where's the joy? Unless she's counting on my mother returning to us as I do every single day.

Mostly, my grandmother relies on her memories and trinkets of the past to make herself smile. When I started college out on the Pacific coast at the "renegade university" as my grandmother called it, I couldn't image my world shrinking down to fit between four walls. I only saw the world as an immense place. I couldn't wait to fly away and all over the world.

At the present time though, my mind weighs my body dead to the couch and except for slurping down my summer drink, I don't think I've moved in five hours and can't find sleep during the daytime hours like I used to. Maybe I should go back to the sleeping pills and my doctors…maybe I'm suffering from chronic depression, which is the cause all of my other symptoms.

The burr of a neighbor's lawn mower and the occasional rock his machine spits out momentarily jolts me back into this particular place and time. Who's mowing their lawn, again?

Slowly, as my neighbor rolls his loud machine to his backyard and the noise diminishes, my mind rewinds the events in my dream last night. Once again, nothing makes sense.

I remember Dr. Hall and Dr. Reid are huddled together against the paneled wall inside a dark coffeehouse; it's one I don't recognize, but they continue to provide irrelevant commentary to what's happening to me, not intervening like good doctors would, just taking slow notes and speaking to each other as if I'm not there.

The song, *Diamonds and Rust*, by Joan Biaz, coos from the ancient speakers tucked up in the cobwebbed corners of the shop's ceiling. I know it's a coffeehouse because the sleeve of Nile's red flannel shirt that I wear smells like the roasted beans and its aroma hangs in the air. Why am I wearing Nile's clothes, again? I look around for Nile. No one else is here, except a barista behind the counter.

I try to listen in on what my doctors make of all of this, but I'm losing my ability to read thoughts, and even to read lips ever since I stopped taking the "mind-expanding" pills, the ones that were too regularly and too easily prescribed to me.

Nile still believes the combination of all of these pills, each with its own long list of side effects, gave me these special powers. Maybe it's a good thing that he's not going into medicine…my wild imagination has rubbed off on him.

The haunting beautiful song is getting louder, so I blame it on the music that I cannot hear them talk about me and my persistent condition. My mother loved that song, and that artist, and whenever I hear her voice, I think of my mother. She would play her eight-track over and over again when I was a little girl and when I had first moved into my grandparent's house. I picked up her same habit of never tiring of a song whereas Nile, my grandmother, and Rosalyn do and do something about it when the song repeats for the eighth time.

This song makes me sad and in spite of my thirteen motherless years, I cannot fathom that she has died. There was no funeral since there was no body. My young mind did process these facts and came to the conclusion then that she did not die. She was just missing.

My grandparents never refuted my logic because they knew I was right.

Also, there was no "celebration of life" gathering like they do these days. I was simply told that I was too young to appreciate or understand such an occurrence. There was no further explanation, just the black fact: "Your mother is gone."

I didn't believe this statement then and I don't want to accept it, today or tomorrow. The more I looked into her disappearance, the meaning meeting her at the statue of *Cristo Redentor*, and the comforting shrine for Mother Cabrini and Jesus here in the states, and all of the Virgin Marys that live with my grandmother and I plus what Nile just found about origami paper cranes, I do believe in fate now. Nile had rushed into one of industrial design classes 'Prototypes' with the new news.

"Tess! Big news!" He whispered to me from the hallway.

My professor granted me permission to step out into the hallway.

"Did you know that there's a statue of Sadako, the little girl, who died from the "atom bomb" disease, holding a crane in Hiroshima Peace Park? Origami paper cranes are also a symbol for peace worldwide just like the *Cristo Redentor* and his efforts to summon peace with his outstretched arms. Everything is pointing to peace. Your mom must still be really busy."

Maybe Nile is right and my mother is trying to do her part in putting peace back into her world and I should just be patient.

I reach for the last piece of origami paper. It's purple—of course. I fold this one without looking, I don't need to now. My hands know what to do. Besides my mind is still thinking and remembering my latest dream in greater clarity while my fingers fold and fold and fold nineteen times.

Dusk particles float randomly in the stale air in front of me. At first, I think it's the floaters, again, the irritating spirals of whiteness that skews my vision and creeps into my eyeballs whenever they feel like it. In my dream, I'm glad it's just dust.

A fruit fly darts at my nose. I swat at it, but miss. The buzz of the espresso machine as the barista blows out the excess water sends my body into an achy pain from my temples to my toes. I fail to wave that noise away and try closing my eyes to stop the vise grip on my head. It does help stop my brain from processing the "every things" and the "nothings" that do not matter.

The glass-paned door of the coffeehouse swings open and the brightness from outside enters along with a silhouette of a woman. The darkness of the shop masks its second customer of the day minus the doctors, who stand more like a Greek chorus portrayed as a hologram against the back wall. They continue to mumble to each other.

I sense someone sitting in the other leather chair across from me. Our knees practically touch. I feel the heat from her body and can make out the fuzzy headshot of a woman's hairstyle, long flowing hair sans bangs and flipped naturally at the bottom where it skims her collarbone.

She does not move, so she looks more like a full-sized, black-and-white photograph placed in my view. Since my head no longer pulses with medication and allows me the perks of being brilliant for the moment or hearing other people's thoughts, my dreams remain hallucinatory in their nature such as this daytime version of last night's travels. With my palms against the warm leather, I push myself up to eye level with this statue-like stranger and then her perfume hits me. Her perfume is fresh with a flurry of aromas that include citrus, water lily, and the fruit lychee, although its scent evaporates as quickly as my mother does in all my dreams.

I breathe in deeply and know.

"Mom?" I don't know why I ask her for confirmation. I know she's here before me again, and at the age that she would have been if she were alive today: forty-one. Originally, when my night travels started and I had suspected the younger version of this woman might indeed be my mother, and I had formulated more than one-hundred questions to ask her when I had this chance, but now find I cannot remember a single one…

"You know, Tess, if I would have kept you with me in Rio…you, too could have been killed."

"They would kill a child?" This definitely was not one of the questions I held for my mother.

"The cartel was ruthless. They aimed to send their message that they would tolerate zero interruptions in their dealings—no matter what the age of their targets. They wanted our family to hear their message very clearly and children were not immunized to their retaliation. They just got rid of everyone in their way."

"My father?"

"Your father, and my father, your grandfather." She wipes at the corner of her eye. "They had mapped their flight patterns and made sure that neither man ever left Rio."

I want to reach out and touch her like Nile suggested that I do to make sure she's a three-dimensional person, not just an apparition I keep holding onto in my heart and in my hope to make her real.

"I remember when Grandma begged him not to go." Her father is gone, too. I forget sometimes to think of her loss. I'm only fixated on my loss.

"But your mother, Grandma, is still alive. Waiting for you. So I am."

"She's why you're safe; you know that, right? She insisted that I hide in the states with you, too." My mother pushes her hair back from her neck like my grandmother does and then looks across the room as if she just noticed my doctors, who are now frantically taking notes down on the pad of paper tucked onto their clipboards. "But I didn't stay in the states for long."

"So, how did I get to North America?"

"I flew you and Grandma here."

"You're a pilot?"

"My father taught me."

"Why didn't you save yourself?" I ache to touch her shoulder, to hold my mother's hand, to be closer, but I don't dare move, believing that I'll erase her and this moment if I do.

"There were still others that I needed to get to the consulate in Washington D.C. We needed to enlist America's help against the drug lords that ran our city and held a noose over its officials or paying off those without a conscious. These key people I evacuated knew of the cartel's secrets and their knowledge could have started to change Rio."

The coffeehouse employee approaches to ask if I want anything to drink and looks to the empty chair that I'm talking to.

I wave him away.

He shrugs and leaves me.

My mother laughs.

My doctors look up to see who laughed, but obviously see no one, either.

I don't want to know the true answer to my next question, but ask anyhow, "Have you finished your assignments yet?"

"I did get almost all of them out of the country once I convinced them they could make a difference from afar. Our city was done, gone, and destroyed more each day by the raging street warfare. Thirteen years, Tess, I gave away thirteen years of my life to those monsters, but I couldn't leave until I saved her."

"Who?" I sit up and bump knees with her. She is real, but why can only I see and hear her?

"My aunt. My mother's sister." My mother looks out the window and smiles as the toddler presses her nose against the pane.

Her mother is mortified and dashes to peel her three year old off the glass. She tries to wipe the smear off the window with the corner of her shirt.

"But she refused repeatedly to come with me. She said, "Who will watch over the street children? And my husband's grave?"

"Uncle Regis?"

"Yes. I didn't have an answer for her, so she dug in and stayed despite the dangers every day. "

"She's still there?"

"Yes. Sometimes, she hides at the beach, but mostly in the *favelas*, in the heart of the cartel's land, but ironically she's safer there, and can offer food, shelter, and medical care to the *"menino de rua"*."

My mother lets her head rest against the back of the chair and sighs. "They expect their opposition to be in the affluent neighborhoods, on the beaches in the mansions where we once lived, not among their customers. That's where you lived, on the streets until I could finally get you to the states. I'm so sorry about that. Luckily, you had Tino to watch over you, too. "

"Menino de rua." I repeat what my mother just said under my breath and instantly know what that means and without resorting to my electronic foreign dictionary: "children of the street" the undesirables, those who did what they had to to survive.

And Tino…she doesn't know?

I close my eyes, again and let my head fall back onto the chair, too; I can see, again the dark wet alley where I ran in one of my first dreams. Was that my house behind the locked gate?

"Yes. That was where you were born." My mother's voice reaches my ears, but I can't be sure that she isn't just talking inside my head.

"And I'm so sorry about Tino." She reaches out and holds my hand.

"And the little girl, who brought you to me, yes, that is, was you. As a seven-year-old, little girl."

My mind does back flips to try to compute what I felt was true, but now she has spoken aloud. I close my eyes and remember, but am having a hard time realizing I have also met the Brazilian me at sixteen, the brave one, who followed Tino around the parade, drank his beer, kissed him on the beach…

How can that be? Is there another earth where I'm alive and living a life, a different life than this one?

I do need to call Dr. Vendall about this possibility. It's the only explanation—if there's an explanation to what I've been experiencing all of these months…years.

Finally, I do remember one of the most important questions I wanted to ask my mother before she vaporizes like she usually does.

"When are you coming back to me?" I keep my eyes closed, afraid if I open them she'll be gone, again.

"Tess, I'm home."

The evening breeze has intensified and blows back my hair from my forehead.

I'm not in the coffeehouse, the doctors are gone.

I'm on the couch in the living room in my grandmother's house, once again.

As I sit up on the couch, the screen door squeaks close behind a woman—the same woman, who climbed the hill above the *favelas* where I sat and waited with my little friend, the same women, who drove with sheer resolve to outrun the pursuing car above the black bay, the same woman from my coffeehouse dream only seconds ago—is here at my grandmother's house, and not in my dream, but here with me. I'm no longer in the coffeehouse, in my dream, or in the memory of my latest dream, but here in my grandmother's house with her, my mother.

As she approaches me, she ages from twenty-four, the mother I barely remember when I was only three and living with her in Rio to forty-one in a matter of seconds, the age she is now.

Her red sandals flop across the floorboards and bring her to where I lie on the couch.

I squint at the figure before me. But it can't be…yet I smell a familiar fragrance a blend of citrus, water lily, and the fruit, lychee—her perfume.

She wears the same white dress with small red poppies embroidered around its square neckline and hem. Her large, silver hoop earrings shine against her dark hair. This is what she was wearing when I saw her at the top of the statue of *Cristo Redentor*, but today I know she's home.

I bolt off the couch and into my mother's embrace.

She's taller than me, so she can wrap her arms around my shoulders.

I know she's finally safe.

"Mom!"

[Morse code message: HOME]

-. . .-- .-.. .. ..-. .

I balance a stack of pink- and white-candy striped, beach towels in my arms wearing a modest, American-made bikini and walk pass my grandmother's Virgin Mary altar. Something new in her collection makes me pause.

I look over the bright towels. Next to an ivory figurine where Mother Mary holds baby Jesus, there's a polished silver frame with a black-and-white photo of my mother as a young woman holding an infant—that must be me, maybe at one month old?

I wonder, When did my grandmother, or mother, put that photo there? I push the screen door open with my butt and head out to greet two of my favorite people in the world.

Nile is in the kitchen talking to Rosalyn, my other, two favorite people.

I unload the towels into an empty wicker chair and slip into the kid-sized, blue inflatable wading pool in the center of our wide porch.

"I can't believe my nineteen year old still likes to wade." My mother smiles and then splashes me.

"Hey!" I wing a handful of water at her bare feet.

My grandmother laughs.

"Thank you. I was beginning to heat up." My mom sips her frozen limeade through a straw, holding the frosty glass with both hands.

Maybe that's where I get my preference for all tart beverages. I close my eyes and let the hum of their conversation lulls me into a state of contentment. I go over the details in my mind, again, what I remember and what the doctors confirmed.

During the sleep lab studies of me, two graduate students pieced together my story while they watched my body's chemical reaction to my mind travels. Along with

Dr. Hall's and Dr. Vendall's interpretations, my questions were finally answered and accepted by the medical professionals assigned to my case. However by that time, I already knew where I was going and why.

Once I stopped taking all of my pills, I could see the answers more clearly, at least in my dreams. I saw my parallel life. I saw myself as a small child, a street urchin left behind without a mother and sometimes without food, running, trying to escape the evils around me. I do remember the kind people, people from other countries, those from the local churches, who would come and sit on the ground with us offering food and medicine or even just Band-Aids. I remember my great aunt trying to care for me the best she could when she wasn't running from the cartel herself.

I remember Tino.

Parallel universes do exist.

I lived my second life at mostly night, traveling back in time to be with my mother whenever I could and regardless of the perils. But my mother was in constant contact, sending messages to my grandmother and to me if I would only listen—telling me why she could not come back to me right now. Through my dreams when I appeared in her world, I was a witness to what would have happened if I stayed. For years, she had been communicating with me through my dreams. The evidence was in my childhood journals and recently in the incessant beeping going on inside my head. She sent Morse code messages to my grandmother and me—if I would have only listened and then perhaps I would have understood my dreams sooner. Perhaps I was more in tune to what I thought I heard and what I was told in my dreams as a child, but because I was a child, I thought they were just that: dreams about meeting up with my mother, once again.

I did die in my other universe that night at the hotel, but discovered I could still be alive in this life. I shudder once again, as I did that day, when I read about my death in the foreign newspaper.

As Dr. Hall placed the pieces of my life's puzzle together with what I had sketched now and what I recorded as a child, she amazingly did admit my night travels as a real possibility of living in two parallel universes and as hard as it was to say it aloud, she said it, "Your dreams are real, playing out in real time elsewhere".

Her long conversations with Dr. Vendall made her a believer.

I had hoped that she told Dr. Reid this, so he would stop giving Nile dirty looks whenever he saw us together on campus. My souvenirs, the bodily marks, I brought home were real, not from Nile.

Dr. Hall and Dr. Reid and their panel of experts including my geology professor, Professor Wilson, who did identify the grains of sand being from the beaches of Rio de Janeiro finally agreed the mix of prescription medication made it possible also for my brain to expand its learning capabilities. They labeled it "hyper-intelligence". Nile prefers to call it my Google brain.

These days, my college's campus is a beehive of activity. With new grant money bestowed by the pharmaceutical industry and the constant arrival of new media people and their camera crew. They come from all over the globe, trying to leak the latest findings about parallel universes and the expansion of what the mind's capable of believing and knowing.

New teams are now studying several other cases of the "instantly-gifted" individuals like me, who suddenly achieve what normally takes a lifetime to master.

International grants to my university are already causing a paradigm shift in scientific thinking and its new, promising results are at the forefront of the way diseases will be treated.

However, right now the cognitive scientists and psychologists and, of course, the media are taking a longer look at people, who are even younger than me and their DNA.

They now believe in the possibility of "memory inheritance", which is an indicator of what immediate skills and talents these individuals will possess—like being a grand master at a musical instrument or speaking a foreign language fluently without any lessons. These candidates, who are naturally inclined to this reality and never questioned it or are aided by the right mix of prescription pills such as myself, can see and hear through their great, great, great grandparent's eyes and ears. Their fingertips intuitively know how to play the piano or cello. Research scientists and doctors from other universities are trying to find a way to make this possible for all people—to tap into the mind's vast treasury of knowledge and its conduit of aptitudes or click on the dormant DNA to activate such talents.

Nile steps out on to the porch, balancing a tray with two bottles of beer and frosted mugs from the freezer. He smiles and squeezes into the small inflatable pool beside me.

I look over and offer a sincere smile of gratitude that he's here again with me. He decided to return to his study of medicine since the field offers fascinating new dimensions to explore—the brain.

Things around my grandmother's house have changed, but have changed for the better.

We took down our house number and disconnected our landline to have some privacy. Rosalyn said we should get a German Shepard, a friendly one, though reasoning his presence would make the tenacious reporters hesitate before launching across our front yard and stepping on my grandmother's flowers.

Nile is forever picking up the pink flamingos knocked over in their haste.

My grandmother's solution was to just let her garden grow wild, so it looked like no one lives here. In late summer, our house can be barely seen due to the explosion of wisteria hanging down from the front porch's gable and the twisting, dark brownish-purple vine with its white blossoms entwining itself between the trellises on both ends of our long porch. My grandmother continues to call this plant her "chocolate vine" due to its color and even when I try to tell her its botanical name…I only wished it smelled like chocolate.

I watch as a shimmery-green hummingbird works its way around the trumpet-shaped white flowers. The busy little bird ignores the morning glories as they're closed due to the afternoon heat. Since I have kicked the lack of sleeping problem, I've taken on the challenge of trying to find ways to embrace summer. Most hot afternoons, I can be found planted on the front porch, sketching my latest invention. I'm not sure if I can ever love this season like I do its icy cousin, winter, but my wading pool is doing the trick today as the mercury in the thermometer climbs to the very top of the meter.

Nile just poured a microbrew into a frosted mug and hands it to me. I can now count two ways to like summer. The ice pulls off the thick side of my heavy mug and plunks into the beer's frothy head. I sip and then smile again at my bartender. I'm so glad he decided to return to our "circle of crazy women"—that's what he calls us, but means it in a good way.

We sit undetected by any reporters on the wide front porch and catch up on the time missed over the years…although I wonder if we ever can. Behind me, my mother and grandmother stretch out and share the daybed, which is, of course, filled with pillows.

Nile fills out our silences and brings my mother up to speed on my loving quirks: the good and the bad, and my past accomplishments from when she wasn't in this life to witness, and my faults, which they all find hilarious. He has known me longer than she, through all the time she went missing.

I sit next to him in the pool, happy to hear his voice when he speaks, and not before in my head like I used to be able to do. I have learned how to turn this ability 'on' and 'off' based on when I want or need to use this talent. Nile has asked me not to use it around him. He said he couldn't surprise me if I always knew what he was thinking.

I'm happy now.

My mother's here. My boyfriend is here and my grandmother, too. I look at her and smile. She has taken to my habit of wearing my ski sweaters over her dresses to ward off her perceived chill of the approaching evening hours. She's slipping away from us, but is happy, too to be here now with her daughter.

Rosalyn is crashing around the kitchen. She has threatened Nile to make another hot and spicy meal. He's a bit wary, but will try her culinary creation. He's such a sport, loving the women, who make up my little family. He says we're the spices he needs in his bland life since nothing ever changes at his house. He now calls me, "Peppy" due to my returned energy.

I did like when I was his 'Cinnamon Girl,' but Neil Young sang a sad song and my sad days are long gone. My new nickname does suit my outlook on life much better now.

My night travels have ceased since I have no need to travel. Everyone I need is here, except Tino…there's still a hole in my heart for him.

Recently, grandmother added another silver crescent moon for Tino in her altar.

Nile says nothing. He knows I can't escape who I'm supposed to be.

I'm sleeping at night, a full lovely and uninterrupted eight hours.

Nile tells my mom. "She can sleep like a rock and only the strong aroma of hot coffee under her nose can arouse her."

"A good morning kiss from you would probably do the trick, too." I rock in the pool to roll little waves over his thighs.

Nile wraps his arm over my shoulder.

I play with his mop of wet hair. He needs a haircut. Maybe he'll let me play with scissors, tonight. He takes my hand from his head, knowing what I'm thinking and shakes his head, but holds my hand. I'm better at drawing than cutting and he and I both know this fact.

Since I'm enrolled in my classes again and engaged in life, too, I need to make something that's happy because now I can feel this emotion one-hundred percent and it lasts. Maybe I can make something for my grandmother's yard—tackle another kitchen gadget that can be improved.

During the last year and thanks to the love from Nile and my grandmother, I felt happiness whenever I could see them, but it always faded too quickly, replaced by a dread of not knowing and that held little hope for the future.

Today, I feel the buoyancy of being happy all of the time. I flash a huge smile at Nile.

"What? Are you happy? Again?" Nile rolls his eyes and does not believe that I can maintain such a state of bliss. "You and your suspended state of happiness."

I counter. "Many people mull around in depression, another state found within the brain, so why can't I choose to be happy?"

"She got a point there, Nile." My grandmother breaks into a large smile that doesn't fade.

My mother joins her in our happiness argument against the sole male on the porch. "I like my happy Tess."

Nile slowly lets his mouth turn into a grin. "Okay. Okay. Okay. You win. Besides, I'm outnumbered."

I sense someone staring at us and I'm right.

Through the slats in the railing, I can see a reporter along with his cameraman in tow, standing out on the sidewalk trying to see if we're home. Months ago, I gave up trying to hide from them since they never go away if I don't acknowledge them. I stand up, dripping wet, and wave them up to the porch.

"Is it a good time to ask a few questions?" The reporter looks like he just graduated from high school. "I'm Rob from CNN and this is Charles."

My grandmother points to the empty chairs, the ones that I made out of old skis with my grandpa a long time ago. I wonder if he knows and can see that we're all together again…

Charles sets up his camera and shotgun microphone on a tripod.

Rob sits and flips open his notepad.

Nile stands up from the pool to leave.

"No, you can stay. Actually, I would prefer if everyone stayed and participated."

Nile plops back into the water. The cameraman holds onto to the legs of the tripod of out nervousness that his camera might topple over due to the quake rippling across the porch.

I smile. Nile forgets how big he is sometimes and his mass makes an impact no matter what he does or where he goes. I think he has been over six foot tall since he was fourteen.

The reporter launches into his questions. "Tell me what you know about parallel universes."

Nile loves this new topic of the day and will answer the reporter's questions more frequently than I do. "The belief in parallel universes wasn't comprehensible without understanding reality and to know of our reality was crucial in order to make some sense of the bizarre findings with quantum physics and general relativity."

"How so?" Rob slides back into the deep chair ready with his pen.

"Currently, what's being explored is the belief there's a parallel universe similar and possibly, a duplicate of our own universe or another earth, the other world."

My mother leans toward Rob. "Not only are there other human beings, but human beings, who are exact duplicates of ourselves and are connected to us through mechanisms only explainable using quantum physics concepts."

The reporter looks at me.

Finally, I add to the conversation. "This is why I could be in two different places at one time because it was me or a duplicate of me at different stages in my lives. At the ages of six, seven, sixteen, and nineteen."

"This is getting really complicated." Rob looks to Charles to make sure the camera's working and then puts down his pen.

Nile gets a very excited look in his eye. I know what he's going to say next.

"If you think that's confusing, what do you think about this new finding? 'The future may play a role in the present.'" He says this often to reporters to watch their eyes cloud up in confusion.

I get confused, too.

He cups my chin, "Is it possible? Am I smarter in one subject than my girlfriend?"

"Yes, I have to admit you are."

He grins and continues to lose me, and probably the reporter and cameraman in his explanations. However, my mom is drinking in his words perhaps finally understanding what she has been living for the last thirteen years.

"Our minds can sense the presence of parallel universes, yet most people ignore the inkling—unlike Tess, who jumped into her parallel universe almost every night."

"Brave girl." My grandmother clucks and clutches the prototype tea cup that I created for her.

I was mystified as to how to keep tea or coffee warm for at least fifteen minutes after I poured a cup. I played with different kinds of materials and added them to the clay before I found my answer. Along with the help of a long-time resident artist on campus and my ceramics professor, we came up with my grandmother's new cup. Actually, only after repeatedly visiting museums when the Greek and Roman treasures were on display, did I see this obvious answer of making a vessel to hold hot water in between its outer and inner shell.

She smiles and nods to her drink, indicating that her tea and hands are still warm.

"As far as the laws of mathematics refer to reality, they are not certain; and so far as they are certain, they do not refer to reality." Nile is quoting Albert Einstein, who confuses me with his words more than my boyfriend.

I splash Nile to get him to stop talking science and return to me and this shady summer day, and to get the reporter to leave, but with no luck. They're getting a story, but not the simple one that they had expected. These notes are going to require additional research, fact checking and conferring with other scientific and medical experts before my story can be aired.

Nile continues to baffle the majority of us collected on the porch. "What Einstein meant was the mathematical laws of quantum physics can only describe the possibilities of reality, but never reality itself."

The reporter taps his tablet with his pen. "Both you and Einstein sound like a Zen koan. Who else has the university studied?"

Nile smiles in the direction of my mother. "I might need to study you in the sleep lab."

My mother tucks her legs up onto the day bed. "No thanks, Nile. Let Tess continue to be your guinea pig."

"Thanks, Mom as if I haven't been covered in multi-colored wires and stuck with needles enough already."

"You and Nile know that I'm still getting my feet used to being in this universe."

Rob sits up on the edge of his chair to turn his attention to my mother.

Nile intercepts the reporter's next question. "But will you let me later—once you have time to adjust?"

"Yes, of course, but not tomorrow or the next tomorrow, okay?"

To me, her answer sounds like an indefinite maybe.

My grandmother laughs and sips her tea. She knows that my mother's answer was just that.

"Nile, you know I didn't send Jules Verne's time machine to pick up my daughter each night, right?" My mother hugs a pillow across her lap.

"I know. Parallel universes exist between our ears." Nile smiles.

The reporter closes his tablet and looks perplexed, again. He's not the only one.

"You're losing me again, Nile. How can my mother and I both be experiencing the same experiences?" I scoot closer to my waterlogged boyfriend, sending ripples of clear water over our legs.

He leans close to me, "You aren't. No one sees life exactly the same way. Again, it's like that Zen garden in Japan I told you about. Remember? There are thirteen stones and no matter where you stand around perimeter of the garden, you can't see all of the stones. How you experience life and how your mother does, or how anyone else experiences it, it is never exactly the same for everyone."

The cameraman peers around the eye of his camera to confirm what Nile just said. I guess Charles the cameraman knows this sentiment better than most as he is someone, who goes around life with only one eye opened.

My grandmother puts her teacup down on the end table, "But Nile, we do experience the same life-affirming or life-shattering events, right?"

"Yes, you're right and you're wrong because you're in your own universe and are experiencing the death, the loss, or the happiness, the reunion at the same time, but not at the exact same time."

"Nile, I think it's Miller Time." I hold up my empty beer mug. Let the reporter think what he might. It is Saturday and it's after four in the afternoon.

"Oh, I can go from being a neuroscientist to bartender in a matter of minutes? Fine. Anything else you would like while I am up?" Nile stands and a shower of water rains off of his large frame.

Charles hugs his camera, again.

"Anyone else?"

Both the reporter and cameraman decline Nile's hospitality. He slops water out of the wading pool, crosses the porch, and heads into the house.

I can hear Rosalyn scolding him for leaving wet footprints around the kitchen. Through our grand windows leading into the living room and into the kitchen, I can see him ice skating on two pieces of paper towels to mop up his mess.

My grandmother peers into windows. "He's going to break his neck."

"Or spill my beer."

The screen door slams behind Nile. "I'm not going to spill your beer. Just mine." He races his lips over the top of his bottle as the foam shoots over the edge, stopping the geyser just in time and plops back into the pool with me.

We barely fit. Most of the water is squeezed up and over the sides again. My grandmother raises her feet to stay dry. My mother lowers her feet to welcome the coolness across her bare toes.

The cameraman grabs his tripod and looks to the reporter as if it's his fault.

"Tess has become the case study for modern neuroscience." Nile smiles at my mom to win her approval. "That what I'm going to be now, a neuroscientist."

He should have known ages ago that he won my mother's and grandmother's approval, based on what my grandmother repeated hinted about him being "the one".

My grandmother just nods her head, not surprised to hear anything new these days. She knew. She cheated and asked her magic mirror one night for me after I sank into a heavy depression about my missing my mother and constantly peppered her with questions about her imminent return.

Since she had no answer for me on that matter, she told me that Nile, my childhood friend, would always be in my life. What she didn't tell me is that she saw Nile and I as an elderly couple happy together living in her house long after she passed to the other side of reality…wherever that may be. This is what Nile wants to study for his Ph.D. thesis, the afterlife or maybe it's our next parallel universe.

Although at the age of seven, I had no idea that she meant he would be my husband, but now looking back that's exactly what she meant.

The reporter looks at me since he's here to interview me and all he has heard is Nile. I recognize that look. They, the media people, have been here before.

"What has been discovered after studying my childhood journals, the Morse code messages, and all of my doctor's recording and notes is that the altered states of awareness such as schizophrenia and lucid dreaming do point to the closeness of parallel universes—

"Do suffer you from schizophrenia?" The reporter picks up his tablet, again.

"No, she doesn't." My mother answers this time.

Nile points to his head with his beer bottle. "What we have learned is what lies between universes is perhaps only a measure of atomic dimensions, or a superspace, as the physicists that have been studying this reality call this extension of place and time, the worlds parallel to our own."

"So, Sybil wasn't insane, just ahead of her time and the rest of the science world." My mother adds.

"Sybil? The book written in the seventies about the woman, who possessed sixteen different personalities?' asks the reporter.

"Exactly. She could see all the realities no one else could." Nile confirms what I was just thinking about inside my head. That book was freaky. I read it at the library all in one day when I was only fourteen to try and answer some of my questions surfacing in my mind even back then.

"Poor woman. So misunderstood." My grandmother refills her cup from the small teakettle nestled on top of a heating coil that I also designed for her. She smiles at me to thank me for the hundredth time.

I smile back, but wonder, How can she drink hot tea on such a hot day and how does she know about Sybil? Did she read the book, too?

"I do read a lot, Tess, including many American stories in English. And hot tea cools you on a hot day. You should try it."

"I just didn't see that book around the house, and no thanks on anything hot today to drink."

"It's in my collection of paperbacks in the attic."

"You collect paperbacks, too?" Nile pours his beer carefully into the mug, so not to overflow it into the pool. He knows I don't like beer floating in my pool.

"I don't collect them anymore; they don't last as long as hardcover books. I do like my books to last as long as me. They're like old friends that always stay around."

Maybe it's the beer or the heat of the summer afternoon, but all this talk about parallel lives and universes is making me drowsy.

My grandmother, although she drinks hot *yerba maté*, appears to be experiencing the same effect of this hot hour.

"Thank you for your time, everyone." The reporter signals to the cameraman to pack up his camera. "It was enlightening."

The media guys step down the well-traveled stairs and across the cracked sidewalk. A small crowd of neighbors are paused by their CNN van parked curbside. You would think they would be indifferent to the media circus by now, but I guess not.

I lean against Nile and smile at my grandmother and mother.

The engine starts. They drive away, down our quiet street—for the moment.

"See? I was right, again." My grandmother smiles at us. "The future is good."

[Morse code message: NEWLIFE]

. .--. .. .-.. --- --. ..- .

TESS: I can't believe you're gone.

.. -.-.-.--.- .- -... . ..-. ..- ..-. ... -.-- --- ..- .-. . --. --- -. . .-.-.-

MOM: Can you hear me?

-.-. .- -. -.-- --- ..- ....- . .-. .-. -- . ..--..

TESS: I'm scared.

.. -- ... -.-. .- .-. . -.. .-.-.-

MOM: I have to get you out of here.

.. ....- .- ...- . - -.-- --. . - -.-- --- ..- --- ..- - --- ..-. ....- . .- . . .-.-.-

TESS: I'm all alone.

.. -- .- .-.. .-.. .- .-.. --- -. .

MOM: But I have to stay a while longer.

-... ..- - .. ....- .- ...- . - -.-- ... - .- -.-- .- .- -- ....- .. .-.. . .-.. --- -. --. . .-. .-.-.-

TESS: Can you come back?

-.-. .- -. -.-- --- ..- -.-. --- -- . -... .- -.-. -.- ..--..

MOM: I have to return.

.. ....- .- ...- . - -.-- .-. . - ..- .-. -. .-.-.-

TESS: Will you ever come back?

.-- .. .-.. .-.. -.-- --- ..- . ...- . .-. -.-. --- -- . -... .- -.-. -.- .-.-.. .

MOM: I will come back to you.

.. .-- .. .-.. .-.. -.-. --- -- . - .- -.-. -.- - --- -.-- --- ..-

[Morse code message: EPILOGUE]

288

<u>Watch for the next books in this trilogy:</u>

The Other Earth by Jill Murphy Long

Tess refuses to believe her long-time friend, Tino, is actually dead and leaves the safety of her home in the Colorado Rocky Mountains to go deeper into the other earth, her parallel life she lives in Rio de Janeiro.

While her mother, grandmother, and her stateside boyfriend Nile try to convince her it's a bad idea to keep going back and forth, she's determined to stay as long as she has to until she find Tino—or discovers what happened to him. Her time traveling back and forth between her two lives is causing havoc in hers and the lives of others, but she won't stop until the truth is known.

With the further interpretations provided by Dr. Vendall and her new doctors, Tess learns what lies between universes is perhaps only a measure of atomic dimensions, or superspace, the extension of place and time where the worlds parallel to our own do exist. Due to his direction and encouragement, Tess goes to the other earth.

Another World by Jill Murphy Long

Somewhere between the parallel lives that college student Tess is living in the snowy Colorado university town and South America's *favelas* in Rio de Janeiro, she finds yet another world where all of her family and friends exist. Her grandmother, who just passed over, her Brazilian boyfriend, grandfather, and her father, the man she never met...

Every time that she enters this surreal sanctuary, she finds someone, who has left both worlds, but meets them at different ages from their lives and from hers.

Tess is becoming increasingly aware of the infinity of time and finally listens to her heart to determine if what she's feeling or possibly experiencing in another dimension of time can be true. Can she be in love with Nile and Tino? Is the human heart large enough for both? Are the worlds where she travels permitting of such celestial romance?

By learning their stories, she begins to piece together her life, both her past and her future with greater clarity. She discovers that her grandmother was right all along when she said: "The future is good," but what she cannot seem to answer is, "What is the future?"

About the Author

Jill Murphy Long is the author of novels and a non-fiction book series. She also writes screenplays and teaches creative writing. She has been a book editor and advocate for dozens of other writers, helping them to publish their books, too.

Prior to writing books, she worked in advertising as a creative director and copywriter for several LA agencies before opening her own: The Ad Group and Murphy & Watt Advertising.

Her first best-selling book, *Permission to Nap, Taking Time to Restore Your Spirit* received the Excellence Award, a distinguished recognition presented by the *Chicago Book Clinic* and the Benjamin Franklin Award by the *Publishers Marketing Association*.

The author has appeared on *CBS* and *Fox* television stations and has been interviewed by other stations throughout North America. Interviewed by NPR and other major metro radio stations across the country, the author has been the keynote speaker at symposiums, conferences, universities, libraries, and spa resorts including *The Golden Door, Canyon Ranch*, and *Red Mountain Adventure Spa & Resort*.

Her other titles, *Permission to Play* and *Permission to Party*, received press coverage in: *USA Today, Better Homes & Gardens, Dallas Morning News, Los Angeles Times, American West In-flight Magazine, Chicago Sun Times, EPregnancy*, and the international spa magazine, *Pulse*, to name a few.

Her books have been sold in gift catalogs such as: *Isabella, Femail Creations, Paragon, Victorian Trading Company* and *Jessica's Biscuits*.

Jill has e-published *Skiing With God*, which will be released as an audio book in before ski season in 2014.

The Conduit will be available as an audio book and a printed book. This author, now screenwriter, is adapting this novel to the big screen next, mainly because she wants to film in the snowy Rockies and Rio de Janeiro.

When she is not writing, she's skiing, cycling, or making a movie.

To book this author for your next creative engagement, email: TheConduitbyJillMurphyLong@gmail.com

Also by Jill Murphy Long

Permission to Nap
Taking Time to Restore Your Spirit

Permission to Play
Taking Time to renew Your Smile

Permission to Party
Taking Time to Celebrate and Enjoy Life

Skiing With God

www.ingramcontent.com/pod-product-compliance
Lightning Source LLC
Chambersburg PA
CBHW060407260626
47160CB00006B/2469